FLEDGLING

BOOK ONE

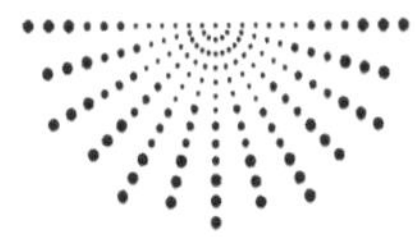

KATRINA COPE

very much entertained. I am hoping this is part of a series and if so, I can not wait for the next chapter.' - Julie

'I adored the fight scenes that happened through out the book. It made me feel like I was there watching them.' - *Shaun*

'What I am asking is when will the next one come out because I really just want it now. - *Owen*

Praise for The Taking

'I always try not to get too hyped up about a book. However, having read the first book in this series, I was eager to read this one, and had high hopes for it. I was not disappointed! This book was a fantastic read!

I enjoyed getting to know more about the characters, and watching the relationships between them grow and evolve. Plus, the plot was both interesting and exciting; it grabbed your attention quickly, and kept you guessing until the end.'
- Toriz

'The Taking doesn't disappoint; avoiding the sequel slump that can often stymie a series. The story has a gradual build up in intensity ending in a great fight scene finish. The ending was full of action packed surprises.' - Will Wortner

'Must Read! I loved this book, and the prior one. I want a

third. The creativity was amazing and it was well written.' - Erika

'Great Read! Action, adventure, and to love stories. I can't wait to read book3. You will be on the edge of your seat.' - Helen

'These are not serene angels gently guiding their human charges through life. These are kick-ass super heroes who are not afraid to put themselves in the way of extreme danger for what they believe is right. Overall a second strong showing in this series and very recommended.' - Phil

Praise for Angelic Retribution

'I thought the the first two instalments of the Afterlife saga, following the exploits of human-turned-angel Aurora, were absolutely terrific. With this third instalment I feel like I need to invent some new superlatives as all the existing ones seem somehow inadequate.' - Phil

'This book is an excellent addition to the series, which makes for an enjoyable read. It is well-written, and has an interesting plot that moves at a nice pace.' - Toriz

My Guardian Angels

PROLOGUE

Breathe, I tell myself. Breathe. I try, and my body doesn't respond. It simply doesn't have the energy. The icy hardness of the tiles presses up through my clothes and onto my skin as I lie on the bathroom floor. Under my head is a sensation of warm liquid. My eyes are open but remain still, and tunnel vision sets in as they start to glaze over. Breathe, I command my body, and it struggles.

Towering above me, I see a man. He's strong and muscular, his jaw set in determination, and his teeth clenched. The wrinkles framing his muddy-brown eyes are deep and straight, pinched with anger.

I want to move, but I can't. I can barely hear my heartbeat—and it's fading.

Not again, my soul screams. It can't be happening again. I was only trying to protect my mother.

Images of two similar scenes flash before my eyes. My soul is reminding itself that this's happened before. This's the third life I've lived and the third time that my life has ended. I'm only eighteen, but this's the longest life I've lived.

Unwillingly, I watch from my fixed vision as the man raises his olive-skinned arm again. The short length of his dark-brown hair flicks around with force. He's flinging the ceramic soap dispenser at my head— again and again and again and again. Surely he must know I'm already dying.

My vision narrows to a tiny circle framing the face of my attacker, the man—my father.

CHAPTER ONE

"Are you ready, fledgling?"

In front of me stands a tall, tanned male. Dark-blue pants define his muscular legs, and his olive-skinned torso is bare. He stands with his legs shoulder width apart, holding a firm stance. My eyes drift up his muscle-bound chest. In another world, I may've ogled over how his muscles bulge from his thin form. As my eyes reach his shoulders, they glide up a little more, observing the top edges of his majestic wings. Although strong, like his physique, they're soft with thick, royal blue feathers. He opens them out to full extension, showing off their magnificence, and flaps them several times, raising him to hover above the ground. They're a pair he should be proud of—the largest in the training group and a reflection of his character.

He chuckles. "Hello," he says slowly. "Are you ready?"

I glance at his face, and he greets me with a playful grin. From under his dark-brown hair, his ocean-blue eyes study my expression. Right from day one in our new lives, he's seen past my facade, reading my emotions and possibly even my thoughts. His handsome features hold wisdom beyond his human years, taking the sharpness from his chiseled looks.

My face turns slightly warm under his gaze. I realize I've been staring. I smirk at him and clear my throat. "Ah, yes. I'm as ready as you are, fledgling," I say, trying to hide my embarrassment, and I stand ready. Like me, he doesn't carry an individual name.

He lowers to ground level. We stand face-to-face, studying each other, waiting for one of us to make the first move. As his feet touch the ground, he steps closer and circles toward me. I step back so I'm always facing him while he continues to circle me. After a moment, he steps in; his leg thrusts out in a roundhouse kick aimed for my head. I dodge it and have my hands ready to block his next move, aimed at my leg. I retaliate with a flying backfist to his temple. He narrowly avoids this by stepping slightly aside, blocking my roundhouse.

A slap sounds from the connection of skin on skin. Pushing my leg aside, he's airborne in the same instant, causing me to dodge a jumping outside crescent kick aimed at my head. I retaliate with a sideways kick to his stomach that he twists to avoid, and I move in for an uppercut. My hand glides up his facial skin, narrowly missing its target. He'd seen it coming again. This time it was close.

He spins around and grabs my wings from over the top, scooping his arms down my back and embracing the full connection where my wings attach to my body. I extend them and flap with strong, expansive strokes. The heat from his body awkwardly reminds me of his closeness. I see the tips of my feathered wings fold in front of me as I push. They shine golden yellow in the sun. We rise off the ground while he still grasps me from behind. From his added pressure, my strokes are labored, but my wings are strong, capable, and reliable.

The grassy ground shrinks away as we rise farther and the deep-blue ocean expands. Below, I can see the small tropical island. Palm trees line the edges and separate the sand from the vegetated areas. On the ground are several other colorful winged beings. They're just like us. The island has been our training ground for the last six months.

As I rise, I continue my fight to remove the attached being from behind me, yet he continues to grasp my wings' attachments. He's in a place that's hard to reach. Farther and farther we rise. I reach over and grab his hair—it doesn't faze him. We're not fighting to kill, so I don't use the finishing actions, and it makes it harder to remove him from my back.

I look around. The sky is a crisp clear blue. We've risen into the clouds. Beyond this, I can see the mainland of Australia in the distance. In our winged form, we're to keep out of sight of the humans, or there will be consequences.

I stop rising then tuck in my wings. With my head tilting toward the ground and my body straight, I allow myself to fall. As we descend, the speed increases rapidly, and I twist. Long dark-brown strands of hair paste across my face. I twist hard enough to begin a spin and each turn increases in speed. My hair is now securely wrapped over my eyes, blocking all vision past its silky dark strands. I feel additional pressure from his body still trying to grasp the connecting point of my wings. I also feel his body pulling away from mine with the force of gravity. The wind wisps around my ears, and the force makes it hard for him to keep holding on.

With a sudden movement, I untuck my wings. I extend the tips directly behind my back, pointing them in the opposite direction of my face. As soon as I do this, his grip slides down my golden feathers and off the ends, projecting him from the force of the spin. I'm free.

Extending my wings out to the side, I stop my spin and turn my body so my head points to the sky. We stop falling only sixty-five feet from the ground. I look in the direction of my captor. I watch as he spreads his royal blue wings and applies pressure to the surrounding air, stopping the force that's pushing him farther away. As he flies toward me, his face wears a smile.

"That was an impressive tactic," he congratulates me. "Very effective."

Before I can answer him, I hear a whoosh of wings from behind. I turn to see the concerned face of my female friend. Her long golden hair is pushed back from her face as she flies in our direction. Her lemon-colored wings spread wide, framing her yellow, figure-hugging bodysuit.

"What're you doing?" she asks, her voice sounds

panicked. "Are you trying to be seen by the humans? You're not even in your invisible forms."

"It's okay. No one could've seen us." I try to reassure her.

"You never know." She shakes her head and crosses her arms. Her wings flap enough to stay level with us. "They have technology that can see very far these days. Remember, we must remain invisible in this form or else we'll face punishment. We've only just graduated. You don't want to end in the abyss before we even start." Her face etches with worry.

I lower to the ground, and they follow. The other graduates are training around us, paying us no attention.

"It's okay, really." I say. "They couldn't have seen us." I shake my head and turn to my male friend. "Do you think they saw us?"

He shakes his head. "No. Stop worrying, Yellow, we're fine."

Yellow isn't her real name. We've given each other a reference until we receive our proven names, making it easier for us. We only use this within our little group.

Yellow races forward and gives me a hug. "Good," she says. "I want you to be around when we leave for our first missions."

I return her hug. "Hey, don't worry about me. I'll be fine," I whisper in her ear. While pulling away, I add, "You stress way too much."

Blue cocks an eyebrow. "Are you sure you should listen to her?" He looks me up and down. "A multicolored being. They're unpredictable."

"I'm not that multicolored." I defend myself. "I'm only a few colors." Holding out my golden-yellow wings, I look at my formfitting clothes and study my pants. The colors reflect our aura. "I'm green, blue, and golden yellow."

"Not to mention the black hair and gray eyes," Blue points out.

I look at his dark hair and screw up my mouth. "Have you looked in the mirror lately?"

He smiles. "There seems to be a shortage on this deserted island."

"Hmm!" I say. "And have you ever thought that maybe my eyes are silver, not gray?"

"Silver eyes," he says looking thoughtful. "Now that'd be an interesting color."

"Fledglings!" The deep voice is stern, sounding over the noise of the group.

I look up. We all look up—all ten of us. In this place, we're all called fledgling—new and ready to test our wings in the expansive world. We're nameless, freshly graduated angels after an intense six months of training. Our human names lost to us forever. All of us were chosen from our unique human lives.

Yes, that's right. We were once humans. How? Well, that comes to the age-old question—What happens after we die? Do we go to heaven or hell, reincarnate, become reborn, spend our days floating around as spirits, or do we turn back to dust, never to be seen again?

My story is different. I've lived three lives. Yes, that's right, three. For the people who believe in reincarnation or rebirth, this isn't news. What makes my lives different is that they all ended abruptly and in violence. Each life was ended by murder. In fact, every newly fledged angel here was murdered three times as an Innocent—pure of heart and doing the best they could to live a worthy life. It's the only way to be chosen to serve and protect the current Innocents. To be honest, it wasn't something on my list of jobs to do as a human—die three times by murder so I can spend the rest of my days in service. Though now that I'm here, I'm glad to have been chosen to protect people who're like I was as a human—innocent.

I study the figure that descends in front of me, the owner of the stern voice. He's tall and built like a warrior with muscles well-defined on his bare arms. His medium length hair flows loosely, and glows golden-brown in the sun. His jaw is chiseled on his handsome face. While standing in front of his new graduates, his blue eyes observe every detail as he calls for our attention. He wears the outfit of an old-style Roman warrior tunic, cut off short above the knee. He's our leader, Michael, the great archangel. Not only is he the leader of our group, but he's also the leader of all the archangels. For six months, he's been training us for this day.

Physically we're ready. We've been training hard. Our mission is to make the world a safer place for the Innocents, but it's what we have to do to the alleged guilty that may be a problem. Ruling someone to be evil, a ruling that'll affect them for the rest of their life, and punishing them is a hard gig, even if we're just being directed to those who must receive the judgment.

The punishment is to insert a conscience into them. Sounds painless, but I have my doubts—after all, it's a punishment.

Today is the day we begin putting our training into practice. We've been waiting for this moment, when Archangel Michael, our trainer, descends to give our instructions. Today is the day we're released to begin our new role as protectors of the Innocents.

By the time Archangel Michael has descended, we're all crowding around him and waiting for his instruction. I look around at the other fledglings' faces. Their different auras are shining in different colors. Some of them look eager to start, and others look apprehensive.

"Fledglings," Archangel Michael says again. He stands firm in front of us with his white wings held out wide. His angelic form is intimidating enough, but the outspread wings give him a godlike appearance. As he studies the faces of his ten newly graduated angels, he continues. "As you know, today is the first day for you to fulfill your missions and duties in your angel life. You have all trained well, yet I know that some of you will struggle with your new role. You trained for a very important mission. It is imperative you insert the conscience, mentally maiming the evildoers from continuing in their ways. These orders must be followed closely to create a better and safer life for the humans on Earth."

He tucks in his wings and paces in front of us, his voice laced with authority. "Note well, if you do not follow these instructions—which we have proven for thousands of years—your trial will be before the board of archangels, and your fate decided. I am the leader of that board; however, if you break the rules, you will not get any leniency from me because you were my student. Due to the large rise in crime, it is only recently we have started employing the innocent humans of three deaths to train as future angels." He stops pacing and turns to face us. "If you do not do as commanded, you will be punished and placed in the abyss for as long as your ruled penalty—if not for life."

He turns and studies his students one by one. When it's my turn, his eyes bore into me as he examines my face. Even though I'm uncomfortable, I turn my eyes to his and hold my head high. It's not an act of defiance. I know I've trained well, and I'm happy to serve and protect. The muscles along his jawline ripple as his face remains expressionless. He continues to step forward and analyze the remaining graduates.

I breathe a silent sigh of relief as his eyes turn away. Archangel Michael stands for protection, justice, and strength. If you're pure of heart, he'll fight for you, but I'd hate to be on his bad side. As he studies the other graduates, I watch. They have a similar reaction to mine, so I know that I'm not alone in how I feel.

Once he's finished his final study of his graduate's faces, he turns and stands in front of us. He holds out his hands, and a small cloud appears within them. Balancing the cloud on one hand, he reaches in the center with the other. When he pulls out his hand, he holds a small glowing bean and approaches me. He holds it out, and I take it from him gingerly. It feels smooth and warm. I look at him with confusion.

"This is a bean of life. Once you receive your bean, you must swallow it for it to reveal to you the life you are to protect. Any person with ill intent who is surrounding your person must receive a conscience. Your mission is to insert a conscience into that person so they will stop pursuing the one you are protecting and possibly others. Once you are successful in completing a mission, you must return to receive another bean. Remember, you are not on Earth to kill." He finishes handing each one of us a shining bean and says, "You may proceed."

I slip the bean in my mouth and swallow. It slides down with ease, just like a tablet would with a little water. When it reaches my stomach, warmth starts to spread through my abdomen. At first, it reminds me of that feeling of swallowing a large amount of coffee; then the warmth grows. It's an unusual feeling. Visions of a face and a name start to reveal themselves to me, along with the country and precise address.

I close my eyes for a moment, taking in the instructions. When I receive them, I open my eyes.

Archangel Michael watches until we complete the digestion of the instructions. "Now is the time to leave. Remember, once your mission is complete, you are required to return here ready for your next. Serve well." His image disappears, leaving the fledglings to process the information.

I look to the side to watch my friends. Blue is watching me. He almost looks sad. I give him a little smile, trying to cheer him up.

Yellow interrupts my thoughts. "I'm so going to miss you guys," she squeaks.

I turn to look at her. "Where're you off to?"

"Bridgeport, Connecticut, in the United States of America." The edges of her mouth are turned down.

I turn to Blue and raise my eyebrow. "Paris, in France," he answers. "Where're you going?"

"London. I'm so glad we can't get cold anymore." I smile weakly. "I hope we see each other soon."

Blue places a hand on my shoulder. My heart sinks. I'll miss him and Yellow. I look up into his eyes, and a thought crosses my mind. Holding out my hand I close it into a fist. After a moment, I open it to reveal three small charms. They're golden with three angels standing together arm in arm: one blue male, one royal blue-and-green female with golden wings, and one yellow female angel. "Hopefully these will remind us of each other until we meet again." I lace one on Yellow's necklace and clasp the latch behind her neck. I study Blue's physique briefly in search of a location to fasten the charm. He's not wearing any jewelry. The heat rises to my ears, as I'm aware that I'm studying his form again. It's a strange sensation because I don't wish for any romance from him. He's my new best friend, and, besides, romances are strictly forbidden. Still, I can't help the heat from embarrassment rising to my face. My eyes finally fall on a metal loop on his long pants—the little amount of clothing he wears. It's near his hip. Glad that the awkward search is over, I lock the clasp over the loop. My eyes wander up to his. He's wearing that cheeky grin again. I back away and my fingers grab my bracelet and fumble with the clasp of the charm.

After I attach the charm, Blue steps forward and embraces me. Awkwardness mixed with comfort fills me while in his firm arms. With a large smile, he steps forward, dragging me backward, and opens his large arms to embrace Yellow. I reach out to embrace her as well. She wipes a stray tear from her cheek and returns the embrace. "Bye guys," she squeaks through her sobs, and then she disappears, leaving Blue and me in our embrace.

I step back. "Best of luck," I say as I lunge into the air without looking back. I hate goodbyes, I always have. Spreading my golden wings, I allow the wind to carry me. I'm in the mood for flying today.

A brightness glows from the buildings and streetlights below. I'm here. I've reached London. It took a little while because the Coral Sea, where the island sits, is near the northern parts of Australia. The flight was long but completely invigorating. I enjoyed feeling the wind beneath my wings and the clearness of mind that comes with that freedom. Since I began as a trainee angel, I've had little time to ponder what's happened. I had this time while flying to London. When I think back over my three lives, I'm glad I've been selected for this role.

It's early evening in the middle of December. It's cold, and many people are already indoors settling in for the night. During my short lives, I didn't have a chance to travel, and I'm looking forward to seeing the various parts of the world.

Beneath me, I spot the street of my destination— Brick Lane. Its road and buildings are finished in brick, and only some of its walkways consist of concrete. Even at this time of night several lights are shining from the lower level of the buildings, and cars are parked out front. Curry restaurants and bakeries are still open for business. As I look for a discreet place to land, I fly over the street, making sure I'm high enough to remain out of sight. My vision is stronger now that I'm not human. The lane is lit too brightly to land there. I rise and circle the area, doing my best to keep my golden wings away from the light. Not too far away, I spot a dark alley. Quietly, I land in the darkness and transform myself by folding away my wings. That way, I look human.

I walk out of the cramped area and into the light, passing some closed shop windows. I stop and pretend to look at the merchandise on display. It's the first time I've seen myself since I've become an angel. As I ignore the people walking past, I observe the young lady in front of me. I look to be about the same age as I was in my past life—eighteen. My skin seems pale, my facial features are well-defined in the right places. My lips are full, and my eyes are intense between the long, dark eyelashes. I watch as the elegant hand in the reflection reaches up and strokes the long, dark-brown hair. There isn't a curl in sight.

Wow. It would've taken me ages to style my hair and face to look like this when I was a human. The image looks similar to me in my last life but better, as if I've been photoshopped.

Letting my eyes wander over the reflection of my body, I see I'm wearing long pants and a long-sleeved shirt. It looks kind of like a bodysuit. I glance down my body for a better look. It's a mixture of royal blue and a deep-green, with a few flecks of golden-yellow I'm certain would match my wings. Glancing back at the window, I turn sideways to have a brief look behind, I look to be in perfect shape. But then I shouldn't be surprised, as training camp is a hard workout with all the fighting styles we learned from Archangel Michael.

I turn back to the window and do one last final check, establishing it's me.

Making sure no one is watching, I focus on my eyes and make them glow. Within the dark shadows of my eyes, a silver gray light emerges. Yes, that's me. Happy knowing what I look like in this form, I turn to continue walking toward Brick Lane. My deep-blue high-heeled boots click softly on the pavement.

I find the street and walk down the lane. It's completely different from any street of my childhood. The buildings are a mixture of shops and homes, or sometimes both together. I walk past some open restaurants and continue under the brick bridge. I pass two men on the street, and they stare at me strangely. I've confirmed that I look like a normal human, so I assume that it's odd for a young female to be walking alone in these parts. I'm not frightened and have no need to be, but I need to get off the street soon or become invisible.

I keep walking and pass a few more cars. It's a very long street. Hearing laughter in the distance, I notice that it's coming from one of the open restaurants. As I walk past the restaurant, I notice it's full of people. I catch sight of a calendar and realize that it's Saturday night. Glancing up at the sign, I see it's called Aladin Restaurant, spelled with only one d. Pondering the reason for the incorrect spelling, I shrug, it's probably just an eye-catching gimmick. Some of the smaller signage is claiming it to be "One of the Top 10 Greatest Indian Restaurants in London . . . Ever!" I don't know if that's true, but it sure smells good. It's a pity that I don't need to eat anymore.

I pass the restaurant and search the street for numbers. I'm not too far away now, so I find a dark area and make myself invisible. I find the apartment and teleport inside.

It's a cramped little place with more people living inside than there are bedrooms. I step around the furniture in search for the person I'm to protect. With so many people around, it's hard to believe this person needs protecting, though I won't question my instruction. The archangels must know that this person is in danger.

It's not ideal living conditions, but at least these people have a roof over their heads. The smell of incense fills the air. I pass a living room, and my eye catches the circular motion of smoke rising from the incense stick.

The conversation is too active for all the occupants to be permanent residents. I get the impression they have guests staying, making the small apartment seem more crowded. I can only see adults, so I assume that the younger members of the house have already gone to bed. The person I'm to protect is young.

I move on past the living room and climb the stairs. My person is here—I can feel her. When I reach the top of the stairs, I see two doors. One of them is closed. I feel a pull toward the closed door, but in case someone's awake, I don't open it. Instead, I transport myself silently into the room.

I'm in a child's room. It's dark with only a dim light shining from the nightlight. Sounds of several children's deep breathing fill my ears. I relax and turn off my invisibility, letting my eyes skim the room. There are two sets of bunks and two mattresses on the floor. The room is overcrowded, though the sleeping children don't seem to mind. As they sleep restfully, I step around them, studying their faces.

Each face is adorable. My protective instincts instantly awaken. These are very young boys and girls with the oldest girl being about ten years of age. Each child has the look of Bangladesh descent. The dark hair and dark features of these sleeping children are melting their way into my heart. There's nothing more adorable than a child deep in sleep.

I notice the blanket's fallen off the youngest child on one of the lower beds. He must be only three years old. By the appearance of the house, it's clear the families have little money. The heat isn't turned on, or, if it is, it's not on very high. The added heat from the extra bodies in the room helps, but the boy's arms are getting goose bumps.

I bend down and pull his blanket up around his neck. He stirs slightly, without waking from the different sensation on his skin. I stroke his hair lightly then leave him alone.

Standing up, I look at the other children. It's then that my eyes fall on her. She's on the other bunk bed at the bottom. Joya. She's the one I'm to protect. I step across the small open space and sit on the edge of her bed. Her naturally tanned skin is flawless under the pale light. I sit and study her features. Her long eyelashes fall over the tops of her cheeks. Her dark eyebrows pucker with the change of a dream. Long dark-brown hair flows loose on her pillow and frames her face. Embraced within her arms is a small plush toy. It's hard to see what it is within her clasp. A long pink ear falls over her arm.

Laughter floats up the stairs. I glance briefly at the door wondering what's so humorous.

I look back at the girl; she's only six, and for some reason she's in danger. It's difficult to believe when looking at her. Her family seems poor but caring. As I remain sitting at the end of her bed, I watch her sleep, listening to her faint heartbeat, and wait.

"I won't be leaving your side, little one," I whisper.

She stirs slightly and turns her head in the other direction.

CHAPTER THREE

The next morning, she wakes, and I make myself invisible. Her eyes open and I catch my breath. Oh, the sweet innocence swimming in those dark-brown puddles. As soon as the light hits those eyes, they fill with joy and happiness.

She throws her blanket off, flips her feet over the side of the bed, and scurries over to the nearest mattress on the floor. A pale-pink, flannelette floral nightie flaps around her ankles. She kneels on the mattress and shakes the sleeping girl in front of her.

"Sadia, Sadia. Wake up," she calls with excitement.

The young sleeping girl's eyes open a tiny crack. The girl moans softly.

"Sadia, wake up," Joya calls again while shaking her a little more. "Today is market day. We get to look at all the goodies in the market."

Sadia's eyes open wide, and she sits up straight. Excitement gleams from her face as she leaps out of bed. The hem of her long blue nightie falls toward the carpeted floor when she stands, and soft ringlets of dark, matted hair tumble around her shoulders.

I watch as the two girls preen themselves and get ready for an exciting day. They dress in the bathroom and hurry downstairs. Joya's mother has breakfast ready for the excited girls.

Looking at the two young girls brings back memories of when I was a young human. In my second life, I wasn't much older than Joya when death snatched me away. My upbringing was different from these two girls, but the excitement and innocence of childhood were the same.

I remember, even though I was only young, I'd already met my true love. I sigh deeply. Ah, yes, my first and only love. We'd met in the life before. Both of us emerged in a new life after our first innocent lives were taken away. It's unusual that both of us were killed at such a young age in our first lives, and introduced again in our second after living for a only few years. It's like we were destined to be with each other.

While the girls eat and talk excitedly with each other, I watch in my invisible state, and my eyes glaze over. I wonder where he is now. He reemerged with me in my third life, yet now we're separated. Last I knew, he was still a human—something I'll never be again.

The two girls finish their breakfast, and their mothers prepare to leave with Joya and Sadia to the Sunday Markets on Brick Lane. The need to focus on Joya and why she's in danger pulls me from my thoughts. As they leave, I follow behind, keeping myself invisible.

They stroll down the gray brick road toward the center of the markets. The crowd grows thicker with each step. Tired of people running into me, I discretely become visible. There are too many people wandering around for the girls and their mothers to notice that I'm following them. I watch as the girls touch and fiddle with everything within their reach. They giggle at the different items that are foreign to them.

As a stall owner glares at the girls, Joya's mother calls, "Joya, stop touching everything."

While putting the item down, Joya's face drops into a pout as she presses on toward her mother, her pretty sari rubbing around her legs. For a moment, the crowd blocks me. I can't see her.

Frantically my eyes search as my heart rate rises. A few minutes pass, and I can't see her or her friend. I begin to worry. I cannot fail on my first mission, especially with such a sweet young girl to protect. I start to push the surrounding people a little harder, trying to force my way through the crowd. I ignore the annoyed side-glances directed my way and maneuver through the tight gaps by twisting my body. The dark-brown hair of a little girl about the same height as Joya comes into view. My heart races—perhaps this's her. The little girl's head turns. She's not Joya. I give the girl a half-smile and push past her.

I continue pressing through the crowd. There's another young girl a few people away. This time I know it's Joya. It's her dark-brown hair, and her sari is the same. Right after I spot her, Sadia appears next to her and grabs her hand. I breathe a sigh of relief. She's still safe. I've not lost her. Sadia leads Joya back to follow their mothers. They stop at a sari stall admiring all the different colors and textures available.

I lean against a wall and observe them from a distance, watching closely across a less-condensed patch of people. As I watch the interaction between the mothers and daughters, my thoughts wander. Memories of my mother from my past life resurface. I remember the tender touches and hugs she gave me, the arms that'd embrace me affectionately over and again. I miss my mother. I wonder what happened to her after I died. She cared for me greatly, and day after day she put up with my abusive father. I could never understand why she didn't leave him.

He abused her mentally, verbally, and physically. I could see the bruises under her makeup, and I knew she hid the tears from me, expelling them during quiet times in her room. After I'd turned sixteen, I began trying to convince her to leave my dad. When he was absent, I'd plead with her to run away and start a secret life away from him—if that's what it'd take to keep her safe.

After two years, I was finally starting to get through to her. I could see the different look in her eye each time he abused her and the changed expression after he'd gone. It was slowly changing from hopelessness to defiance. She was about to leave when I visited from college. He started hitting her again because of some stupid reason. This time he'd hit her so hard that he'd knocked her unconscious in a matter of seconds. That's when I stepped in to defend her, and that's when he ended my life. The heat of anger swells inside me at the memory. He's the reason I'm here. He ended my third life. It's this memory that fuels my drive to protect the Innocents. People like him shouldn't be allowed to wander freely and unpunished, taking innocent lives whenever they choose.

I can feel my eyes tighten with anger. When I remember the reason I'm standing there, I refocus. I realize that Joya, Sadia, and their mothers are looking at me. They look haunted. I guess my face had a look of hatred on it, and they probably thought I was another racist staring at them in anger. I blink and rub my temples and give them a little weary smile. I hope this will convince them I'm not a racist or in any way casting hate in their direction. In any case, it would've been unnerving having a stranger watching so intensely. Because of my carelessness, I have to look away.

Turning a little to the side, I start to reprimand myself. I have to work on my skills and learn how to focus better. I've just made my first mission much harder. Now I've to be especially careful that no one notices me following Joya. The mothers would certainly be watching me closely.

I watch through my peripheral vision as they start to fold into the crowd. Having to face in another direction is proving difficult to keep a good eye on them, especially now that they're starting to move among many people. I'm considering turning invisible again when I hear someone calling.

"Joya! Joya!" It's young Sadia calling. She sounds lost.

Maybe Sadia has been separated from the small group. I know that she's not the one I'm sent to protect, but I'm not about to let Joya's friend come under danger. I turn, stepping closer to where I'd seen them not long before. I search the crowd for the group. Finally, my eyes fall on Sadia, beside her are the two mothers. She's safe. I see Joya's mother turn to see why Sadia is calling. After spotting Sadia, her eyes start to search for her daughter. Panic crosses her face.

She calls, "Joya! Joya!"

Trepidation begins to rise. She must be here somewhere. I search the crowd, scanning face upon face with each additional one becoming a blur, but still no Joya.

I begin to move around to search, and the large crowd hinders me. It's too thick. I can hear the mothers and Sadia still calling out as I press farther away, searching, but there's no response. I'm starting to panic. Where's she gone? I can't lose her. She's only a little girl and my first mission.

I call out, "Joya! Joya!" My concerns over being noticed vanish as I call louder. "Joya!"

All that I receive for my effort is stares from strangers. I continue to search frantically. Finding an alley, I stop on the corner. Searching this way isn't working. Leaning against the cold brick wall, I breathe deeply, trying to think. I still feel panic, but it subsides a little, so my breathing becomes more normal. My eyes start to clear, and my body calms. Something twinges from my core. A warm glowing sensation starts to build. Curious, I continue to breathe deeply, feeling the warmth grow. When it consumes my entire midsection, I feel the urge to walk farther down the alley. I follow the sensation. I don't know where I am, but I don't care. Following the pull, I pass a couple walking hand in hand, lost in their personal world.

I stop them. "Excuse me."

They look at me, alarmed that a stranger would approach them. Ignoring this, I continue, "Have you seen a little girl pass this way?"

The man looks to be in his twenties. He's freshly shaven and wearing strong cologne that makes my eyes water. Clearly he's trying to impress his lady. Doing my best to hide my reaction, I look farther up the alley, then back at the couple.

The young lady is shaking her head, and the man answers in a strong English accent. "We haven't been here very long and haven't seen anyone else but you."

Not wanting to waste any time, I mutter, "Thanks." But the warmth is still pulling me down the alley. I continue. I don't know where the warmth comes from—perhaps it's from the glowing bean that Archangel Michael gave us before our mission. Perhaps, just perhaps, it's Joya's life essence—a connection to her that helps us find our Innocent if we become separated. I'm going to go with this hunch; it makes sense.

I rush farther down the alley. I can no longer hear the desperate cries of Sadia and the mothers, but if my hunch is correct, they're still calling. A chilly breeze whips past me. I look at the bit of sky I can see through the gap between the buildings. The day has turned overcast. How fitting, it's just like my mood.

Suddenly, I feel the urge to stop and find myself looking at a weathered door with peeling paint. I reach for the knob and am surprised when it turns. As I push the door open, the hinges squeak. I grit my teeth and hope that the sound didn't alert anyone. Afraid, I remind myself I'm no longer human, and I press forward.

I close the door behind me, and surprisingly, it doesn't squeak. I search the entrance. Strips of wallpaper fold toward the floor. Underneath are exposed patches of the original plasterboard. Mold is growing on the wallpaper strips and the wall. To the left is a tight corridor leading to a dingy kitchen in the back. A stale stench hits my nose. Unwashed dishes are piled on the bench. Before the kitchen, doors veer off to the side. They don't look to be in any better condition than the one at the entrance.

To the right of the entrance is a staircase. Torn carpet with pulls hanging over the stair lips attempt to cover the wooden steps. At the top, the protective railing is coming loose and falling to the floor, leaving the edge of the next level exposed to the danger of the ledge.

I hear a creaking sound from the level above. I work my way across the entrance, glad that it had remnants of carpet buffing any sound from my heels. I progress up the stairs, trying to step where the nails are secured to avoid making noise. When I'm near the top, a light cough and sniffle sound from the room on the far left.

The door is slightly ajar, so I creep up to it and peek through the gap. I hold my breath.

I see Joya sitting on the dirty, carpeted floor. Her beautiful, dark-olive face is streaked with tears, and puffy red walls surround her eyes. She looks confused and scared, but for a six-year-old, she's handling the situation well, although I think the full reality of being abducted hasn't set in.

Next to her, I see movement. I push the door open the slightest bit, praying for no creaks. I exhale. No creaks, but then I hold my breath again. Sitting beside Joya is another little girl about the same age. This little girl is very pale skinned. Her light, pink dress is dirty, and her curly blonde hair falls matted to her shoulders. Smudges of dirt cover her cheeks, with lines running directly from her eyes along the inside of her cheeks to her jaw. The two girls are holding hands. They know they're in this together whether they like it or not.

Inside of me, the anger is welling. Emotions are something I haven't mastered even though I'm an angel. I'm supposed to be objective and follow the rules to protect the Innocents. My anger begins to boil. I shrug. I guess I've a lot to learn. As I barge into the room, I'm no longer worried about being quiet. The two girls glance up in shock.

Standing in the middle of the room, I take in the surroundings. Near the two girls is a mattress against the wall. It is dirty and sagging in the middle. There are no clean sheets or blankets. In fact, there are no sheets or items of warmth. Above the mattress is an uncovered window. It's closed but has no curtains or blinds to keep out the cold. I turn to the right in time to see a man stand up. He's alarmed but plasters a sneer on his face. He looks me up and down. I want to be sick.

"Hello, gorgeous!" He smiles and shows his astonishingly clean, straight teeth.

He wears new blue jeans and a black leather jacket. He appears to be in his late twenties and doesn't look poor like this house. In truth, if I saw him on the street, he'd look like a semidecent person. It pains me to think this way, knowing what he's done. I'm confused.

He steps toward me, still wearing that horrid smile. The girls scurry backward near the mattress under the closed window. The man continues my way. I can see on his face that he thinks he can dominate me.

Turning to face him, with my feet firmly placed, I ask, "What're you doing with these girls?" Anger is still churning inside of me. The closer he gets to me, the more it rises.

He clicks his tongue away from the top of his mouth and scoffs. "Oh, darling. You don't need to worry your pretty face over them. They're my nieces."

I can't believe he's trying to charm me. Yeah, right! Like that's going to work. I know he's lying. This guy is getting on my nerves. I step forward and say, "Of course they are—the family resemblance is so strong." I shake my head and screw up my face. "Seeing we're telling the truth, let me tell you my truth." I slowly take another step. "I've been sent by Archangel Michael to protect this little girl." I point at Joya. "The angels foretold that she'd become exposed to evil."

He looks at me like I'm crazy. To be honest, I don't

blame him, but that was my tactic. I step closer. His eyes start to hold some uncertainty.

He laughs, and it sounds a little nervous. "So, sweetheart, you're telling me that you're an angel?"

I nod.

He slaps his thigh and chokes out a laugh. "Well, would you look at that? You really fill in the cliché of looking like an angel. You may be a little nutty, though. Don't worry, I like them a little on the crazy side." He winks at me.

Grr! He's giving me the creeps. I step even closer and smile sweetly. "Wow, so quick to believe me. I never thought it'd be possible." I make sure I wiggle my hips. "Tell you what, seeing you're so happy to accept what I am, let me pass on the special message to you from the archangels." I hold out my hands and place them on his temples.

An anxious look passes across his hazel eyes. He steps back quickly and swipes my hands to the side. He shakes his index finger at me.

"Ha, ha, no touching the head, sweetheart. That's only a privilege for people I trust." He reprimands me while stepping back. He strokes his dark-brown hair into place while looking a little jumpy.

"What's wrong?" I ask. "Don't you want your message from the archangels?" I feign innocence. "It's just a simple message." I take another step forward.

He steps back and stands in a defensive mode. "I'm starting to think you're a little crazier than my type, so it's time to leave." He points to the door.

I sigh. "I wish it were that simple," I say, with my

expression turning serious. "But I can't leave until I've passed on this message." I take another step forward, closing him into a corner.

Panicking, he starts to lash out and throws a fist at my face. I twist slightly to the side, watching it pass without hitting its target. His mouth drops. It's clear to me already that he's not trained to fight. He tries to kick me, but I catch his lower leg and scoop it up, breaking his knee with my other hand in a downward strike. The sound of bones cracking and tendons ripping reach my ears. He screams out in pain and clutches his knee, falling to the floor.

Now is my opportunity. I'm not here to kill, no matter how deviant the person is. I lean over him, my long dark-brown hair falling forward, blocking the edges of my view. I'm no longer under threat and neither are the girls. I place my hands on his temples. Ignoring his screams of pain, I continue. I release the "message" with a white light that penetrates from my fingertips into his brain. He throws his head back, and I see his eyes properly for the first time. They play me his life story, including the horrible plans he had for the two little girls and many girls following them. I want to be sick, but I continue passing on the message.

The message I'm giving this man, and will be giving many others in the future, is a conscience. It doesn't sound like much but try to imagine living without one for a night and then waking up with it the next day. Imagine your torment when you remember all the bad you did that night. Now picture what it'd be like for a person who's lived without a conscious for a very long time and then was suddenly given one. Their conscience would be burdened by all the horrible things they'd done.

After the white light fades and the unforgivable parts of his life have passed before my eyes, I release my hands. Backing away, I look at his face. He's spooked. I rummage through his pockets quickly for his phone and dial the emergency hotline, calling him an ambulance. I place his phone back in his pocket and see he's not moving. Yes, his leg would be in excruciating pain, but the look on his face says he's not going anywhere soon. The torment is eating him inside. This look concerns me. It makes me feel queasy and unsettled. I saw all he did in his past, along with his plans for the future. I agree 100 percent he used to desire evil, but I still saw some good. Perhaps, given the correct guidance, he may change.

After casting him one final glance, I turn to the girls. I give them both a cuddle and look them in the eyes. "I'm taking you back to your families, girls." I smile. Joya looks relieved, and the other young girl lets a few happy tears run down her face. She throws her arms around me again. When she releases me, I ask, "How long have you been here?"

"Three sleeps," she croaks. Her eyes are hopeful.

A mixture of sadness and happiness floods through me. "Then let's get you home. I'm sure your mommy and daddy will be missing you." I stand and take both girls' hands, and we walk down the stairs and out the door.

CHAPTER FOUR

By the time I return Joya to her home, her mom and visitors are frantic. The wailing travels to the street. They've given up the search outdoors, leaving it to the police. I step forward, knock on the door, and then retreat while watching Joya, making sure she remains safe. The door opens slowly, and the tear-streaked face of Sadia's mother appears. She looks down and sees Joya and starts to yell into the house while scooping Joya into her arms.

The warmth in my stomach explodes to full capacity, heating my whole body, then dies away. It is like it's telling me I've completed my mission. I return to the street, grabbing the little blonde-haired girl by her hand. I turn back to Joya's house. Her mom is there, hugging her and crying tears of joy. Next to her is Sadia's mother; she spots me, and I can see the recognition in her eyes. Her face is full of questions. She can see that I'm not going to stay, so she mouths the words thank you. I smile and walk away, hand in hand with the remaining girl.

An enormous joy fills my heart, knowing that I've succeeded with my first mission. Not only that, I've also managed to save another little girl as a bonus. Her angel hadn't made it in time, if she'd an angel allocated to her. The world is short of protection angels these days, with the rising corruption and lack of people with a conscience. I shake my head. What's happening to the world? It used to be a more caring place.

I pick up the girl and cuddle her, placing her head against my chest and cover her eyes. "Sleep, little one." I say. "You need your rest. I'll carry you there." The girl must be exhausted. In no time her body goes limp in my hands and heats up, her breathing becomes deep and even. Now she's asleep. I turn myself invisible and spread my wings, cradling her in my arms as I fly her home. She needs to get home as soon as possible.

As I fly, my mind wanders back to their captor. I did what I was instructed to do by giving him a conscience. I agree he needed intervention and needed to learn to do the right thing, but the whole process is unsettling. Something seems off about it all. Something makes me feel as though it's a cruel way to punish him. I know I shouldn't have any feelings of sympathy for him, as he was the scum of the earth, but there's something else I saw during the process. I don't know why I'm concerned. I guess it's the way he looked after I'd finished transferring the conscience.

The girl stirs in my arms, and I hug her closer. The breeze is much cooler up here. My eyes search around below. It looks to be the place. I lower myself to the ground, fold my wings away, and in a sheltered place I turn visible again. With the girl still in my arms I step forward and onto her street. Her house is in the distance. I kiss her on the forehead, which is still full of dirt with the tear marks still evident on her face. I've thought about cleaning her up before taking her back, but I know her family won't care—they just want her back. Her eyes, as blue as a clear sky, flutter open.

"Hey," I say. "Time to wake up. I think you have some people who want to see you."

She turns her head and looks around at the houses. "Home," she croaks. A deeper peace spreads across her face.

I nod and stand outside her house. After putting her down I knock on the door. "Take care little one," I say. I kiss her on the forehead again and walk away, keeping an eye on her to make sure she stays safe. When I reach the corner of the property's fence, the door opens. A pale-skinned man in his thirties stands at the entrance. He's thin, and his face is downcast and worn. When he first opens the door, he looks annoyed at the intrusion. The irritation is replaced with excitement when he looks down at the little girl. Instantly he bends down and scoops her into his arms. Tears of joy run down his face. His eyes search the street, but he doesn't see me. I've turned invisible. Happiness fills me while watching the homecoming.

I turn to leave. I'm supposed to go back to the remote island base, ready to receive my next mission. I still can't shake this pestering feeling. If I'm quick, maybe Archangel Michael won't know I've taken a detour. I know there will be penalties if I don't have a good reason, but I have to risk it. I have to check on the girls' kidnapper. I need to see how he handles his newly acquired conscience.

I open my wings and fly. I can't resist the urge even though it's slower than teleporting. I love feeling of the wind beneath my wings.

As it's still daylight, I remain invisible and fly toward the Royal London Hospital. It's the closest to Brick Lane, so I assume that's where he is.

Once there, I make myself visible and search the newly admitted patients from the emergency ward. Looking for the familiar face, I study each patient. My shoes click softly on the polished floor, mixing with the noises from the health staff and patients. It's a depressing place, with all the sickness and injury. Thankfully for most of the people here, they're only in for a temporary visit. I continue to travel among the rooms. I've checked every room, and I'm certain that I must look lost or suspicious.

A nurse in her blue uniform stops and asks, "Are you looking for anyone in particular?"

She's slightly plump. Her skin is fair and her eyes hazel and kind, but they also threaten consequences if someone aggravates her or her patients. Her unspoken threat doesn't bother me, but I'm not here to cause trouble.

I answer, "Yes. Actually, I'm looking for someone who was admitted this morning—a man with a broken knee."

Her eyes cloud. "Oh."

"Did he not get admitted here?" I ask, wondering why her expression became somber.

She sighs. "If it's the man I think you're talking about, then follow me."

She leads me past a few more rooms and stops in front of a closed door. She turns to me and says, "We had a no name admitted today with a broken knee. I hope he's not the one you're looking for." She places her hand on the door handle and balks. "Prepare yourself."

I frown, wondering why I'm preparing myself. Curious, I stand in front of the door as it swings back revealing a room with only one bed. Lying on the bed is a figure underneath a sheet. I stare, wondering why a sheet completely covers a man with a broken leg. I look at the nurse. Her face is sympathetic.

"Why's he covered?" I ask. "Didn't he just have a broken knee?"

She nods and looks me straight in the eyes. "That was his only major physical injury, but there was something wrong with his mental health when the ambulance picked him up." She sighs and places her hands over her stomach.

"What do you mean?" I ask. I can feel the fear rising within me.

"He seemed spooked or something—like he'd witnessed a real-life horror." She steps toward the bed. "Before I tell you anymore, come and see if he's the man you're looking for."

I step closer to the bed, crossing my fingers behind

my back and hoping it's not the man I saw this morning. I watch as she grabs the top edge of the white sheet and slowly folds it back from his face. With each bit revealed, I find it harder to breathe. It is him. He looks ghostly white. I stare at the lifeless form in front of me while lost in dark thoughts, trying to understand how he has died. He was so full of life this morning.

I hear a faint voice beside me, but I don't truly hear it. I think I hear it again, but I'm not sure. I continue staring. A hand lands on my arm, and I jump from the contact.

Looking at the owner of the touch, I find myself looking at the nurse's sympathetic side. "Is he the one?" she asks.

I nod.

"I'm sorry, dear. He must've been close to you. You look horrible."

I shake my head. "No, not close, but I knew him." I choke remembering the evil and the potential for good that was within him. "What happened?"

"He committed suicide. We think it was because of the mental problem he had that I told you about."

"What? How?" I stammer.

Her eyes divert to the floor. "He had a mobile phone on him. He smashed it and slashed his wrists with the glass from the screen. I'm so sorry . . . we couldn't save him."

I feel my jaw drop. I had returned his phone to his pocket after I called the ambulance. I thought I was doing him a favor. I'm devastated. I gave him a conscience, which had put him in a mentally unstable state, but I also gave his phone back. It was his weapon.

Wishing to be alone with him, I turned to the nurse. "It wasn't your fault." I try to reassure her, not wishing to cause any more grief today. "Thank you for letting me know." I look back at the kidnapper and sigh, allowing my shoulders to droop. "Do you mind if I've a few minutes alone with him." I'm confused. I need space to think before returning to the base.

Thankfully she nods. "Of course." She turns and leaves, closing the door behind her.

I stand over the body and study his face. Everything looks normal. Nothing looks weird or out of place. They warned us that people react differently to receiving a conscience, yet I didn't expect this.

Did he really deserve to die? He was far from innocent, but I struggle with the idea that a life was taken because a conscience was forced inside. He died instead of being guided and taught a conscience.

If the person given a conscience doesn't commit a crime too extreme, then what happens? Are they still unable to handle the guilt of what they did? They, too, would have the opportunity to kill themselves. What if the person was doing these bad things only because they're stuck in a bad place? I shake my head. Their conscience would take over, and their guilt would be more than they could handle. There has to be a better way.

My eyes wander down his arm. I move the sheet and reveal the puncture marks that ended his life. I couldn't shake the thought that he had good in him, too. Doesn't that make me a murderer? I thought angels are supposed to protect and teach love, not kill people.

I stumble over to the chair in the corner and cover my face with my hands. It doesn't seem right. I shake my propped head. It just doesn't seem right, I think again. There's got to be a better way.

Tears roll down my face. I should go, but I can't get up. I can't find the energy to go back to base. Guilt and confusion have zapped the energy from my body. And I've to sort out my emotions before facing Archangel Michael again. He can't see me in such turmoil.

I don't know how long I sit undisturbed in the dark room. I've lost all track of time. With my head planted in my hands, potential solutions run through my mind. Then I feel an atmospheric change within the room. I look up. Standing in the far corner is my favorite being in my new world.

"Blue," I say as I stand and throw my arms around him. I'm so happy to see him. "Weren't you sent to Paris?"

He nods and wraps his arms around me. His warmth and comfort seep through the skin on his bare chest, and I move in deeper, trying to get more. He wraps his royal blue wings to encircle both of us.

"If you're meant to be in Paris, then what brings you here?" I look up, and his ocean-blue eyes greet me— they're always so welcoming.

"You," he answers. "You bring me here."

"What do you mean?" I ask puzzled. We're friends, nothing more.

He releases me and steps back . He looks at his waist

and clasps a metal loop on his pants. My eyes follow his movement and fall upon the little charm I gave him and Yellow before we left the base. For some reason, the angel in the middle with gold wings is glowing.

I watch it glow, then fade, and then glow, and then fade. It's impressive, but I don't understand how it's happening. I look at my own charm. Nothing. It isn't doing anything. "What's happening?" I ask as I look at him confused.

"I placed an enchantment on the charm you gave me." One edge of his mouth lifts in a smile as he watches the understanding flow to my face. "I did this so it'd tell me if you're in trouble."

"Really?" I ask. The attention slightly embarrasses me, but at the same time I feel special.

He nods.

"Did you do it for Yellow, too?"

He wobbles his heads slightly from side to side and shyness emerges on his face. "Well . . . yeah." He runs his hand through his hair. "But yours burns as well, just in case I miss the glow."

I feel my face heating up.

He grabs my hand and says, "Here, feel it."

I allow my finger to touch the surface, and I'm surprised by just how hot it is. "Doesn't that burn you?"

"Not really." He shrugs. "The heat needs to penetrate through these pants first, but I can still feel the warmth. Anyway, what's going on with you? Why're you glowing?"

I pull away and look down. I should be so ashamed, but all I want to do is tell him everything. If he tells

Archangel Michael, I could be in real trouble, maybe even thrown into the abyss.

He touches my chin lightly with his fingers and pulls my face up so my eyes meet his. "You know you can tell me." His eyes are sincere.

I think for a moment, and then I begin to spill my secret. "I . . . I'm struggling with our mission."

"What do you mean?" he asks. "I thought you wanted to protect the Innocent."

"I do," I say. "I really do. But my first mission has resulted in the perpetrator killing himself." I study his face to watch the changes in his features as I tell him my problem. So far, I don't see any judgment.

Pointing to the man on the bed, I say, "He couldn't face the guilt of his conscience, so he ended his life." I look at him searching again for judgment. I can't see any. I continue, "He had good inside of him, too. Maybe, just maybe, with the right circumstances, he might've changed."

Blue shakes his head, but I still don't see any criticism in his eyes. I hold on to hope that he might understand.

"But we've been trained and are under strict instructions to fill these wrong-doers with a conscience," Blue says. "We can't deviate or else we break the rules."

My hopes crash, and my heart drops. I turn away and face the bed. "It's okay. I shouldn't expect you to understand." I shake my head. My heart is crushed. My best friend doesn't understand, so neither will the rest of the fledglings at the base. "Why don't you go on ahead to base? I'll follow soon."

My arm is pulled gently from behind. "Hey. I do understand. You've just been through a lot, having your first mission ending in a death, and all, because of something you did to follow your training. I get that. I really do." He spins me around to face him and looks me in the eyes. He reaches his hand up and strokes my hair around my ear. "But you can't just not obey the rules. It'll be the end of you. I don't want to lose you . . . my new best friend," he says.

I look at him and try to smile. His eyes hold concern.

He continues, "We'll work it out together. Okay?"

I nod. I haven't come to a conclusion, but having someone who understands and share my concerns with —well, that's a good start.

"What about Yellow?" I ask.

He shakes his head. "This's to be our secret. Leave Yellow out of it."

I nod in agreement.

He grabs my hand. "Come, let's fly back. Despite your unhappy ending, we did good today. You should be proud."

CHAPTER FIVE

Down below, our tropical island waits for our return. I scan our old stomping grounds and see that Yellow is back, along with a couple of others. Blue and I land and let our wings air. It's nice not to have to put them away. We approach Yellow, who's standing at the edge of the island looking over the water.

"Hey, Yellow," I say trying to sound casual. "How'd it go?"

She spins around to face us. "Hey, Blue and ahh . . . Multicolor." She squeals and runs forward to give us a hug.

I smile. They still haven't figured out what to call me. It'd be a lot easier if the archangels would allow us to use our human names. They have their rules, and they're to be abided, even if they're old-fashioned. The archangels had been around since the beginning of time and know best, so no name it is until we earn one.

"So did you protect the human?" Blue asks, stepping back from her embrace.

Her eyes sparkle. "I sure did. It was so satisfying." Her eyes fall on Blue's bare chest. "Didn't you go to Paris?" She crosses her arms.

He nods.

"And you still didn't grab a shirt?" She cocks an eyebrow while scrutinizing him.

He shrugs. "Hey, I went to work, not to shop."

She shakes her head, and her blonde hair flicks into her face, aided by the wind. She retrieves a gold hairpin from her yellow bodysuit and pins some of it back. "How'd your missions go?" She looks at both of us.

"Like you said—satisfying," Blue says without a pause.

Her eyes turn to me, and I do my best to concentrate on the joy of returning the girls to their families. I look at her and smile. "It was such a wonderful feeling to help the two young girls back to their family."

"You had children?" Yellow squeals. "Oh, how exciting and rewarding." She runs forward and throws her arms around me. "And you said two?"

I finish the hug and step back, trying to get some air. "Ah, yes. Well, no. I was to protect one child, and when I was protecting her, I was able to rescue another approximately the same age. It was just luck. You know, at the right place, at the right time." I feel awkward under the friendly interrogation, and I don't want to let on about my conscience receiver. I try to change the subject. "So, is Archangel Michael here yet?" I turn away from her to look around and to hide my face. I don't want to force the happiness anymore.

"I believe he's coming back every afternoon to give

out new missions to the returned angels. You've come back just in time. From what the others were saying, he should be here shortly." She gazes around the immediate island as if she were looking for him.

"Have you talked to the others who've returned?" I ask.

"Sure have. Everyone seems happy with how it all went. How'd you find the whole transferring of the conscience thing?"

"Ah," I say hesitantly, I don't want to go into the details.

"It was a little strange," Blue answers for me.

She reaches forward and touches Blue on the forearm. "Wasn't it just? I saw pieces of their life. It was fascinating seeing someone else's life flash before your eyes."

"Fledglings." The call sounds behind us. We turn our heads to see Archangel Michael standing nearby.

"Jeez! Where'd he come from?" Yellow blurts out and giggles, placing a hand over her mouth.

All the other fledglings are surrounding him. Butterflies fill my stomach, and a tightness forms in my throat. He stands still, watching us intensely as we move forward. I stick by Blue. For some reason, he makes me feel safe.

When we're in our positions, Archangel Michael steps forward to the first being on the left. This fledgling is Orange. He stands straight and tall with the orange tints in his auburn hair glowing in the sun. His clothes are different shades of orange, and, unlike Blue, he wears a deep-orange T-shirt.

Archangel Michael looks him in the eye and places a finger on his forehead. A white light shines from the tip and into Orange's head. It only lasts a couple of seconds, but it makes me feel uneasy. I don't understand what he's doing, but it can't be good.

Archangel Michael steps back and places a hand on Orange's left shoulder. "Good work, fledgling. You have served well."

A smile creeps onto Orange's face. He looks relieved.

Archangel Michael summons the small cloud in between his hands and reaches in, withdrawing a shiny bean for Orange. Orange takes it and swallows as our leader moves along to Blue.

Blue stands straight with his royal blue wings folded down his back as the archangel approaches. He places a finger on Blue's forehead while he looks deep into his eyes. A white light passes through the finger just as it had with Orange.

I'm panicking. He's reading their minds. How am I going to bypass this? I can't let him see my conflicting thoughts over the conscience implants—he'd be so angry. I have to find a way to block it, and quickly.

Blue's finger probe lasts only a few seconds. Archangel Michael pulls away and places a hand on Blue's left shoulder. "Good work, fledgling. You have served well."

I'm happy for Blue, but I roll my eyes. Blue always does well. Archangel Michael prepares the bean for Blue's next mission and then steps toward me. My palms are sweaty, and I'm glad I don't have to shake his hand. I'm still wondering if I can block my conflicting thoughts.

His sapphire-blue eyes are boring into mine. It feels awkward, but I've no choice. The finger touches my forehead, and a warmth seeps into my skin around that point. I can see my mission in front of my eyes. I see the replay of the man's life, bad and good, pass in front of me again. I feel the sickness that came with the visions and then the face, the haunted face of my perpetrator. The vision passes to the two young girls and their families and the joy of returning them safely home. I then see the hospital and the perpetrator who'd taken his life.

The warmth leaves my forehead, and I realize the archangel has removed his finger. He did not see my conflict over the inserted conscience, but I'm not breathing a sigh of relief yet. I study Archangel Michael's expression, trying to pick up any emotion. He's unreadable.

He reaches forward, rests his hand on my shoulder, and says, "Good work, fledgling. You have served well; you saved an extra Innocent as well as the allocated one. But you should never check on the victim of our punishment. You may not like what you find."

I can't hide the frown. I'm confused, but he doesn't seem to notice. He holds his hands together and forms the cloud. He reaches in to grab my shining bean and holds it out for me on the palm of his hand. I take it and swallow it, my stomach warming the second the bean reaches it. I hope this mission won't turn out with such a bad ending.

Archangel Michael progresses along the line of fledglings. Even though I passed, I'm the only one with a correction. The others all get the simple "Good work, fledgling. You have served well."

Am I the only one curious about what happens to our perpetrators, or am I the only one who had someone die? I had to see what happened to my perpetrator. The look on his face after the process is plastered across my mind.

With the final fledgling completed, Archangel Michael stands in front of us. He almost looks proud.

"Well done, fledglings. You have all protected your Innocents. Go forth and complete your new mission with confidence." He looks at each of us individually. "Might I remind you to come back to base as soon as you have completed your mission." His eyes fall on me. "It is not wise, or encouraged, to visit the receiver of the conscience."

I try to hold his gaze, but so many mixed emotions are flowing through me. How can I care for one person but not the other when I see goodness in both? His gaze finally leaves me as he paces in front of the fledglings.

I sneak a quick look at Blue. He turns at the same time. His eyes express concern, but he puts on a smile for me. I can see he's trying to make me feel better.

In my peripheral vision, I see Archangel Michael turn back and head our way again. I spin to face him and so does Blue. We're soldiers, fighters for the Angel Army. We're supposed to stand at attention.

"Fledglings, you are dismissed," Archangel Michael finishes.

I exhale, glad it's over. At the same time, I worry about my new mission and how I'm to handle the conflict of interest.

Blue moves closer. He's about to talk when something barges into me on my right side. I turn to see who it is. Yellow is inches away from my face.

"You went to check on your perpetrator?" Yellow blurts out in a whisper. Her eyes are wide with shock. "Are you mad? You're going against the rules and good advice, causing yourself trouble."

I take a step back, gaining some personal space. My shoulders slouch forward. "I know. I shouldn't have done it." Forcing a smile, I try to look sincere. "Don't worry. I won't do it again."

"Well, I should hope not. You're playing with fire doing silly things like that. I'd hate to lose you, or know you're locked up in the abyss. I can't think of anything worse. Promise me you won't do it again."

"It's all right, Yellow. Stop stressing. I won't do it again." I look deep into her golden-brown eyes, making a promise I know I won't be able to keep.

CHAPTER SIX

My next mission is in Prince Albert, South Africa. The atmosphere couldn't be more opposite to the city of London. It's a small town in the middle of a desert. I've gone from cold and cloudy weather to hot and sunny. The streets are empty of vehicles and people. It's a quaint little town in the middle of the rolling hills at the gateway to the Great Karoo.

I land in a secluded place behind some trees and fold away my wings. I'm greeted by the fresh smell of early morning mixed with the scent of blossoming flowers. I walk down Church Street past the Dutch Reformed Church. My intuition tells me I should walk this way. Despite the place seeming so dry, established bushes grow between the buildings. The street is lined with a mixture of shops, galleries, antique stores, and a handful of restaurants. The surrounding houses are a mixture of Dutch, Karoo, Victorian, and French homes as well as other styles with which I'm not familiar.

As I walk past the Swartberg Hotel, a farmer's

pickup truck with an open bed drives past. It's full of day laborers, their skin a blended colour mixed between dark and pale. They're being taken to a farm for the day's work. Mesmerized, I watch as it drives past. Laughter and chatter fill the air. There must be at least twenty standing people crammed in the back. It's such a contrast to the country of my last life. In Australia, this is illegal, if not highly frowned upon, but each of the workers seemed happy and grateful for the lift.

A couple of males yell out in Afrikaans. It's not a language I understood as a human, but as an angel I've the privilege of understanding all languages. I don't quite catch what they say through the rattling noise of the truck and chatter from their companions, but the gist seems to be a little inappropriate. I looked down at what I'm wearing. My full-length bodysuit isn't a good way to blend in. As soon as they're out of sight, I make myself invisible. I don't want to stand out.

Then I see her. Riding a bike down the street, going in the direction of the pickup truck, is my next Innocent. Her high cheekbones are pushed higher thanks to her smile. A soft churning and clinking sound comes from her bicycle pedals as they respond to the commands of her feet. Her hair is braided in cornrows. It looks gorgeous on her, accentuating her face. Her happiness is catching and seems to make her even more beautiful. She's in her early twenties and is clearly happy with her life. Wait, is that singing I can hear coming from her direction?

Dressed in long blue shorts and a simple black T-shirt with sneakers on her feet, she continues past me along the road. The bike looks brand new. From the information I received of Louisa, it's a recent gift from her boss. Noticing that she's riding at a fairly fast pace, I release my wings and fly above her. She doesn't slow down as she rides past all the main buildings and out of town.

I don't know where she's going. I believe it's not the usual path to her work. Perhaps she's just getting some more practice on her new gift.

I follow as she continues to travel along the lonely road. The distance is nearly an hour's drive by car to the next town. We're half a mile out of town when she stops and turns around. The temperature is rising despite the early hours of the morning. The air holds a dry heat, not like the tropics, but this doesn't stop beads of sweat from trickling down Louisa's face. She raises a hand, wipes it away, and presses along happily on her new bike.

A faint rumbling approaches from behind. I flick my wings and spin around. I can see my wings' golden feathers glowing in the early morning sun. When I'm invisible, they're slightly transparent, which helps me see if I've turned on the invisibility correctly or not. Through my wings, I see the outline of a white car. I spread my wings out wide and assess the car. It's a new Mercedes. Squinting at the license plate, I see it's not from around here. Even though this place is in the middle of nowhere, it still attracts tourists.

I turn around. Louisa is still peddling toward the town. She must be only a quarter mile away and still going a good pace. The car approaches her, slows down, and pulls over just in front of her. She stops singing and stops before she reaches the car.

A pale man opens the car door and steps onto the road. He's a stocky build and looks to be in his midtwenties. The sunglasses he wears covers a decent portion of his face, and he flashes Louisa a broad smile, showing off his straight, white teeth. Stroking his fingers through his pale-brown hair, which is long enough to touch the tops of his ears, he walks in her direction.

I circle above, watching. So far, the man just seems friendly, but my hair is rising on the back of my neck. If I've been sent here at this moment to protect Louisa, this could be the perpetrator.

I can hear the engine still running as Louisa slows to a stop. She doesn't look comfortable. There are no choices available to her out in the middle of nowhere with only on a bicycle. Even in a trusting country town, it's good to see she's had enough exposure to the outside world to be wary. She waits for him to speak.

Still smiling, he says, "I'm wondering if you can help me."

I recognize his English accent as Afrikaans. Does he not know he's in a mostly Afrikaans-speaking area?

"I think I'm lost." He pulls out a paper map from his pocket. It surprises me in this technology age, and he steps closer to her to show her his map. "I'm looking for this turnoff here." He steps closer again, making sure she can see.

Louisa leans forward. Instantly, he reaches out and places an arm around her shoulders. The gesture seems friendly enough, except he walks her to the car. From where I am, I can see her body tense . She's not comfortable with his embrace. She twists in the opposite direction, escaping his hold. Stepping back away from him, she trips on a clump of desert grass on the side of the road.

He reaches behind his back and pulls out a gun. He aims it at her and demands, "Get in the car."

Her face turns pale. She stares at him unmoving and in shock.

He steps forward, holding the gun firmly in his two hands, pointing it at her. "I said, get in the car."

She looks down the main road to Prince Albert. Not one car is in sight. Slowly, she crawls to her feet.

When I've seen enough, I land softly on the ground behind him. Folding my wings away, I make myself visible. Louisa spots me and stares. I don't blame her, considering I've appeared out of thin air. Giving her half a smile, I hold a finger to my lips. She's going to be in shock later and will probably think she imagined this. I indicate to her to move to her left at the count of three. I hope she understands, but if she doesn't, she should still be safe—it's just a precaution. I hold up my hand in a fist, the inside facing her. I lift my index finger —one. I lift my middle finger—two. I lift my third finger—three.

Instantly she dives to her left. At the same time, I step to his right. His eyes catch sight of me and then bulge. He's too late. With a palm strike, I slam straight into his outstretched hands, sending them pointing to his left. A shot fires, but it lands in the desert more than three feet away from Louisa. Before he has time to react, I jump, spinning around and my heel connects to the side of his head. I land balanced on my feet. As he falls to the ground with a thud, I stand over him to assess the damage. He's knocked unconscious.

Straightening up, I look at Louisa. She's still in shock. "It's okay now." I try to reassure her. "I'll handle him from here."

She says nothing. Her face is still a pale-coffee color as she stares at me with her full lips stretched open.

"Are you okay to ride home?" I ask. I understand her shock, but I need to deal with the man, and I don't want to rush it this time. I can't do that and help her get home.

She nods and staggers to her bike, picking it up from the side of the road. She throws a leg over the bar and then turns to me at the last moment. "Thank you," she mutters.

"Hey, that's what I'm here for." I smile. "Now go and keep living your caring, open life. Okay? Don't let this change you." I sound like I'm preaching, but this isn't my intention so I flick my hand in an off you go movement and say, "Take care."

She nods and steps down on the pedal, riding back to Prince Albert.

The warm exploding sensation fills my body. I've protected my Innocent.

My eyes wander over the desert plains and hills. There isn't a soul in sight. I squat down and touch a finger to the man's forehead. I shouldn't be doing this. I should be giving him a conscience, but I need to know.

A white glow exits my finger as I look into his mind and soul. I witness bad, lots of bad, especially in the recent past. I dig a little deeper, and I begin to observe traces of good and innocence. I see days when he used to be happy and willing to help people. What changed? I search deeper. I can see more good, but I can't find what caused him to change.

I remove my finger and sit back. How am I supposed to insert a conscience into him that could kill him, when it's clear he used to be good? Maybe he could be coerced into being good again and grow a conscience, rather than being bombarded with one right after he's committed many evils.

Conflicted, I stand and pace next to his body. I need more time.

The car is safely pulled far enough off the road. Placing a hand on it, I make it invisible, then pick him up, release my golden wings, and fly to a place out of sight in case someone passes. I place him down in the middle of a small cluster of hills. A snake sees me and disappears into the desert grass. Happy to be left alone, I sit and observe the man while he lies motionless.

What am I supposed to do? If I don't force a conscience on him before returning to base, I'll be in a lot of trouble with the archangels and possibly sent to the abyss. But on the other hand, if I do as required and insert him with a conscience, he might kill himself or go insane from the guilt. What about all the good inside him?

I place my head in my hands. I don't know how long I sit there. A hawk screeches overhead, briefly casting a shadow over us. I look up just in time to see it scoop up the snake that'd slithered away earlier.

The desert is warming up as the day progresses, and the man is starting to sweat under the sun. I see a medium-size tree not far away, so I pick him up and carry him to it, placing him in the small amount of shade. As I stand up, a whoosh sounds behind me. Surprised by the sound, I turn. My eyes fall on Blue. His dark-brown eyebrows are crushed together with worry.

"What're you doing?" he asks. His voice leaks concern. The sunlight catches on his magnificent wings.

My shoulders slump. I look past his bare torso to the charm hanging from his pants. The colorful angel is glowing again. I try to stall for time, so I point to it and ask the obvious, "Did the charm report me again?"

He raises an eyebrow and nods. "Hey," he says softly as he walks forward. "You're concerning me. Why haven't you finished your mission and headed back?" He looks at the unconscious man lying under the tree. "Clearly you've succeeded in your mission up until the final part."

"I . . . I . . . What if there's another way?" I stammer.

He looks at me and the worry creases in his forehead deepen. I'm putting him through stress he doesn't need. He probably thinks I'm about to lose my sanity.

"I don't want to say this because I know you've heard it before," he says, "but we have to do what's expected of us. It is why we were created. These people won't stop." His arms are spread out to the side with his palms up. "Please, just finish the mission and let's go. I couldn't bear it if you were exiled or sent to the abyss."

"I know . . . and I'm sorry that I'm putting you through this. I was trying to work it out on my own. I've had a look into his mind and soul, and again I see good. It's in the past, but I see it. Do you not wonder what made these people change?"

"I haven't really thought about it. I've been concentrating on what I'm trained to do—be a good warrior, obey orders, and protect the Innocents."

He steps forward, holding my shoulders gently; his voice is pleading. "I know this's what you want, too, but somehow you seem to get emotionally involved. It's messing you up. There are casualties in war, and this's a war to protect the Innocents."

In many ways he reminds me of Archangel Michael but with a modern, softer side. He'd be an incredible warrior if he ignored me.

I look deep into his eyes. "Just humor me, please. Take a look into his soul."

He studies my face, releases my shoulders, and strolls over to the unconscious man. Then he crouches down and places a finger on the man's forehead. A white light glows from it.

I study his face. It's etched with sadness.

A few minutes later he releases his finger and looks at me. Hesitantly he says, "I understand what you're saying."

"But?"

"A conscience must still be inserted into him," Blue says slowly.

"What?" I cross my arms. "After all you just saw, you still want to take the risk?" I'm not happy. Maybe Blue isn't the sensitive guy I think he is.

His eyes are pleading. "The way I see it, both ways are a risk. If we insert a conscience, then we risk him killing himself or going insane. But, if we leave him and try to get him to regrow a conscience, then he may not change, and I'll lose you." He sits back on his feet. "I'm certain the archangels won't smile down on you for disobeying their orders." He stands and makes his way over to me. Looking me in the eyes he says, "I know you're not a weak soul, but if you can't do this, I'll do it for you."

I'm shocked. "But, you can't do that. They'll find out."

"We don't know that. Maybe they'll not see it." He shakes his head.

"I don't want you to put yourself on the line for me—this's my problem, my mess."

Lifting one side of his mouth in a half-smile he says, "That's what friends are for, right?"

I turn away to ponder while looking at the desert plains. It's a strange desert—dry but not completely barren and used as good farming lands for produce and ostriches. After a few moments, still undecided, I turn back. I see Blue crouching over the man. He's already inserting a conscience. I remain torn, but he's made the decision for me.

When completed, he scoops up the man and flies him back to his car. Following, I assist him by making the car visible again, so he can return him to the driver's seat. I'm sure this man will be in for a shock when he wakes.

When Blue finishes, he turns to me and says, "Come on. Let's go back before our absence is noticed."

I want to hang around and see what happens to the man, except Blue has already grabbed my hand. He pushes into the air, and we start to fly. I flap my wings with my eyes on the car until it's no longer visible.

CHAPTER SEVEN

With each stroke of the wings, my guilt impales its piercing claws farther into my conscience. Blue has broken the rules all because of me. I'm dragging down my best friend. A sickness fills my stomach. He can't be dragged down because of me—he just can't.

We're almost back to our base. The smell of the salty seawater is strong. I look down and see a small gathering of rocks pushed up in the ocean where seagulls and other seabirds are squawking and chattering. A thought hits me. I look to my right and see Blue flying strong and steady.

"Blue," I call out.

Before now, our flight has been silent. Not a word has been uttered between us. He looks at me with a curious expression.

I point down below. "Let's land for a minute."

He nods and angles his legs so he lands feetfirst on the rocky island. I do the same and land next to him amid a spray of feathers and dust stirred by our wings.

A couple of birds nearby take flight immediately, startled by our presence. The remainder of the birds on the island continue on with their business. They know that angels are not a cause for concern.

"What's up?" he asks. His dark-brown eyebrows are pushed together.

I see the worry on his face, and I sigh. "I've been thinking; there must be a way to block the archangels from seeing everything in our mind. I think we should stop for a bit and give it a go."

He raises one side of his mouth in a half-smile. "There you go again, thinking outside the box with the rebel's heart." He shakes his head. "And to think that the last six months I thought you were a good girl."

"Hey!" I pretend to be hurt. "That's rich coming from someone who just broke the rules."

The smile drops from his face, and I shut my mouth. I realize what I've just said and shake my head.

"What I mean to say . . . is . . . thanks." I stumble out. "What you did means a lot to me, but I don't need you getting into trouble."

A solemn look is on his face. "It's okay. I'll deal with it," he says. His eyes have turned the deepest shade of blue.

I shake my head. "No. I can't live with that. We have to try." I lift my hand and place my index finger on his forehead. "I want you to try to block what we just did."

He nods, and I probe his mind, searching only the recent events. I catch glimpses of his day.

I see his Innocent and the mission that he completed well—following the rules and completing his mission by inserting the conscience into the perpetrator. I see the perpetrator's life flash before me. A deep nauseating feeling penetrates my stomach. The task overwhelms me, and my knees want to give, but I don't let them. I'm puzzled why this feeling is stronger than the others I've had, until I realize I'm picking up on Blue's feelings. The two stomach-churning feelings combined are working out to be a powerful force. He's hidden it so well, sticking to his training and obeying the rules, but I've seen it now. I've seen his true feelings. He feels the same way I do.

Pushing past my disbelief of my new discovery, I continue probing. I travel with him as he discovers the charm flashing, up until the moment he sees me in the desert. I'm hit with a wave of emotions as he looks at me. I get the impression that he's fond of me and wishes for more than friendship. This puzzles me. We're not allowed to have anything more than friendships, nor are we supposed to even feel that way. Out of curiosity I want to dig deeper, but I won't. I feel awkward as I stare into his eyes, especially because my heart already belongs to another. I leave it. I'm also not supposed to be digging into his personal feelings. I search the next few minutes after we meet in the desert to see if I can find what happens next. As I follow the wavelength, all seems complete, but what I actually see I know didn't happen in that order. There were parts missing. What I see is me standing there when he arrives. The next scene is Blue grabbing my hand as we take off together.

I release my finger and focus on his eyes. A strange

look is on his face. He almost looks embarrassed. Not knowing how to respond to his emotions for me, I only comment on his success. "You did it. You blocked me." I smile. "And what was that I saw about your deep-centered beliefs being compromised by your missions. You feel the same way as I do about inserting a conscience," I lightly accuse.

He breathes out a deep sigh. "I have you and your last mission to blame for that. Before that I was on the straight and narrow."

The guilt washes over me again. I look down. "Sorry," I mutter. "Now I've got you in a deeper mess."

He shakes his head. "No, that's my fault. But if I managed to block you, then there's hope." I lift my eyes to look at his. He continues, "It's your turn to practice. Let's see if you can block me." A slight smile stretches across his face.

I lift an eyebrow. He looks as though he's going to enjoy this too much, but I know I should practice, so I nod my head. He lifts his hand and touches his index finger to my forehead. I can feel the probing warmth immediately begin to spread. I track his moves as he goes through my day. When it comes to the part after I'd dismissed Louisa, I direct my memory to when Blue lands in the desert, skipping the parts between. I then direct it past the next stage straight to when Blue grabs my hand and we take off to fly. Knowing the probing is finished I relax a little. I'm surprised when I feel Blue probe other emotions. Not knowing where he's going, and not wanting to expose more than I'm ready to part with, I immediately put up a wall. The warmth leaves my forehead as Blue removes his finger.

"What was that?" I ask.

He looks down. "Sorry. I overstepped my mark. I was just trying to get to know you better." His face is a mixture of sadness and embarrassment.

"Well then, you should do it the old-fashioned way, not by probing in places uninvited. I'm your friend, not one of your perpetrators." My words are harsh, but the sternness doesn't carry through my voice. I nudge him with my shoulder lightly. "Come on. There's hope for us yet. We both managed to block each other."

He relaxes and looks at me.

"We'd better get going," I suggest.

He nods, and we both push off the ground together. Another couple of seagulls squawk and scatter from the sudden movements.

Our base isn't far away. As we fly the final stretch, I feel as light as the clouds surrounding me. I'm more positive that Blue won't be caught for completing the final part of my mission.

I see our base and prepare to land. A few of our fellow fledglings are down below, waiting for Archangel Michael's blessing and new task. I wonder if any of them are struggling with the final part of the mission.

I land with a soft thud on the grass, and Blue follows behind. A couple of the others look over briefly. The afternoon is young. They're probably hoping it's the archangel so they can have something to do. I quickly scout around.

"Can you see Yellow?" I ask Blue.

He looks around and shakes his head. "She might've already been here."

"Let's check the edges near the ocean. She's always had an attraction to the sea."

He nods, and we walk together away from the other fledglings. The sun is peeking behind a cloud, but the rest of the sky is a clear blue. The only sound is a couple of distant calls by seagulls and pelicans that can be heard over the roaring waves.

Growing up, I didn't mind being alone. I enjoyed the peace. This's probably a good thing because an angel doesn't exactly lead a social life, though I'm glad for the friendships I've made with Blue and Yellow. They really care.

This was often not the case when I lived in the city of the Gold Coast. I always felt insignificant and invisible around the people and the area. But there was one exception—Ethan, my only love. I wonder, What's he up to now? Is he still living? Has he found a new girlfriend? I can never go back now as my days as a human are over. A wet sensation trickles down my face. Deep in thought, I lift my hand and wipe the tear away.

"Hey," Blue's soft voice pierces through my thoughts. "What's up?"

I blink and realize what's happened. I focus on his eyes feeling slightly embarrassed. I give half a smile. "Nothing. I was just thinking about my past life and what I'm missing."

A look of understanding passes across Blue's face. I haven't told him much about my past, we're not supposed to share, but he nods as if he understands. He puts an arm around my shoulders and squeezes them lightly. I rest my head against his shoulder and look out over the sea.

"Is there room for a third?" a voice calls from behind us. "I hope this isn't a secluded club."

We release our embrace and turn around. Yellow is standing behind us. Her usually bright face looks unsettled.

"Of course there's room for you," I say as I hold out my arm inviting her.

Her face relaxes, and she dashes forward for a group hug. "I so need this," she says.

"What happened?" Blue asks.

I look down and notice that the yellow angel on his charm is glowing dimly. Something must've upset her.

I feel a little selfish as I turn and look at her. "Is all okay? Did something happen?"

She sighs deeply and releases the embrace. "No, not really. I just had a really creepy evil person. I find it so hard to believe that people can stoop that low and do what they do to our Innocents."

I nod. "It's upsetting, especially when all of us come from a background of innocence—not once, but three times. Doesn't it make you wonder what made them become that way?" I ask.

Her blonde brows crease together and her face puckers. After a moment's pause, she shakes her head. "No. I'm just glad that we're giving them what they deserve." Her shoulders shudder as she lets out a sound of revulsion.

Blue grabs my arm firmly from behind and pulls. I know that he's trying to tell me to stop. I can't help myself. "What if there's still good inside of them?"

Her eyes study my face. "Nah. That's not possible. These people are pretty much born evil. They deserve whatever the conscience does to them."

I feel more pressure from Blue's hand on my arm. My insides are about to explode. I want to argue and convince Yellow that there is possibly good in everyone, even though I know I shouldn't, but I don't understand how she could be so blind. As he watches me closely, Blue digs his fingers in deeper again.

I'm about to open my mouth to speak when I hear the call, "Fledglings." Our leader is here. We can't see him, but we can still hear his call within our minds. We begin making our way to the meeting place.

As we turn the corner, we see him. Standing in the center of our grassy meeting spot is the great warrior— our guide—who trained us to be the toughest of the new angels. He waits with his hands on his hips defining his bulging muscles. He looks tough in the skirt of his Roman warrior uniform. His feet are shoulder width apart as he examines the new angels in front of him with his piercing eyes. His no-nonsense demeanor is rather intimidating, even to the rule followers. Considering he's the head of all the angels, and the greatest warrior since the beginning of time, the intimidation is understandable.

I'm starting to feel nervous again. After seeing him, my confidence in being able to pull off the deception is wavering. My concern for Blue heightens. He shouldn't have become involved. It's my battle. I glance at him as he walks beside me toward our meeting spot. His face is a blank canvas. If he feels concern, he's not showing it. I can't read any emotion.

I look back at our leader. His eyes are studying me. I try to hold an honest stare, but I'm not sure I'm pulling it off. He turns and assesses the gathering few as we line up and wait.

"All right," the archangel says. "Let us begin."

He walks up to the first in line. It's Yellow. Glancing to the side, I can see she looks completely relaxed, but I know that she doesn't need to worry. Her mind is on the straight and narrow, not willing to divert from our training. Archangel Michael places a finger on her forehead and it lights up. After a moment, he pulls it away.

"Good work, fledgling. You have served well." He produces the cloud in his hands and pulls out the shining bean. She smiles and takes it between her thumb and index finger and places it in her mouth. I watch as she swallows. I'm half-jealous that she can follow the angel law without remorse, but at the same time I'm happy for her. She's earned it.

When she's swallowed, Archangel Michael says, "Go, young one. I believe your mission is of an urgent matter."

Yellow nods once and disappears, teleporting to wherever she needs to be.

With Yellow gone, it's Blue's turn. The flutter of wings fills my stomach. Our leader stands in front of him. With his legs firmly apart, he places a finger on Blue's forehead. I sneak a sideways glance. Blue still doesn't show any emotion. I wonder if he's stressing right now or if he's redirecting the probing light to avoid the unwanted areas. I feel faint and realize that I've not been breathing. Taking deep breaths, I try to calm my stomach. After a few moments that seem to take forever, Archangel Michael removes his finger.

He says, "Good work, fledgling. You have served well." He turns and looks at me. "But, we have some issues to discuss."

I try to swallow the large lump that's suddenly formed in my throat. It doesn't go away. I look at Blue. His eyes darken as he looks at me. He shakes his head, and his face shows deep concern. Great. That isn't helping me relax.

The leader of the archangels stands in front of me. He's forever in fighting stance, standing balanced and strong. His eyes are piercing as he looks into mine. Is that disappointment I see in those sapphires? He raises his hand and touches his index finger to my forehead. I feel the light as it spreads into my mind. I don't know what went on with Blue, but I'm not going down without a fight. I'm going to do my best to redirect the probing.

I allow it access to where it wants to go. As it begins to progress past the part where I save Louisa, I put up my barriers and begin to direct it to the last moment, when Blue and I take off to come back to base. My diversion begins to work. I'm feeling confident, but there's a sudden push from the white light, and it penetrates my barrier, exposing all the secrets I want to hide from my judge.

I'm still looking into the archangel's stoney eyes as I fight to rebuild the wall, but I can't find the strength to raise it from the ground. Before I know it, everything I want to hide has been seen. Now I know why Blue looked so defeated. The pressure lifts slightly as the probing light is removed, yet the archangel's eyes turn to an eerie color of ice.

CHAPTER EIGHT

"You have disobeyed me, fledgling," Archangel Michael snaps. My eyes look to the ground as I wait for his judgment. "Not only have you disobeyed me, but you have also disobeyed the standing rule of the archangels. And because of your disobedience, you have dragged down your fellow fledgling." He looks at Blue. "But this fledgling is not without fault."

Out of the corner of my eye, I see Blue bow his head to face the ground.

"He should not be chasing you and finishing your work," our leader continues.

Blue lifts his head and focuses his eyes straight ahead and says, "I felt she was in trouble, sir. I was making sure she was okay."

"That may be so, but she should be strong enough to complete her own mission." He turns in my direction, and the glare is scrutinizing. Then he turns back to Blue.

I lift my head and look at Blue. His jawline ripples

as he clenches his teeth. He looks strong again, but I wonder if underneath he feels petrified.

"You know the rules. You are not to finish another fledgling's work if they choose not to complete it themselves." Archangel Michael turns and glares at me again.

Blue is clenching his fist by his side, and I wonder if he's having second thoughts about helping me. I turn my head to look at our leader I feel terrible.

"Esteemed archangel," I say.

The cold eyes assess me silently as he stands only inches away. After a moment he says, "Speak."

"It's my fault. Please punish me as you deem fit. Blu —I mean—he's not to blame."

The archangel's eyebrow lifts. "You have named each other?"

I've put my foot in it again. We both remain silent, and I try swallowing that persistent lump. I think I can see steam coming out of Archangel Michael's ears as he clenches his jaw.

"You know this is forbidden. You were both clearly breaking the rules even before this incident," he snaps. "I'm taking you to stand in front of the panel of archangels straight after this meeting. Your fate is up to the archangels." He turns to his left and continues down the row of fledglings to finish the checkup.

Riddled with guilt, I sigh and look at Blue. His eyes are so sad when they look at me. He seems disappointed. I mouth the words, "I'm sorry."

He shakes his head and says quietly, "It's not your fault. It was my choice to step in. I was—"

"No talking." His voice is harsh. Archangel Michael's finger is pointing at us, but he's looking the other way.

With adrenaline exploding through our veins, we fall silent and wait for him to finish and our trial to be over. It seems to take forever for the remaining fledglings to be cleared and given a new mission. I watch them disappear or fly away after they've cast both of us a sideways glance. I'm sure this isn't helping me make any new friends. Like Yellow, the other fledglings have done the correct thing. I hold a tinge of regret I can't do the same. But I also know if I did not start to question what would happen to our perpetrators, I wouldn't be happy with myself, and my conscience would eat away at me.

As we wait silently, watching the last fledgling disappear, Archangel Michael turns to us and demands, "Follow me." He pushes off the ground and flies into the clouds. As I lift off the ground and into the air, I hear Blue do the same behind me. My wings flap back and forth, and I listen to the dull whistle as the wind pushes away with each stroke. The rhythm of the sound is comforting, and at this moment, I don't want to lose the sound.

Within moments we're in the clouds, rising farther up. I don't know where we're going. We've never been to wherever he's taking us. The temperature is dropping rapidly as our wings quickly take us higher. It's not long before I see a strange-looking platform on the highest cloud. We fly directly to the platform, rise over the edge, and follow our leader as he drops to land.

I take a look around. If I weren't so nervous, I'm certain I'd have found this humorous. The area looks like the typical cliché of angels living among the clouds. The entire place has a fluffy white-cloud finish. In different parts of the platform, there are large cloud chairs that resemble lounge chairs. They're large enough to lie on and are empty.

We step forward following Archangel Michael. Walking on the platform is a strange feeling. It's like we're walking on the semifirm cloud, but we don't fall through. I hear a slight rumble of an airplane underneath us.

Up ahead there's movement, and from behind a cloud wall I see an angel step into the small gap of a doorway. The blue angelic gown flows softly to the angel's feet. It's a slightly darker color than the sky. Majestic white wings fan behind the angel's back. I haven't met any of the other archangels before, and I'm not sure what to expect. If they're all like Archangel Michael, then I'm sure we're in for a rough time.

I look apprehensively at the angel's pale face. The features are handsome but soft, so I can't tell if they belong to a male or a female. And the gown is too loose to make out any defining shape of either sex. Allowing my eyes to meet the angel's, I'm surprised to see that they're the color of a welcoming crystal clear spring, rather than that of a hard sapphire. I begin to feel confident in my decision again, and I've an overwhelming urge to go and do something creative and express my emotions—this isn't like me. I'm not the creative sort.

Turning to look at Blue as he walks on my right,

slightly behind me, I see he also has a more confident look on his face. He makes eye contact and gives me half a smile. My hopes rise. Maybe we'll be okay after all.

As we step closer to the archangel, my drive to want to protect the Innocents becomes stronger. I know that I've done all I can. The happiness settles until my thoughts pass to the perpetrators and how I don't want to insert a conscience into them and purify their minds. My confidence starts to slip away. Guilt begins to take over. I know what I wish to do isn't abiding by the archangels' rules, but at the same time I know that I can't just insert a conscience into the evil ones. To have them kill themselves or go insane when they, too, have an innocent side is an undesirable consequence.

"Michael," the blue one says. The voice is firm, but it's not masculine or feminine. Considering the position that I'm in, I know that I won't be asking which gender this angel is.

"Yes, Gabriel," Archangel Michael says.

"What's the meaning of this? Why do you bring two young fledglings to our meeting place?"

"I have brought them to be judged by the council. They have broken the rules." The disappointment is prominent in his voice.

The blue eyes survey us as we approach. The softness pushes away from the eyes. "You have two in your small group that have disobeyed our instruction. Have you lost your touch? Is the warrior softening?" the archangel asks.

"I have not done anything different," says

Archangel Michael. "These two have chosen their way despite the stringent training." He almost sounds annoyed at Archangel Gabriel.

We reach the doorway where Archangel Gabriel is standing, and Archangel Michael says, "Now if you would please stand aside so I can bring them through to Uriel and Raphael. The four of us will decide their fate."

Archangel Gabriel moves aside, and we follow Archangel Michael through the cloud doorway. Archangel Gabriel continues to study us. Even up close I still can't tell if Gabriel is male or female. Awkwardly we pass, and I focus my eyes on the room. It's about twenty feet square and simply decorated within the white cloudy walls. In the center is a large white-cloud table surrounded by white-cloud chairs.

Standing in one corner of the room is an angel in a green gown that reaches the floor. It reminds me of the deep-green color of leaves. He stands tall and straight, and his pale-green wings fall majestically behind him. He has dark-brown hair that's cut just above his ears. I study his face. It remains serious as his green eyes assess us.

Next to him is another angel whose clothes are white and flow to the ground. His majestic white wings blend in with the clouds. Squinting, I try to work out where his wings end and the clouds start. Draped over his shoulders is a large golden shawl that falls past his knees. His dark-brown midneck-length hair has a slight curl. As his golden-brown eyes study us, I can't help but think his look reminds me of descriptions of Zeus.

We've stopped just inside the room. I stand next to Archangel Michael with Blue on my right.

The white angel speaks, "Who do we have here?"

"Uriel," Archangel Michael begins. "We have fledglings that have gone against our instructions. I have brought them here, so we can decide their fate as a board."

Archangel Uriel's wings rise with the points angling up. The tips finish in a golden color close to the color of my wings. He looks at the green-clothed angel next to him. "Come Raphael. We must decide what is best for the Innocents."

Archangel Raphael's face appears apprehensive as he steps forward with Archangel Uriel. From all the angels, I'm sensing a mixture of feelings. As I look among the angels, I see Archangel Gabriel standing close to Blue.

Archangel Gabriel steps forward directly in front of Blue, glances at me, and says, "I hope what you've done isn't worthy of the abyss. It's a horrible place." Archangel Gabriel then places a finger on Blue's forehead, and it lights up.

Before I peel my eyes away, I sense my forehead become warm. I turn to look directly in front of me. The smoldering golden-brown eyes of Uriel greet me. His finger is firmly on my forehead. He's already beginning the process of my assessment.

An overwhelming sense of clarity and intuition flood through my body. As much as it distresses me, I know there's no point in trying to divert his probing. After the attempt with Archangel Michael, it's clear an archangel's experience surpasses barriers against seeing truth.

The seconds drag until he removes his finger, and Archangel Raphael follows his lead. I want to melt into the comforting greenness as my inner turmoil softens and begins to heal. He removes his finger, and the feeling subsides. Gabriel steps forward to view my disobedience.

As much as I try, I can't get a reading of what they're thinking. The wait is tearing me apart, but I don't have a choice.

After the removal of the last angelic finger from our foreheads, the four archangels walk to the table and take a seat. I glance at Blue. This makes me feel worse. He shouldn't be here, it's all my fault. He looks at me, and there isn't a hint of regret in his eyes, but I still don't feel any better. He should hate me right now.

I hear voices coming from the table. I turn my attention back to our judges. The verdict discussion is beginning.

"I believe they should be thrown in the abyss," Uriel states without a hint of remorse. There he goes again reminding me of Zeus, an instantaneous decision maker regarding those who go against the rules. "If we do not make an example of them, many will follow in their footsteps. Then we would have a huge problem on our hands. We would have to eliminate all the nonabiding fledglings and would lose years of work and progress."

Archangel Gabriel speaks up, "I know what you're saying, but the abyss is a very harsh punishment. I don't think that they deserve the punishment of permanence in the abyss. I think they have uses for the future."

My initial confusion over Archangel Gabriel's thoughts is corrected. Male or female, I don't care. I'm now glad that Gabriel is here. Maybe it's the creative energy of Gabriel I felt earlier that is cause for a more open mind.

Raphael speaks, "As you know, my first goal is to heal. Heal the body and the mind of all living creatures. If we let the perpetrators stroll freely among the Innocents without a conscience, then this will harm the world, not heal it. We must rectify these two fledglings, despite the outcome for the perpetrators. This one," he says indicating me, "cannot make that decision. Her decisions are immature and without direction. It is a recipe for disaster. And this one," he indicates Blue, "cannot go and do this one's work for her. It is not allowed."

Archangel Michael speaks. "Well, you know my position when it comes to enforcing the angelic law. We must uphold the strength of our justice system. It was ruled thousands of years ago to protect the Innocents. We must sustain the law." He looks sternly in our direction.

Our outcome isn't looking good. As much as I don't wish for my inevitable fate, I can't stand having Blue punished as well. He was only trying to protect me from punishment. Instead, he's ended up in the line of fire with me.

Uriel begins to speak, "So it is to the abyss—"

"Please," I interrupt Uriel. I swallow hard realizing

what I've done, but I must continue. "Please, let him go." I indicate Blue. "It's my fault, and he was just trying to save me from punishment."

"I can see what he has done, child," Uriel says as his eyes survey me without compassion. "You need to control your emotions and have respect for the angelic law, including not interrupting while your archangels are speaking." He raises his chin.

I try to swallow that lump in my throat again. "I do apologize for my error. I'm nervous for my colleague; he doesn't deserve to be punished for protecting me." I falter, realizing that I've told the archangels what they should or shouldn't be doing. I take a deep breath and suddenly I've a surge of confidence. Looking into his eyes, I watch the smoldering pots of gold-colored pupils constrict. "I also believe that there must be another way to treat the perpetrators." I hear a gasp from Archangel Gabriel, but I continue. "They also have innocence inside. It may be deep, but it's there. Something's happened to them to cause them to do evil to the Innocents."

"Enough!" Archangel Michael demands. "You do not speak to your superiors this way. I am certain I have taught you this. You need a harsh lesson. I rule that you both be thrown into the abyss until you feel the effects it will have on you." He looks around at the other three archangels. "How do you rule?"

My eyes quickly look at each face. They're all nodding. I bite my bottom lip to stop from saying more. I've done enough damage. Glancing at Blue, I still feel guilt, yet I'm relieved that I won't be in the abyss alone. A very selfish thought, I know.

Someone grabs my left arm from behind. I look over my shoulder to see Archangel Michael. This meeting has come to an end.

Guided by my arm, I'm taken through the open cloud door to the edge of the cloud's platform. Blue is being escorted by Archangel Uriel. As we stand at the edge, I'm readying myself for flight when a big hole appears in front of us. I gaze in and see nothing but blackness. My muscles tighten.

"You are first, fledgling," Archangel Michael says. I look and see that he's talking to me. His eyes are emotionless. This's only business to him. He's doing his job. I don't feel hate for him or the other archangels. I'm only sad their beliefs in the long-standing law are so rigid, that they're not willing to see another option. Taking a deep breath, I know I've no other option, so I brace myself and then jump into the hole. There's nothing in here. No walls, no floor, just blackness. I'm continuously falling. I spread my wings and flap while I wait for Blue. At least I'll have someone in here for company. I flap, and I flap. Soon the hole should open just above me, and Blue will appear.

I wait. Time is passing. I don't know how long it's been, but it's beginning to feel like an eternity. I continue to hover. Surely they'll be putting him in here straightaway. Perhaps the hole has this feeling of time going slowly. I'm hoping this's the case, but I can't help feeling anxious that Blue won't be joining me. I wait . . . and wait. Nothing.

CHAPTER NINE

I t feels like weeks have passed, but I don't know. I don't have a watch, and there's no day or night. There isn't even a place I can land and feel secure. It's just an open nothingness. The blackness engulfs me. It's so dark that I can barely see my golden wings. I wish they'd projected me into space. At least then I'd have the stars and moon surrounding me, something to observe.

I've been waiting outside the place where I'm certain I entered. My wings are tired, and I'm weary, as if I could use some sleep, but angels don't sleep.

There's still no sign of Blue, and this splits me in two. One side of me is hopeful that the archangels had a change of heart and did not put him in here. The other side is disappointed that I don't have the company I'm yearning. I'm ready to give up waiting. After all this time, he can't be coming.

I relax my wings, and start to fall with no hope of reaching the bottom. I feel weightless as I fall but I also seem to be floating. It's like being stuck in an anti-gravity zone. I hope they won't leave me in here for long. The place isn't uncomfortable—just so lonely, so empty. It's not the kind of aloneness I enjoy.

I lie back and let go, reflecting on what I did to get thrown into here. The strange thing is that I'm sure I'd do it all again. I guess I'm not repentant like I'm supposed to be. The only thing I'd do differently would be to keep Blue out of it.

I fall and float in this antigravity zone. It's a disturbing feeling. I'm helpless to do much else. There's no sleeping, eating, talking, nothing to even observe. I begin to feel helpless. I try to picture Blue and the Innocents I've saved so far. The perpetrators also enter my mind. What could be changing them and making them commit these horrible crimes? I long to check on my past perpetrator to see what the conscience Blue inserted into him did. Is he still alive?

I'm still buoyant. The time is dragging on. It feels like I've been in here a couple of months. I close my eyes. My mind begins to wander to my previous life. We're forbidden to associate with our past families. It may be so, but it can't make me forget them. No, their memory is still engraved in my mind, especially my true love.

We'd lived three lives together, but his third is still in progress. I reached my hand up to my lips. I miss him. I wish he could join me in the angel world, except that'd still not fix the problem. We're not allowed to have romantic relationships. Besides protecting the Innocents, there isn't much going for the life of an angel.

Thinking back to the people I've saved, I'm still glad I became a protection angel, despite its restrictions. I just need to get out of here.

I don't know how long I've been in limbo. I keep blacking out and it seems as though my mind is beginning to shut down. I thought I'd go crazy before my mind shut down. Perhaps it's a way to preserve my sanity. I start to fear that I'll be here forever when a bright light opens up before me. It shines through my closed eyelids.

Instantly I become alert. It's hard to open my eyes wider than slits because I'm no longer used to the light. Groggily, I straighten my position to face the bright hole. A hand grabs my arm at the elbow and yanks me into the light. I can't see the owner of the hand because my eyes still haven't adjusted to the brightness of the light.

When the darkness disappears, my feet hit solid ground. My knees buckle at the unusual feeling, and I land in a half-kneeling, half-sitting position. I place my hands down next to my knees, and the feeling of short grass prickles my palms. My eyes are adjusting better, and I can see that I'm surrounded by nature. The area looks familiar.

"Fledgling," a stern voice calls over me.

After blinking I look up. Archangel Michael is standing over me. He offers a hand, I accept and I stand. "I hope you have learned your lesson."

I don't say anything. I'm in no hurry to go back into the abyss, so I nod. To me, my lesson was that the abyss stinks. It's a horrible place to be for such a long time.

"Good," he says. He doesn't place a finger on my forehead to check. This surprises me. "We need all hands on deck, and at the moment we don't need you to be locked away."

I look around the area. We're at our training base. I've missed the view of the ocean and the palm trees swaying in the breeze. A seagull squawks in the distance. I've even missed their unpleasant cry. I don't see any other fledglings. They must all be on a mission. Turning back to my leader, I see that he's studying me with his arms crossed.

"I know going into the abyss is not pleasant, but if you do not follow our rules, it will be your punishment. You were in there for only a few days."

I almost fall over with the reality. "Really?" I ask struggling with the information. "It felt like months."

He nods. "It pains me to do it. Not only are we in need of all the angels we have, but we especially need the help of the gifted and more powerful ones."

I frown. I'm not sure where he's going with this.

He uncrosses his arms and cups his hands in front of him. The cloud appears in his palms, and he reaches in, pulling out a shiny bean. Handing it to me he says, "Go and serve as instructed. The Innocents need you, the evil of heart do not."

I take the bean and swallow. The warmth fills my stomach, and I relish the feeling. I'm needed again. As I let the warmth spread, I look at my instructor.

His eyes are studying me with a concerned look on his face. "Remain here for a few minutes until you are ready to proceed. Your mission is not completely urgent, but do not dawdle."

After I nod, he disappears, leaving me alone again. I'm not fond of being alone at this moment. A thought crosses my mind. It's my first moment of freedom, and I've been itching to find something out. I push off the ground and open my golden wings. Flapping consistently, I begin to rise into the sky. Each stroke pushes me rapidly forward. Before long I've crossed the mainland of Australia. I look beneath me and observe the Indian Ocean. It's so nice to be free again.

It takes only a little while to reach the coast of South Africa, and I go to see Louisa's attacker in Pretoria. I stop at his home and am surprised to find a mansion. I enter through an open door off the balcony on the first floor. I can hear his maid downstairs in the kitchen. The smell of food cooking wafts up the stairs and into the living area on the first floor. It smells divine. Following my instincts, I walk quietly toward his bedroom, and I enter.

Lying on the bed is a sorrowful sight. I see a body of someone like a man; at least, I think he's a man. Scratches cover his face, and his hair is in disarray. He's nothing like the man who was driving a luxury car not so long ago. I look around. It's a lovely place, modern and equipped with luxuries. Standing near the window, I hear digging in the garden. I look outside, and below is a man with colored skin. He's digging out some weeds and redefining the garden edge.

I sigh. This is a place filled with almost everything

that a person could want, yet not so long ago, he was traveling the countryside, hunting down innocent victims. I turn around and approach the bed. The figure moves. He's muttering softly to himself. I walk right up to his side and gaze at the man. His face is torn, and his fingernails are filled with his own skin. He's a mess. I touch a finger to his forehead and watch it light up as I probe into his brain. His eyes open. They're absent of thought. After a few moments, they focus on my face and open wider. I can see the pure terror in his bulging eyes. He has recognized me and is completely distraught.

I concentrate on the probing for a moment and see that the conscience is tearing him apart. He hasn't killed himself, but he's not living, either. His frantic hand grabs mine, and I release the probing. With a sad heart, I gently return his hand to his side and pat it affectionately, trying to reassure him.

Gently I say, "I'm not here to hurt you."

I don't know if this registers because he doesn't respond. He's so lost and traumatized that I feel sorry for him. I'm baffled by how he became so evil when in his earlier life he'd been an asset to society. I stand by my belief—we have to find another way.

I rise, walk to the door, and fly out the way that I came. I've confirmed my suspicions. This's what I wanted before undergoing my next mission. I now have a long flight over the Indian Ocean back to Australia. My next mission was already interesting without the information I'd just collected. My destination—my former life's stomping grounds, and I've a suspicion that I may know the perpetrator.

CHAPTER TEN

There it is. There below is the place where I spent many days during my past life. It is nighttime. While I land between the gardens in the front yard away from the street, I'm confronted with memories. Many happy moments resurface, making it hard to concentrate. I miss so many people from my past.

As usual, the outside light isn't working. The darkness helps me remain unseen as I cross the plain concrete driveway. Making myself invisible, I walk around to the back of the little brick house on Monroe Court, Oxenford. I'm careful to not knock over the many potted plants lining the walls. Looking around I see that it hasn't changed since I was here last. Although the place is neat, it's an older and cheaper house than most in the area.

With my hand on the rough bricks of the house, I make my way to the covered patio. Stepping silently on the terra-cotta-colored tiles, I dodge the mess of a recently smashed potted plant on the ground. Pieces of crockery, dirt, and mangled plant lie on the usually spotless tiles. It's fallen off a tall plant stand that lines the back of the pergola.

Glancing at the house, I notice the outdoor table and chairs lie sprawled across the patio, and the back sliding-glass door is open. It appears there's been a struggle.

I peek around the dark, grassy backyard. I can't see any movement among the vegetable garden boxes or around the steel shed. Remaining invisible, I step inside the house. Memories engulf my mind. This home belongs to Ethan's mother—Ethan, my true love. I had visited here many times even though Ethan didn't live here anymore. He moved out at a young age when his mother remarried and his stepdad moved in. Ethan and Dean didn't get along.

Tonight I'm looking for his kid brother, and I don't like what I see. Looking around at the signs of a struggle, I'm starting to worry that my detour may've been too long. Maybe I'm too late. I hope not. I liked Ryan. He was a good kid. He was very young when his mother remarried. After a quick calculation, I work out that he's about fourteen now—not a boy, yet not quite a man.

I hear a scuffle somewhere deeper in the house. Picking up the pace, I progress toward the noise, walking as quietly as I can on the wooden floating floor, my heels making a slight noise. Somehow, I don't think they'll sound above the noise in the distance.

Walking down the hall, I follow the sound. While passing the main bedroom, I glance through the open door. Lying on the floor is Ethan's mom. Her face is pale. Thankfully, I can make out a small rise and fall of her chest. The pull to check on her is strong, but I know I must first follow the noise. It pains me, but I continue.

My mission is to protect Ryan, and this's important to me in more than one way. After a few more steps, I hear more banging.

"Stop." I hear, followed by sobbing. The person sounds young; he could be Ryan.

I hear more thumping and a half-scream, half-sob. I run the last few steps to the noise.

"You're so stupid," I hear a man shout. I think it's Dean, Ethan's stepdad, but it's hard to tell because the words are being forced through his teeth.

They're in the office. I reach the door and see Dean leaning over Ryan, who's crumpled against the wall. Dean has a solid grip on his shirt with one hand and is shoving him repeatedly against the wall. He raises his fist to strike. Dashing forward, I grab his fist with my hands before it can find its mark.

"I wouldn't do that, Dean," I say.

Dean turns and looks at his fist. "What the—?" He blinks as if he's trying to clear his vision. Then I remember that I'm still invisible, which means he can't hear me, either. I fold my wings away and make myself visible. His angry eyes study my face.

"You're supposed to be dead," he grunts. "You always were a meddling tramp."

I take a deep breath. I wasn't a tramp. It's not important, I tell myself. It's not the time to argue. "And you were never the charmer or adoring father. I see you haven't changed."

He makes a guttural sound. "These mongrels were never my kids." He indicates Ryan with his thumb. "Useless sacks of s—"

"You agreed to be a father to them when you married their mother," I interrupt. I'm a little surprised by his comment. I knew he had a temper, but I wasn't under the impression that he didn't care for them at all.

"Yeah, well she turned out to be a good for nothing ho," he spat. "What the hell happened to you? Where the hell did you spring from? And what the hell happened to your looks? You look like you've had a ton of plastic surgery." He blinks. "This isn't real. This is not real." He shakes his head then turns to Ryan. "What the hell did you put in my beer?" He raises his fist to strike Ryan, and I grab it again. He flicks his fist backward to free it from my grasp. "You're not real. You're dead. Bugger off!" he yells.

I grab his arm again before he can cause any more damage. He turns. His teeth are gritted together as he swings out his fist trying to land it on my face. Leaning slightly backward, I feel the wind brush my face. Stunned that I avoided the collision, he tries again. This time his fist flies past my nose. I watch it pass as I twist to the side. As I do this, I swing out my fist, which lands on his nose. His head flings backward as I hear the crunch of cartilage. Blood flows from his nostrils, and his nose lies crooked on his face.

I turn to look at Ryan. He stands stunned against the

wall. His face is a ghostly white, and his long strands of light-brown hair hang untouched in his eyes.

"Go check on your mother," I instruct. "She's still breathing." He nods and pushes off the wall to leave. "Oh, and Ryan, don't forget to call the emergency service for help."

With Ryan gone, I turn back to look at Dean. His head is tilted back, as he tries to stop the blood flowing from his nose.

"You tramp!" he screams and spits some of the blood from his lips in my direction. It narrowly misses my face. After straightening his head, he digs in his toes, and with his shoulders down, he rams forward trying to tackle me to the ground. I step aside and watch him stream past. I follow him with my foot, landing a sidekick on his behind. He topples forward quicker than he anticipated and struggles to stay upright. He manages to stop just before he hits the wall. Using the wall, he pushes himself to a standing position.

Dark-brown hair falls in his eyes as he faces the wall with his head tilted. His body starts to shake. At first I don't know why his torso is jerking. Then I hear it—he's chuckling into a malicious crescendo.

Shivers run down my spine.

He turns and shakes his index finger at me. "You've changed. You faked your death, and to think I went to your funeral. You even stood up Ethan. You broke the stupid kid's heart. I saw him sobbing to his mother for months." A satisfied smirk spread across his face. "And you think I'm heartless."

I'm on guard. My feet are apart, my body is balanced and ready, just as I was taught. With my fists raised in front of my body, I'm ready to defend or strike if needed. I look in his eyes, ignoring his condescending look, and shake my head.

"You have it wrong," I tell him. "I did die."

He scoffs and shakes his head. "You expect me to believe that?"

I nod. "I'm serious. My father killed me, and now I'm reborn as an angel and trained by Archangel Michael, the greatest of all angels, to defend the Innocents against people like you."

The evil laugh starts up again. "I know—you went to comedian school. Do you really expect me to believe such religious hogwash like that? You, an angel." One side of his mouth lifts in a smirk.

I shrug. "It's surprising to me, too, but that's the way it is. Now as a word of warning, you need to change your ways or else I've to change it for you." I shake my head. "Trust me, you don't want that."

"Ooh, I'm scared. Are you going to send me to church?" He laughs.

"Actually, I've the power to give you a conscience. It doesn't sound like much, but I've seen people kill themselves and go insane from the effect it has on them. I don't like doing it, and I don't want to harm you, so if there's the slightest bit of good left in you, I'm giving you the chance to choose."

Dean holds his stomach and bends forward in laughter. "I swear you've been hanging out in comedian school. Your jokes are priceless, unlike any I've heard before."

I shake my head. "Then you leave me no choice." I step forward.

He immediately holds his hands up to protect himself. "Whoa! What do you think you're doing?"

I sigh. "I've already told you. I'd prefer if you decided to do good."

"Oh, no you don't. You don't lay a hand on me. If you come any closer, I'm going to take you down."

It's clear that no matter how much I reason with him, he's not going to change. It pains me, but I've to protect the Innocents, and this Innocent is Ethan's kid brother. So there's no way I'm leaving him in harm's way.

I step forward with my hands ready to insert the conscience. He swipes my hands away, and his fist comes flying at my cheek. I move just in time to feel it scrape down the side. It wasn't strong enough to be a bruising hit. I grab his arm. He steps forward twisting out of it and throws his fist at my face. Blocking it outward with my arm, I lean in and give him a direct hit to his already broken nose. I pull my fist back. Spattered blood covers it. He stops, stunned for a moment, and I rapidly position myself ready to execute a sidekick to his abdomen. As I release it with full force, I feel his two hands grasp the ankle of my kicking foot. Damn. He's recovered enough to respond. Before I've time to react, he's raised my foot up to the ceiling, causing my supporting leg to slip from underneath me. My upper body crashes to the ground, sending jolts of pain through my shoulder. If I were human, I'd be in excruciating pain with a sore head and neck. But I'm an angel. It still hurts, but not much.

I roll onto my back as I see him charging me. Just in time, too. His foot slams down next to my head in the exact spot it was a split second before. Grabbing my opportunity, I kick up into his groin. His eyes water as he screams out, clutching in between his legs. I try not to smile. His yell turns silent with agony. The look on his face is rewarding.

While I have a moment, I jump up and step forward with my hands ready to insert a conscience. My hands hover over both sides of his temples. I pause. I still don't want to do this. I wouldn't be surprised if he used to be a good person at some stage. My internal struggle continues while I contemplate if I should check his mind first. Then Ryan's face crosses my mind, and I know I can't take the risk.

I begin to move my hands in closer when a fist hits my stomach in a perfect uppercut. I lurch forward and stagger backward out of the room into the hall. While cursing silently at my distraction, I clutch my stomach. A stupid mistake. The pain shoots up to my brain; I know it'll subside shortly. I begin to straighten up when a kick comes crashing into my side, pushing me down the hall. My feet are not centered so I stumble harder than expected. Before I can steady myself, another kick lands on my midriff. With pain shooting down my side, I'm involuntarily pushed farther down the hall and into the living room.

"Yeah, that's right, skank. I used to take martial arts

when I was a kid, too."

He 's still wheezing a little from the blow to his jewels, but he's not giving in without a fight.

"You're going to be toast," he spits before lunging again with another kick.

This time I'm ready for him. I step aside narrowly missing the connection. I jump farther back and twist, landing my foot on his stomach with a roundhouse kick. Tired of fighting inside, I jump and kick into his side, pushing him toward the back patio door with a sidekick. After the thump sounds of the connecting limbs, he clasps his stomach. He stumbles in the direction that I want, and I kick again. He trips on the overturned table leg, just managing to stay upright as he rectifies his position out on the grass.

I look at the man I used to know. Although I had my suspicions before, I did not think that he was a completely bad person. Something must've changed him for the worst. Right now, I can't see the good in him. Maybe I was mistaken. I can't believe that I almost broke the rules for him and risked spending a lot longer in the abyss if I got caught.

Now we're in an open area on the grass, there's more room to fight. In the dark, I can see him clearly. With the lights shining from the house, it's possible that he can see me, too. The shadows cast over his eyes makes him look positively evil. I shiver. I need to stop him now. I can't see a way to change him without inserting the conscience that I'm instructed to give him. I stand ready.

"Dean, you've left me no choice," I warn again.

"Why don't you relax and let me do what I've come to do?"

Bloody drool runs down his face, and with the dark shadows over his eyes, he's beginning to look like one of those zombies or vampires in horror movies.

He shakes his head. "You're not setting a hand on me."

He dashes forward with his fist raised high, aiming for my face. I step and brush it aside with my arm, watching it move past my face. While the same hand clasps his wrist, I step in and flick a hammer fist to his temple. It connects, and he's dazed. I step in with my back toward him and snap his right elbow over my shoulder. The crunching of bones and the ripping of tendons and muscles churns my stomach.

He lets out an involuntary scream, which echoes through my head. I flick my elbow back into his rib cage, letting his broken arm go. His knees buckle in pain, and he hits the grass. I watch as his face turns up, twisting in pain. He attempts to get up but is having trouble pushing past the agony. I could cause him so much more discomfort, but I'm not taking pleasure in this.

I step forward, lean over, and place my hands on his temples. A light shines on his head from both hands as the conscience enters his mind and soul. His eyes are open, reflecting his terror as I see his life flash before him. Yes, there it is. Just as I thought, he also used to be a good person. What's happening to these people? The urge to get to the bottom of their change becomes stronger with each perpetrator.

I release my hands and press my palm to his forehead. I've one final thing to do. I need to wipe his memory. A light shines from my palm into his forehead. With his expression pained from the insertion of the blue conscience, he doesn't seem to notice my palm on his head. I remove my hand and straighten up. I'm about to walk away when I have second thoughts about leaving him in the middle of his dark backyard. I squat down and hoist him up by wrapping his arm across my shoulders. His feet involuntarily move with me toward the house. Pushing aside the toppled outdoor dining set, I take him into the lounge and lay him on the couch, spreading his legs across the chair.

With Dean taken care of, I make my way to the main bedroom where I'd sent Ryan. I reach the doorway and see his mom still lying on the floor. Her head rests on a pillow, and she's still unconscious. Ryan sits on the floor leaning against the bed. He's holding her hand and stroking the back of it.

"Hey, Ryan," I say softly as I enter.

He looks up. Wet lines are running down his confused face. He reaches a hand up and wipes them away. "What's going on?" he asks. "I thought you were ... dead." He struggles to say the last word.

I step forward and squat beside him, wrapping my arm around his shoulders and pulling him gently toward me in an embrace. Resting his head against my chest, I stroke his light-brown hair. I feel a growing moistness on my top underneath his head. "I am. But I've come back, just this once ... to protect you."

His head turns up, and I look into his puffy blue

eyes. His brow creases into a frown. "And how do you do that if you're dead?" he asks.

I smile sadly at his comment. "What I said is true. I've been chosen to be an angel." I expose my wings, letting them unfold. I watch as his eyes open wide. He reaches out and touches the feathers with a look of awe on his young face. "Lucky me, hey?"

He nods.

"But I tell you one thing for sure, I miss you and Ethan." I almost choke on Ethan's name. My eyes start to well with tears as sadness takes over my heart. I'm pulled away from this thought when I hear the distant wail of sirens. The ambulance is on its way.

"What's worse is that I have to wipe your memory of seeing me."

He pushes back from me shaking his head. "No, way."

Tiredness overwhelms me as I insist. "I wish I could leave you with my memory, so you know that I'm okay, but it's forbidden."

He screws up his nose at me.

"I can't leave you with it. I'm sorry." Before he has a chance to react, I press my palm up to his forehead with my other hand holding his head forward. I'm out of time to discuss it with him any further. A tear rolls down my cheek as I make myself invisible during the process.

With his memory wipe complete, I stand and walk out the back door. My torso overflows with the warmth of another successful rescue. This one is extra special to me, and I smile. As the ambulance screams into the driveway, I prepare to take flight, and then I have a change of heart. There's something I want to do before I return to base.

CHAPTER ELEVEN

The darkness engulfs the cloudless sky in the early hours of the morning. In the east along the horizon there's the slightest ray of light. I've made it to my destination. My nerves are on edge. I shouldn't be here, but I can't resist the pull after being so close.

I'm standing outside a small townhouse in Coomera. Except for a couple of community street-lights, the pale brick apartments are in darkness. With a cyclone in my abdomen, I find the spare key and make my way inside. In reality, my current form doesn't need doors or windows to enter buildings, but old habits are hard to break.

Inside the building, the paint and tiles of the main living area are pale beige. A few clothes scatter across the floor and kicked-off work boots lie beside the deep-blue double couch. The sight brings a smile to my face. Warmth fills my heart as memories flood my mind of how these simple acts used to annoy me. I sit down on the couch and run my hand over the leather. The cool smoothness is comforting. Breathing in deeply, I realize I've missed this place more than I thought.

Keen to keep looking, I stand and progress up the stairs, remaining invisible. There are three bedroom doors. Each one is open. I approach the farthest one, peering in each door as I pass. The rooms are as I remember them, a spare double bed in one and a computer desk in another. They're absent of people. I thought there'd be roommates by now.

Nervously, I take the final step to the last door. Holding my breath, I look inside. Lying in crumpled, dark-red cotton sheets in the middle of the double bed is Ethan.

My eyes quickly scan the remaining space on the bed. It's empty. I'm torn, happy and sad at the same time. It looks as though he hasn't moved on to another partner. My heart reaches out to him. I want him to be happy and in love, but I also don't want him to forget me.

I enter the room and sit on the corner of his bed. His body takes up the full length of the bed as he breathes, deeply and quietly. The urge to lie next to him and hold him close is overwhelming, but I mustn't let him know of my presence. I miss him so much. Comforted by his breathing, I watch him sleep.

Hours later, the room fills with light, and his alarm sounds. His light-brown eyes slowly open. Working as a builder, he's an early riser. He's in the final year of his apprenticeship. He throws back the sheet, revealing he's slept in his black boxers. His pale-brown hair is in disarray, making my heart melt. The defined muscles on his chest and arms ripple as he staggers sleepily toward the bathroom downstairs.

Before he reaches the door, he turns and looks at the upper level right at where I'm standing, invisible. A frown creases his brow followed by a blanket of sadness that crosses his face and breaks my heart. I'm sure he can't see me, but that look puzzles me. He turns and steps through the door with sadness still etching his face. His melancholy demeanor concerns me. I decide right then that I'm going to follow him for a while to make sure he's coping well.

By the time he leaves the bathroom, I'm waiting for him next to his white pickup truck. The back is laden with tools and equipment ready for his work day. It's not long before he climbs into his truck and drives to work as I fly above.

My actions are those of a stalker's, and considering my motivation, I know that I'm stalking him. I work hard to convince myself that I'm doing this for him, and I continue to follow. I know I'm breaking the rules again. Considering my mission is complete, I should be heading back to base to report for my next mission.

When he arrives at work, I continue to watch him. He doesn't seem as vivacious with his boss and work colleagues as I remember. Later in the morning, he's sent to pick up a couple of work supplies, and I watch him walk down the aisles of Bunnings Warehouse. The store is busy, and I'm tired of being bumped into, so I find a hidden spot, fold away my wings, and remove my invisibility.

Keeping my distance, I return to watch from the

ends of the aisles. In my high heels and tight blue, green, and gold-flecked clothes, I feel out of place in the hardware store, but not as much as when I was in Prince Albert. Making a mental note to work on changing what I wear when I'm in human form, I watch Ethan. I stand slightly secluded, ignoring the looks I receive from the tradesmen and general DIY customers.

A pretty young lady wearing skimpy clothes passes Ethan. She looks around my human age with long blonde hair flowing loosely around her shoulders. Makeup that could be scraped off using one of the tools on the shelf is plastered on her face. Jealousy rises within when she circles back after seeing Ethan and leans over, pressing in close and brushing up against him to reach for something on the shelf. Ethan looks up at her. I can't resist a smile when I see his eyes are distant and unresponsive, even after she smiles sweetly at him.

A moment later I frown and cast my eyes to the ground, reprimanding myself. It was such a selfish thought. I smile again—an enjoyable one, though.

While looking to the side, I see a bright flash of blue. I turn to look directly at the spot. I'm surprised at what I see, although I shouldn't be.

"Blue?" I whisper.

He's in his invisible form standing a couple of feet away from me. He's moving his wings so that people passing by won't run into them. After dodging a few more people, he gives up and folds them away. I feel the heat rise to my face. He's caught me again.

Avoiding this thought, I say, "Thank goodness

you're okay." I breathe a sigh of relief. I haven't seen him since before I entered the abyss. "Did you end up in the abyss? I waited for you, but you didn't show."

He nods. "I was in there for a little while, but not as long as you. They make sure we don't end up with anyone when we're in there, so the punishment is more severe."

That makes sense. I was so keen to spend the time in the abyss with Blue. It probably wouldn't have been half as bad if he'd ended up in the same spot.

I'm happy until a sinking feeling fills me. "What're you doing here?" I ask.

A couple of people pass and gaze at me peculiarly. I realize that to them I look like I'm talking to empty space.

He gives me a guilty look. "Your angel was flashing on the charm again."

I look down to the top of his pants where the charm hangs and see the angel with golden wings still flashing. "I'm okay." I try to reassure him. "I completed my mission this time."

He shows relief, and I continue, "You did a lot for me and landed yourself in trouble. You can't be here. I don't want it to happen again."

A puzzled look crosses his face. "If you've completed your mission, why're you here?"

I try to hide my guilt as I explain, "I'm just checking up on someone."

One eyebrow rises, and he crosses his arms in front of his bare chest. I get the feeling he doesn't believe me. He asks, "If that's so, then why's your angel flashing?"

Shrugging my shoulders, I say, "I don't know. You charmed the charm."

He raises an eyebrow. I look away and find myself looking directly at Ethan by accident. My heart stops, and I hold my breath—he's looking at me. Anguish covers his face. I lower my chin, pull my hair over my face, and step back completely behind the aisle. Cursing silently to myself, I see that this movement doesn't escape Blue's attention.

Trying to bluff him, I feign innocence. "What?" I ask.

His second eyebrow rises to level with the first, and his blue eyes dance with amusement. "Do you really think I didn't see that?"

"See what?" I ask. I focus on the color of the ocean in his eyes, trying to reinforce my bluff. A couple of more customers pass, and I see them in my peripheral vision look back in my direction. I'm starting to look like a crazy woman standing here talking to myself. "Don't you have a mission to accomplish?" I whisper through my teeth.

"All complete," he says. "This's why I'm checking on the troublemaker." He smirks. "Clearly you're not in danger, so what trouble are you up to?"

A middle-aged couple wandering past and run into the invisible Blue. They stop suddenly and turn to give me a filthy look. I guess seeing me in the vicinity, they think I'm the one responsible for their sudden stop. I hide a smile behind my hand once they turn their backs to me. It's almost comical.

I look at Blue, He's smiling broadly, but he can afford to, considering they can't see him.

"Today is turning out to be quite entertaining. Which reminds me, what was that you just did—hiding behind your hair and the shelving?" he asks.

I can see that he's not going to give up. I try to divert the question. "Look, like I said, I'm just checking up on someone."

"Yeah, I get that. So, who is it?" he asks as he looks down the aisle to where Ethan is standing.

"Nobody in particular. Everything is good, and he's safe. Let's get out of here." I grab his bare arm in a loop then drop it, remembering that this will also look weird to the humans. He shrugs his shoulders. I know I've won for now, and I smile. We prepare to walk outside to find a place where I can transform back into an angel.

A voice sounds from behind, not loud, just audible. "Aurora?"

I freeze. I've been longing for so long to hear that voice call my name, but now isn't a good time. My head barely moves to look up at Blue standing on my right. He's seen my reaction, and whether I like it or not, I've his full attention. I try to step forward as though nothing has happened. As I lift my leg to move my foot, I hear it again.

"Aurora?" The voice is almost pleading.

My heart is ripping in two. I'm not supposed to be seen, and now Blue also knows my real name from my past life. On top of this, if the archangels find out about this encounter, I'm gone for sure. "You should go," I whisper to Blue.

He shakes his head, and his eyes hold determination.

"Get yourself away from here. I don't need you to be in trouble again because of me," I insist as I look pleadingly into Blue's eyes. I can see my words are not convincing him.

Slowly, I turn toward the voice. As my eyes rest on Ethan's face, I can feel the tears welling into the small dams in the corner of my eyes. The only way to tame these dams, which are about to explode, is to think of how much trouble I'll be in if I'm found out.

CHAPTER TWELVE

Across Ethan's face, I see hopeful disbelief. This isn't surprising—I'm dead. Once I completely turn around, he looks me up and down, assessing if I'm real.

"Aurora?" he whispers, almost choking on the words. His pale-brown eyes are cloudy with confusion, and the corners of his mouth edge down as though he knows someone's playing a cruel hoax on him.

I nod. I can see he wants to believe it, but he's not a fool and knows that I can't be real. He takes a few moments to study me, and then his face relaxes. He steps forward and surrounds me with an embrace.

"You look different. Like you—but different," he whispers in my ear.

I hear Blue clear his throat in the background. "Who's this?" I hear a strange tension in his voice.

I turn my mouth away from Ethan's ear. "This is Ethan, my true love for three lives," I whisper.

"What?" Blue hisses. "We have to ditch this dude

and get out of here, after we wipe his memory, that is. You're playing with fire here. Even for you this's extreme."

Blue has never hissed at me before, and it concerns me, but I understand. Releasing Ethan, I turn to look at Blue and say, "You should leave, Blue. I did warn you. This's my mess to deal with."

Ethan steps back and asks, "Who're you talking to? And what do you mean the past three lives?"

I'm about to turn and look at him when I see Blue become brighter. "Me," he says. He's made himself visible. Thankfully there's no one in the area at the time. This isn't how I envisioned my time with Ethan.

Ethan steps back from me and away from Blue. "Whoa! Where'd you come from? And where's your shirt?" He looks back at me and asks. "Are you a ghost? No, wait, I just hugged you." He steps a little farther away, his face losing its color. "How are you here?"

Blue places an arm around my shoulders and stands a little too close. "She's an angel. But I guess you already knew that," he adds in a cavalier fashion. A smirk forms on his face watching Ethan's expression as he registers the information.

I turn to give Blue a glare. "You're not helping."

"And so I shouldn't be. What you're doing isn't healthy. We need to wipe his memory and leave. Angels and humans shouldn't mix, especially past loves. This is going too far." Blue is upset. I've never seen him upset before. He's always so calm and collected.

Hearing raised voices, a male shop assistant looking to be in his fifties, stops. He wears a red shirt and deep gray apron with "Bunning's Warehouse" written on it. He peers down his nose, through his glass lenses and asks, "Is everything okay here?"

Ethan looks at me; his face is contorted, but then his eyes rest on Blue. "Yeah," he says without emotion. "Yeah," he adds with more conviction. "Everything is good here."

The shop assistant looks at each of us individually, and I see him observing the facial expressions of the two males. He looks back at me and says, "Okay then. But there will be no fighting in here." He doesn't sound convinced, but he steps away, remaining within hearing distance.

A few moments of silence pass, and I can see his eyes continually looking in our direction, watching and listening.

"Can we go outside and talk?" I ask Ethan.

Ethan nods, and Blue adds, "Yeah, let's take this outside."

I turn to him. "Actually, you aren't invited."

He shrugs. "It doesn't matter; I'm coming anyway. You need protection from yourself. Hopefully, I'll get it through your head how dangerous this is. The archangels will make sure you won't see the light of day if they catch you."

I sigh and begin to walk outside with Ethan next to me and Blue following too close for comfort. As we walk, Ethan keeps turning his head and looking at me. He seems to want to say something, but then he looks at Blue and the words never come.

When we reach the parking lot, I look for a place

without security cameras. I see a grassy spot just off the tarmac, and I direct the group in that direction. Blue is still hovering around, and I can see that it's causing Ethan to be more on edge. I turn to Blue and ask, "Can you take off for a bit?"

Blue opens his mouth to protest, and I place a finger on his lips. I plead with my eyes, as I look deep into his. I can see his concern, which I'm guessing is the cause of his anger.

"I'll be fine." I try to put him at ease. "You can even stand just over there, near those trees. That way you can see everything that's going on." I know because of his angel hearing he'll still be able to hear what we say, but Ethan doesn't know that. After studying my face, Blue glances at Ethan then back at me. He nods, and I can feel the pressure rising.

"Just don't do anything stupid. I can't bear to lose you to the abyss again. I'd miss you too much."

I smile sadly. "I'll be good. I promise."

He leaves us to talk, observing from a distance. I sit on the grassy mound and tap the ground next to me with my hand, inviting Ethan to sit with me.

He sits, resting his elbows on his knees and his arms stretching out in front of him, joining at the hands. His muscles in his arms twitch as he fiddles with his fingers. He's staring straight ahead. A puff of breeze ruffles his hair, and an alluring smell of burgers and chips wafts by from a local fast-food place. I wish I could eat food again. Ignoring the pull, I look at Ethan.

He continues to look straight ahead. A frown is crumpling his tanned forehead, and his lips press together. I push my body sideways, nudging his shoulder softly with mine.

"Hey!" I say forcing a smile.

His eyes focus on mine. The confusion resting in them hits me with a wave of sorrow. I can feel the edges of my mouth turn down.

"You know, I didn't mean for it to happen this way," I say slowly. I see the lines in his forehead deepen, but he doesn't say anything. "I was only trying to drop by and see if you were doing okay . . . and because I miss you." I finish in a whisper. His creases iron out a little. "But I didn't mean to cause you confusion or heartache."

"How are you here?" he asks. His voice cracks midsentence. "You . . . you're supposed to be dead." He studies my face. "And you look like you, only different."

A tear trickles down my cheek. I lift my hand and wipe it away. "It's true. I did die . . . and I'm . . . no longer human. As Blue said, I'm an angel. I'm chosen because I died an innocent three times." I smile. "I guess that's why I look better now than I did as a human."

"Don't be absurd. You looked perfect as a human." His mouth turns up in a half-smile, while his eyes search my face longingly. I can see he means it. "I want you back," he whispers as he reaches out and takes my hand.

A tear rolls down my other cheek. I don't wipe this one away, rather I taste its salty flavor when it hits the side of my mouth. "You aren't much different than I was." I choke out the words past the lump in my throat.

"What do you mean?"

I want to tell him that if he remains an innocent and gets murdered, he'd be able to join me as an angel, but I don't. I know that this isn't a good thing to tell someone when they're in the sad mental state. If he knew this information, he might jeopardize his chances of dying as an Innocent while in a mad rush to be with me. Oh, how I dream of having him with me.

I smile at him and pat his thigh affectionately. "Just keep living like you do—with a good heart. Maybe one day we can be together again." I cast my eyes to the ground. Time is passing quickly, and I know I have to go. I begin to rise. He reaches out a hand and pulls me back to the ground next to him.

"Don't go," he whispers.

I look deep into his eyes. It pains me as I say, "I have to." I've already gone too far.

He reaches out a hand and lightly grabs my chin, pulling me forward. He leans in and brings his soft lips to mine. I can't breathe. My body is weighed to the spot as I allow his lips to explore mine. I welcome each gentle movement and inquisitive touch. My parted lips taste his flavor after so long—how I've missed his touch. This's making the necessary parting more difficult.

To the side, I see Blue step forward. I raise my hand toward him in a stop motion and give him a look begging for understanding. Surprisingly he stops, but not willingly. He crosses his arms over his bare chest so tightly his pecs bulge.

Ignoring Blue's disapproval, I turn my attention back to Ethan. Tears are now rolling down my face as I struggle with the internal battle that I know I must overcome. With my eyes open, I reach my hands up to his face, gently embracing each side of his head. I caress my fingers through his hair and feel the lump in my throat grow. I miss him already. Fighting against my will, I softly drag my palm over his forehead and my other palm behind his head, gently pulling up. As a warm sensation runs through my front palm, I watch his eyelids fly open. Panic is in his eyes as I begin the process of wiping his memory.

CHAPTER THIRTEEN

Standing together invisible under a nearby tree, Blue and I watch silently as Ethan gathers his thoughts where I'd left him. Tears are still pouring down my face. He looks completely lost and confused, assessing how he arrived on the grass in the first place. After a few minutes, he rises, dusts off his pants, and walks back to the store shaking his head.

If my heart were chocolate, it'd be a melted mess right now. I want to be alone, but I can feel Blue's eyes on me.

"What was that?" His tone is harsh, and it makes me cringe.

I need a hug, but sensing Blue's mood, I know this isn't going to happen. I'm gathering my thoughts when he starts again.

"What're you doing checking up on your past life?"

My heart is torn, and my head is a mass of torment. I'm not in the mood to have this discussion, so I walk away. I hear the whoosh of his wings behind me.

"What you did was going too far. It's bad enough for you to break the rules, believing that our perpetrators may change for the better. But for you to go out of your way to check up on your past love . . . is . . . is . . . beyond ludicrous." His voice has escalated to a yell. There are people going to and from their cars, but they can't hear us when we're invisible and speaking to one another.

I spin around to face him and hiss, "What's it got to do with you? I told you to leave me with it so that you wouldn't get involved. Besides, it's because of you that Ethan caught me. I would've been able to check in on him without him knowing." I wave my arms aggressively at him. "What is it with you and sticking your nose in my business?" I place my hands on my hips and stand firm.

"I'm trying to protect you," he protests.

"I don't need protection?" I snap. "And I don't need you getting into trouble because you keep getting messed up in my business."

"Don't you get it? We're no longer part of this life." His voice softens. "We have to rely on each other, and your friendship in our world means everything to me." His eyes have turned a deeper shade of blue showing his compassion.

He steps forward, and I drop my guard a little. I can't stay angry with him for long. I let my arms fall to my side. "I just needed that time alone." My voice drops to a saddened level. "My last mission was saving Ethan's little brother. I just had to see him." I choke out the words. "I had to see if he was okay."

Blue steps closer and reaches out. He grabs my hand and pulls me to him. Hesitantly, I let my legs stumble forward, and I fall into his embrace. Instantly his warmth makes its way to my heart and comforts me. He holds my head against his bare chest and strokes my hair. "You worry me," he whispers.

"Yeah, well, you worry me coming and getting involved in my mess." I remain snuggled against his skin, enjoying the comfort I'm receiving from him.

After a while, he pushes me back slightly and looks at me. "What was it he called you? Aurora?"

I roll my eyes. "There you go again, getting yourself into trouble because of me. You know I'm not supposed to tell you."

He smirks. "So your name was Aurora?"

I sigh then nod.

His eyes pass over my clothes and wings, and he says, "It suits you. It suits you even now."

I smile and shake my head. "Well, you know we can't have you as the only one in trouble. What was your name?"

"Guess." He lets me go.

I look at him weirdly. "Yeah, sure." The sarcasm is thick in my voice. "I don't know."

"Come on, guess." He grins.

I shake my head. "Don't blame me if I pick ones you don't like."

He shrugs.

"Timothy?"

He shakes his head.

"Andy?"

"No."

"Stephen?"

He shakes his head again.

"Jayden?"

"No." He throws his head back.

"Please don't tell me it was Michael. That'd make you seem so somber." I smile.

"No, I'm not named after Archangel Michael."

"Phew!" I wipe my brow mockingly. "Ethan?"

He rolls his eyes.

"Reginald?"

The look on his face makes me laugh. "Hey, you're making me guess."

He shakes his head. "Yeah, stupid me thinking you'd be smart enough to guess." He cocks an eyebrow. "My name is Ben."

"Really?"

"Why? What's wrong with that?" He begins to cross his arms.

"Oh, relax." I reach forward and uncross his arms. "It's nice to finally meet you, Ben. It's only been about seven months. Now we're both rebels."

"Speak for yourself."

I shrug. "What do you think Yellow's name was?"

"I don't know. Cindy?" He smirks.

"Cindy," I muse. "It suits her. It's a shame we can't call her that."

"Come on, we need to get back. If we hurry, maybe Archangel Michael won't dig into this part after our mission."

I nod. "Maybe we should skip the flying and teleport back." I suggest.

"Great idea. That'll save some time."

I cast a final glance around, looking for Ethan, hoping for a final glimpse before I leave. I can't see him. I wonder if he'll remember any part of what happened. I shake my head. It's better if he doesn't. I teleport back to base before Blue, rather Ben, starts to ask more questions.

When I arrive, Yellow is there, and I appear right next to her. "Hey, you," I say throwing an arm around her shoulder.

She jumps and holds a hand to her heart. "Oh, you startled me."

I smile. "Missed you. What've you been up to?"

"Missed you—" she jumps again.

Ben appears less than a few feet in front of her. "Hey. Cin—Yellow."

I lift my hand up to my mouth, hiding my smile.

"You guys seem chirpy today. And you always seem to arrive together." She eyes us suspiciously. "You're not up to mischief again, are you? 'Cause you know your trip to the headquarters has been the roaring conversation here. What happened?"

"We were sent to the abyss," I lower my voice. The reminder is already dampening my mood.

"Really?" She squeaks.

I nod. "Yes, even Blue. He finished my mission for me, and he got in trouble, too. Take note, you can't finish someone else's work. It's not allowed."

She picks up on my mood. "Sorry, sweetie. It looks

as though I've brought up bad memories." She squeezes my shoulder in a gesture to comfort.

"No, it's okay. I'd be curious, too." I try to sound reassuring. "I doubt Archangel Michael would tell you much."

"Ha, ha! Mr. tight-lipped himself. So, what was it like?"

"Horrible," I say. "I haven't had a chance to ask Blue yet." I look at Blue.

"Yeah, no. I wouldn't recommend it," he answers. "I wasn't in there as long, but I can imagine it being very hard to be in there for a long time. I think you'd go insane. There's no one to talk to, nothing to see. You float around in total darkness."

Hearing him describe it, my guilty feelings surface again. I'm the reason he was in there, yet he acts as though it wasn't my fault.

Yellow screws up her nose. "Sounds as horrible as the archangel's promise. I bet you're not in a hurry to break any more rules." She laughs.

Ben and I sneak a look at each other. After a moment, I answer, "Ah . . . yeah."

She stops laughing and looks at me. "You haven't broken the rules again, have you?"

I look at Ben again, and he answers for me. "You'll be happy to know that she completed her mission this time. I didn't have to finish it for her."

"That's awesome. That must be a relief for you to come back after a successful mission."

"Uh-huh!" I say.

She turns and looks at me while smiling. She opens

her mouth to say something but falters. Noticing that she's gazing past us, I turn to see what has her attention. Standing right behind me is Archangel Gabriel. The archangel's blue gown flows softly to the ground, and the white wings frame the slightly darker blue from the clear sky. My mouth drops open for a moment.

"Archangel Gabriel," I say.

"You know him, um, her?" Yellow whispers in my ear as though an archangel wouldn't be able to hear.

"Yes, that's right," Archangel Gabriel answers for me, not using a condemning tone and in a voice that isn't masculine or feminine. "We'd the unfortunate circumstance of a meeting at headquarters. Didn't we, sweethearts?" The archangel turns to look at Ben and me, the blue eyes kind.

I look sideways, feeling a little guilty, and see Ben look at the ground.

"And as for him or her," Archangel Gabriel continues, turning the handsome face to Yellow. "Archangels are technically androgynous. How we choose to appear to you or humans is up to us. Being more open-minded, I choose to leave that up to you."

"Ah," Yellow says, for once short on words. Her eyes gaze over the archangel's blonde, curly hair.

I remember that Archangel Gabriel didn't want to send us to the abyss and look up. "It's good to see you, but how come you're here instead of Archangel Michael?"

"Oh, yes, that's right. He's currently in the middle of a battle and can't make it here today."

"What?" we all ask at once.

"I know. It's so shocking. Right?" A mock frown creases Archangel Gabriel's ageless brow. "You do know he's the great warrior and leader of all the angels, don't you?"

"Yes, of course," Ben says. "We're just used to having him around. He's never missed training or giving out a mission."

"Well, unfortunately, the demons are getting stronger, and he's leading the archangels against them to squash them before their strength increases."

"Don't you go?" I ask.

"Oh, honey, I'm not into that stuff." Archangel Gabriel tilts a hand at me. "I prefer to be the bearer of inspiration and creativity, not war."

I realize how much that makes sense and why I had the overwhelming feeling of creativity when I was near the archangel at the headquarters.

Archangel Gabriel continues, "But what they do is critical. It's another reason that what you do is important and essential to keeping the demons' strength down."

"What do you mean?" Because of my personal beliefs about the conscience inserting, I'm hungry for the truth behind it. "How does what we do help fight demons?"

"Oh, that's right. You're all too new to know about why inserting the new conscience is so important." Archangel Gabriel places a broad, almost hairless, hand up to their chin and rubs it lightly. "Normally we wouldn't tell you yet, but maybe it'll help you to make the right choice when it comes to finishing your mission." Archangel Gabriel finishes this sentence while looking at me.

"Maybe," I say, not making any promises but itching to know the reason. The archangels and their traditions and secrets, I think to myself. They need to catch up with the times and realize that our generation likes to have full access to knowledge, so we can make clear decisions. "Can you tell us, please?"

Archangel Gabriel casts a brief glance around the small group and sighs. "Okay. But I hope it helps you make the right decision. Each time you insert a conscience, you injure the demon that's made the person evil. The injury weakens it and its cause by flushing it out of another host."

"I knew it!" I exclaim. "I knew there had to be something that made these people evil, especially when they had good in their past."

"Yes, it's true, but we have to enforce this ruling." Archangel Gabriel's eyes are already studying me with a worried look, so I decide to pull back my excitement of the knowledge. "One of the reasons that you're punished when you don't insert a conscience is because you give the demon a chance to remain and grow stronger. It's a shame when humans don't handle the guilt from their evildoings once a conscience is reinserted."

"What's that?" Yellow screeches. "What do you mean that they don't handle the guilt?" Her eyes flick off each one of us, then settle on the archangel.

Archangel Gabriel leans over and strokes the frond of a palm nearby. "Isn't nature lovely?" The wind picks up and blows the green leaves from the archangel's hand.

Yellow looks at us. "Do you know? Is that what you were trying to tell me the other time?"

I look at Ben. He looks uncertain. We both look at Archangel Gabriel.

"I've said too much already," the archangel exclaims. "But clearly I need to tell you a little more as these two are not suitable to tell you. They've a different effect than other angels when they insert a conscience. I saw it when I looked into their minds up in headquarters—especially the colorful one." The archangel is pointing to me.

I frown and look at Ben. He also looks confused. "What do you mean?" I ask.

"Oh, for goodness sake. I'm digging myself into a bigger hole." Ignoring my question, Archangel Gabriel turns to Yellow and says, "When perpetrators receive a conscience after committing crimes, some don't handle the guilt well."

"What happens?" Yellow asks.

"Each one is different. Some of the perpetrators get a mild case of guilt, but some feel the guilt more. It's intensified or dulled depending on the angel giving it to them and the extent of their crime."

"Okay, but what happens to them?" Yellow's eyes are fixed on Archangel Gabriel.

"Well, some just feel sorry for themselves and reprimand themselves for their actions and move on. Some go crazy and become mentally ill to a certain degree.

And some of the perpetrators get so mentally ill or distressed that they end up killing themselves."

Yellow gasps. "What do my perpetrators do? I've never checked up on them. I was doing as I was told." Her face is flat in shock. I feel a little stunned as well, being told I've a special effect on my perpetrators.

"Yes, well, that rule is for your own state of mind," Archangel Gabriel continues. "Let me take a quick look into you." The archangel steps forward with a hand raised and touches a fingertip to Yellow's forehead. It lights up. In only a few moments, the finger is removed. "Rest assured, your perpetrators receive only mild guilt —nothing that'll destroy them in the end. So go on out there, sweetie, and do your work."

Yellow almost smiles, and I don't blame her. "What do their perpetrators do?" She's pointing to us.

"The male has a bad mental effect on his perpetrators."

"I do?" Ben asks.

I move my head up and down. "Yes. I saw it. I went to check up on the perpetrator in South Africa." I watch as the corners of Ben's mouth turn down.

"And what about your perpetrators?" Yellow asks me.

Unsure if I should answer, I look at Archangel Gabriel. I receive approval by the tilt of the head, so I continue. "The perpetrator I checked up on, my first perpetrator, killed himself. I haven't checked up on the last perpetrator. I'm hoping that isn't the case, but now I'm not so sure."

"Oh, gosh! Listen to me jabbering. Enough already. I

have to check your missions and send you on another one—if you've been good, that is." Indicating with a hand, Archangel Gabriel calls me over. "Come on. You first. You're the naughty one."

Great! Now I've a target on my head. I approach slowly. The nerves are already starting to create a whirlwind in my stomach.

"Come, come. You can't have already broken the rules so fresh out of the abyss."

I swallow the lump in my throat, trying to not make it obvious. Archangel Gabriel places a finger on my forehead, and I can feel the warmth as my mind is being probed. I'm tense, but there's nothing I can do. As I found out the hard way, I can't redirect the archangels from places within my mind. I watch as my mission is relived in a flash of time. While looking deep into the archangel's compassionate eyes, I feel the finger being removed.

"Well done! You had a hard mission there, and you conquered it. What an emotional ride that must've been for you."

A tear rises from the memory, and I blink it away. "It was difficult."

Archangel Gabriel places a hand on my shoulder. "You should be proud." Moving the hands together, I see the small cloud forming in the center. The archangel reaches in and pulls out a glowing bean. I take it and swallow, enjoying the warmth. I wait as Ben and Yellow are assessed; both pass the probing and receive their new mission.

When finished, Archangel Gabriel stands back and

says, "Wow, look at you. You all passed with flying colors even with a difficult mission. You're so strong and focused. It's no wonder Michael chose you. My students are softer and impartial."

"I'm sure that they're happy students, though." From the couple of encounters I've had with Archangel Gabriel, I was certain that we'd get along and that the teaching wouldn't be so strict. "I think you'd make an awesome teacher."

"Oh."

For a moment, I thought I saw tears forming in Archangel Gabriel's eyes.

"Oh, enough with you. You have the best teacher for you. Now off you go." We're shooed away.

CHAPTER FOURTEEN

Large drops of water pelt down. The gray clouds blanket the once blue sky, masking the changes as the day turns into night. With gusto, the rain hits my hair and wings aided by the breeze. If I weren't an angel, I'd be soaked.

Over the rain, I can hear my footfall as my boots hit the pavement on the boardwalk lining the Belmar Marina. There's no one in sight, undoubtedly sheltering from the unpleasant weather.

For this mission, my Innocent is at the Jersey Shore, in the US state of New Jersey. I look to the left and observe the recreational boats rocking back and forth while attached to their floating docks on Shark River. I haven't been here before, and if it weren't for the gloomy weather, the scenery fading quickly into the darkness would most likely be enticing.

I hear a muffled scream to my right, and I pick up my pace. There's a four-lane bridge on large concrete pillars, and the sound appears to have come from that direction. I step onto the grassy, uneven bank, keeping my eyes peeled for any movement as I listen for any sound. Deep down I sense that I'm heading in the right direction. As I walk up the slight slope, a flash of blue appears in my peripheral vision. Curious, I turn in that direction, and I'm surprised when I see Ben standing only a few feet away.

"What're you doing here?" I ask. "You can't be checking up on me again, surely?"

He bears a stunned look. "Actually, I was wondering what you're doing here. Are you going to start following me around now?" He smirks. "It's okay. You can tell me that you miss me and can't bear to be without me."

I glower at him, but I can't help but smile. "You're funny. But this's my mission."

"It's mine, too," Ben says. His brow creases. "What're we in for if they sent both of us?"

A gut-wrenching scream fills our ears, demanding our full attention. Without another word, we turn in unison and continue up the hill under the bridge. We've remained invisible, giving us the advantage of sneaking up on the perpetrators. In a secluded corner between pillars, I see movement. I turn to Ben and gesture in that direction. The area is sheltered from the miserable weather and the eyes of any possible passers-by. We hasten our steps up the slope. In the dimness, I see one dark-clothed person moving up ahead, and as we move closer, I see another. With each foot forward I seem to be seeing more people.

What's going on up there? I wonder.

I turn to look at Ben and see a flash of yellow behind him.

"Yellow?" I gasp.

Her pale face mirrors the confusion I felt only a few minutes before.

"What's going on?" she asks.

"We don't know, but it looks like a joint mission," Ben says. "There's movement up there with several people."

"And there's been cries of distress," I say.

"Well, what're we waiting for?" she asks. She spins in the indicated direction, flinging her hair behind her. We quicken our pace to keep up with her.

We reach the secluded corner, and what we find brings us to a halt. I quickly scout around the shadows under the bridge, taking in the horrifying scene. Now it's clear why we all need to be here for a good result.

Before us, I see nine males laughing and jeering. In the center of their ring is a young female being pinned to the ground. She looks only sixteen. There's a man at each of her hands, pinning them to the ground, and a man holding down each of her feet, securing her legs wide. Her clothes are torn, barely covering her private parts. The exposed flesh is battered and bruised. Behind the bruises and abrasions, her face is ghostly white. I don't know if she's conscious. Her eyes are puffy and red. It's hard to tell if she's looking through the slits of her swollen lids.

I've the urge to dry heave as my eyes gaze over her skin. There are deep gashes with blood pouring from the wounds on her face, arms, legs, and torso. Kneeling between her legs is a young man. His dark-brown hair sits neat and untouched, showing signs that the girl didn't have a chance to fight. In his hand is a switch-blade. He holds it tauntingly over a rare unmarked piece of flesh on her body. The crowd is cheering on his actions. From the tip of the knife, drops of blood fall on her skin.

I can't believe what I'm seeing. The males can't be any older than eighteen, some possibly years younger yet still large for their age. They're of different races and seem to be from a variety of backgrounds. What could possess these males to act this way and think it's okay?

I don't know if they intend on violating her sexually, but I'm not about to wait around to find out. I fold my wings away and prepare to turn visible. Noticing a movement off to the side, I turn to see that Ben is one step ahead of me with Yellow not far behind, walking in his shadow.

Ben stands behind the group of boys and crosses his arms over his bare chest. Purposely, he clears his throat loudly. Watching from behind, I see the boys turn around. The expressions on their faces show annoyance.

The man in between the girl's legs turns in his kneeling position and sneers. "Hey look, guys, model boy thinks he's going to be a hero." A caliber of laughter echoes through the group. "Where's your shirt, model boy? How'd you like me to put a few markings on that canvas?" Bearing a sadistic smile, he raises to his feet, still clutching the bloody knife in his hand.

Yellow steps forward out of the shadows of the concrete pillar behind Ben and stands on his left side.

With her wings packed away, she looks like a brilliant Barbie doll. Her face is pale and flawless, framed by her golden hair, and her body is defined well in the tight yellow bodysuit. I haven't seen her in action, and it's strange to see her face so determined. She stands with her legs shoulder width apart and her arms crossed in front of her chest.

Not wanting to miss out on the action and wanting to help the poor girl, I step forward. I stand on Ben's right side, and going with the theme I cross my arms in front of my chest. My disposition is solemn, and I'm in no mood for wisecracks.

The man with the knife continues. "Look, he brought his pretty friends for us to play with. Looks like we'll be in for a treat tonight." His eyes skim Yellow's and my body. "I was getting tired of the other tart, too. These ones are a better class," he announces. "Not to mention that they've plenty of squirm left in them, unlike this one." He indicates the broken girl on the ground. "I'd love to carve some special markings on your bodies."

His voice makes the hairs on my body stand on end, and I cringe with each perverted look he casts my way. I can see his companions begin to circle around behind us. The ringleader focuses on me for some reason. I unfold my arms and clasp my hands into fists. I'm ready. We were trained to be ready for the unexpected as well as the expected. I certainly know which way this's going. The group has circled and is ready to fight three to one.

The leader spots my reaction. "Oh look, how sweet.

This one thinks she has a chance." He laughs heartily, and his minions follow suit. "It's always extra special when they think they have a chance. I find that irresistible." He blows me a couple of kisses.

I'm sick to the stomach, but I play along. I deepen my voice to a seductive level. "Then come and get me, honey."

He nods to his lackeys behind me, and they charge. In one movement, I lean to the side on one leg and plant a sidekick into the one on my right's stomach, sending him backward into a concrete pillar. While doing this, I reach out with both hands and grab the wrist of the one on my left. As I correct my position, I pull his arm toward me and snap it over my shoulder. I hear the crunch of bones breaking right next to my ear, followed by his low-level cry as he slumps to the ground in agony.

On guard, I turn my head toward the leader. He's still standing close to me, but this time I see a tiny crack in his mask of confidence. He doesn't let this overtake him. With the bloodied knife still in his hand, he reassesses the situation. He looks at my attackers one at a time, then says, "I think you just got lucky, sugar."

"If that was just luck, then why don't you come and try yours?"

He licks his lips as though he hasn't had a drink for a while and fiddles with the knife, tossing it between his hands. I watch his eyes. This way I can judge in advance which way he's going to attack. As I stand on the balls of my feet, ready to spring, I see a slight twitch in his right eye. A moment later he lunges forward with the knife in his right hand. I step far enough to the side for the knife to pass by me. I revel in the surprised look on his face, but not for long. As soon as he pulls his hand back, he tries for a strike again. This time it clips my sleeve, narrowly missing my skin.

He regains his posture and holds the knife above his head, trying to thrust it into my heart. I dash to the side and grab his wrist with both hands, helping its natural momentum downward, directing it into his leg. He buckles to the ground screaming in pain with the knife sticking out of his thigh. He reaches for it, and I see a strange tattoo on the inside of his wrist. It's an upside-down pentagram finished with the details of a goat's head inside a circle. A recognized symbol of Satan. I don't know why, but this surprises me for a second. I've a bad feeling about that mark.

In this moment of distraction, a pair of arms grabs me from behind, securing my arms tightly behind my back. I look to the side and see the teen with the broken elbow charging at me. He should still be crippled in pain. Using my captor's strength, I put my full weight into his hands and kick out with both legs. The broken-elbowed attacker involuntarily flies backward as does my captor behind me. Still in his grasp, we stumble together until he trips on something, and we land on the ground, me sitting on top of him. The shock causes him to release my arms. I jump up, away from his grasp. The leader is limping my way with the knife removed, and blood gushing down his leg, but he still keeps coming. I don't understand how they can keep advancing.

In the near distance, I see Ben. He's fighting in his usual confident and strong style. His attackers are covered in blood; one has his whole arm dangling from its socket, and he still continues to lunge forward and attack with ferocity. On the wrist of the loosely flapping arm, I spot the same tattoo.

A blast of wind passes my ear. I move sideways away from the pressure. While turning to see where the gust has come from, I see the leader slashing his knife at my throat. Leaning back, I narrowly dodge the knife. He swings it again toward me. I block it with both arms then slide one hand down to his wrist. Ducking under his upturned arm, I snap it over my shoulder. He drops the knife yelling in pain. My elbow slams into his ribs as I turn and begin to attack his face and throat. My swinging hammer fist brings a final blow to his temple; I watch him fall to the ground.

Before he lands, I feel arms grab me around the waist. I drop to the ground with all my weight and slam one of my high heels into the toes. The hands instantly let go from the shock of the pain. I turn to finish this attacker when I see the attacker with the broken elbow coming my way.

Grunting, I jump and kick him straight in the stomach and then up to his head, directly in his face. I hear the crunching sound as the cartilage breaks in his nose. Blood is pouring down his face, yet he begins to regain his balance to try again.

I can't believe it. These teens are relentless. My eyes skim quickly for Yellow. It wasn't hard to spot her with her yellow colors. She's fighting well, and I feel a surge of pride rise in my chest. I take a moment to study her attackers. One of them has a bone sticking out of his lower leg. When I see him, I feel my mouth drop. He's still continuing the fight, somehow limping forward, ready to attack again. Impossible. I look at his wrist. He, too, has the same symbol. There has to be something that's preventing these attackers from falling.

I quickly turn my attention back to my attackers. Bloody Nose is still coming my way. Behind me, attacker three is getting ready to rush again, and the leader is also starting to squirm. I have to do this fast—this fight needs to end. With my ears on full alert, I hear attacker three approaching very close behind me. I turn quickly, spotting my mark and jump, landing a round-house kick straight to his stomach. Following through with the momentum, I place the kicking foot down and spin on it, jumping again and landing the roundhouse kick on the side of his head.

He leans to the side with the kick. I spin backward and let my heel hit his head in the opposite direction. He falls to the ground. This impact would land any normal person unconscious.

I turn around ready for my bloody-nose attacker. He's almost on me. Spinning, I land a fist in the front of his face, right on his already broken nose. He screams out in pain, and tears fill his eyes. While he's grasping his nose, I jump and land a kick straight on his kneecap. The sound of ripping tendons and breaking bones sends shivers down my spine. His leg bends in half the wrong way. The look, along with the recent sound of the destruction, almost makes me sick. I mentally push the sensation down and turn to find the leader. He hasn't quite made it up, but considering a normal human would be completely wiped, he's achieved an enormous feat.

Swiftly, I approach him before he can stand, and place my hands on both his temples. There's something about these attackers that makes me not want to see what's in their minds, especially this one. His eyes open wide. For the first time, as I watch the conscience enter him, I notice that they're the color of a clear-blue sky.

The battle has drained some of my energy, and I catch my breath while I complete the process. I find it harder to feel sorry for this perpetrator, but as I see some innocence from the past, I'm torn. I hold on to the hope that he won't end his life after I've finished, but after what Archangel Gabriel said, I'm doubtful. There must be a better way to take the evil from a human.

When I retract my hands, he sits stunned and unmoving. I don't have time to observe his reactions, as I've to check on the other two attackers. Revolving around, I see Broken Nose is trying to get up. I shake my head in disbelief. I do a quick check to see if Ben and Yellow are okay. Ben is leaning over his first perpetrator. I can see the white light passing through his hands as he inserts a conscience. His other two attackers are lying on the ground for the moment.

Yellow looks to be in control, although all her attackers are still untouched.

I reach the guy with the broken nose and push him completely to the ground. I step on his broken knee, hindering him from getting up, and his cry fills the air.

He slumps completely to the ground, and I place my hands on both temples. Before I start the process, I look into his eyes. This time I notice not only that there's a weird distant look in them. Hearing groans from my third attacker as he regains consciousness, I know I don't have time to ponder over this look of absence. I release the conscience into his temples. In his eyes, I see my same nightmare again—innocence and kindness wasted. Each time I see this it eats at my soul.

When I finish, I turn to attacker number three. I struggle with the vision of him standing perfectly straight in front of me. I can see the bruises already forming on his head from the knocks that rendered him unconscious, yet there he stands as though nothing happened. He lunges at me. I twist away and land a low back kick into his groin. I know it's a good hit. Once I turn around, I see him gasping for breath. Now is the time to insert the conscience. This time I turn my guilt sensor off and try not to think of what might happen to him later. It helps to look at their unconscious victim still lying in the rain-soaked grass.

When finished, I drop the head gently and look around. Blue is still battling, but from what I can see, he's doing fine. I turn my head to look at Yellow. She still has three attackers, and none of them look very injured even though she's fighting them well. Her face looks drained. Keen to round up the fighting, I step in to help her. She knocks one to the ground in my direction. Before he can get up, I grab him from behind and insert a conscience. At first, he struggles but gives in after a little while. When finished, I lift my head, and I see Yellow has finished her first victim. Leaving only one left. Knowing she doesn't need help to finish the last one, I stand. Ben is fighting his last attacker, so I make my way to the young lady—our mission.

I kneel down beside her. She's a mess. I can't see her chest rise and fall with the rhythm of breathing, and I begin to worry. I run a hand over her chest area without touching her, sensing her vital signs. Unable to find a pulse, my worry intensifies. I inch my hand closer and run it over her chest again. The concern is a tyrant through my body until I find the weakest of beats from her heart. Even though I've found a pulse, she's in no condition to start a celebration. I still don't see or hear any breathing, and her heartbeat is getting weaker by the second.

I open her mouth, placing mine on hers, and start to breathe some air into her lungs. Her chest rises and falls with my help, but when I stop to see if there are any results, her breathing ceases. While touching her lips, I can feel her heartbeat fading. I become very concerned. We're not supposed to lose victims, Innocents. We're supposed to save them; this can't be happening. I throw my head back in frustration. We can't lose her.

CHAPTER FIFTEEN

With anxiousness overtaking me, I look down at the young lady's dying body. I've no idea what I'm doing, but my instincts tell me to place my hands on her chest. I do this with my palms down over her heart. I've visions of an electric shock entering my head. I gasp when this vision transforms into reality, and a shock leaves my hands and goes straight into her body. She doesn't move. I find myself picturing the same vision in my head, and again my palms respond with small bolts of lightning.

Her body jumps. This time I can feel more than a brief heartbeat. I can hear it continually beating softly under her rib cage. I breathe into her mouth a couple of more times and watch as this time the rhythm sticks, and her chest continues to rise and fall. I exhale a sigh of relief. My eyes scan over the numerous cuts and bruises. I can't bear to see them on her anymore. Acting on instincts alone, I begin placing my hand on each wound individually. Seeing the sores disappearing slowly with each touch brings a deep joy to my heart.

I hear a sound close behind me and gaze briefly in that direction. Yellow and Ben are watching me.

"I didn't know we could do that," Yellow says.

A smile spreads across my face. "I didn't, either. But it sure makes me feel good. You should give it a try."

An apprehensive look crosses Yellow's face. "How do you do it?"

"I don't know. It just comes naturally."

She kneels down and touches a sore and waits. Nothing happens. She touches it again. Nothing. Her shoulders slump forward. "It's not working," she whines, the look of disappointment covers her face.

"Maybe it's because you don't have confidence in yourself," I say, trying to be helpful. "Envision it in your head like it's already happened."

She reaches out and tries again. Watching with bated breath, I almost cross my fingers behind my back for her. Right now she needs a little booster in confidence; I can feel it. The sore doesn't heal. Yellow looks devastated.

"Hey, it's okay," I say. "We haven't had training in this."

"But you can still do it." It almost sounds like an accusation.

I reach out and touch her hand while studying her face. "I'm sorry if this upsets you. You do know I wouldn't want that for the world, don't you?"

She sighs and shakes her head. "No. It's not your fault. I just wish I could do something special."

"You are special. You're an angel." She doesn't return my smile, so I return to being serious. "I don't know how I'm doing it, but I'm sure you have talents that I don't have."

"I hope so." She places a hand on the girl's forehead. "It'd be nice to have healing powers, though." She turns to look at Ben. "How about you, Blue, are you going to try it?"

Ben shakes his head. "It's okay. Besides, it's time we turn invisible. It looks like our patient is waking up."

I turn to look back at the girl. She's stirring, and her head is moving side to side slowly. I conceal my form and continue with the healing. After I see Yellow and Ben fade, I remove the bruising from her eyes. Her eyes open, and I smile. She begins to sit and have a look around.

Yellow stands and lets out a yell of happiness, heard only by Ben and myself, her recent grievance forgotten for the moment. My stomach fills with a deep warmth that spreads throughout the rest of my body, and I breathe in deeply. We've succeeded.

The invisible Yellow is smiling, and she stands behind the girl helping her up to a standing position and bracing her when she has a wobbly turn. The girl's hair is matted, and she's recovering from the blood loss with a few cuts remaining. Otherwise, she looks in perfect health. The girl looks down at her torn clothes, barely concealing her body. She clutches them, trying to cover up a little, and then studies the remaining marks on her body.

Touching a couple of wounds, she mutters to herself, "I could've sworn that they did more damage than that."

Something catches her eye, and she looks over, spotting her attackers. They're still sitting on the ground, their eyes unfocussed, as they struggle with the insertion of the conscience. Regaining her balance quickly, she stomps over to one of the males that pinned her down and punches him in the face. The sound of the fist against his skin is quite impressive. She stumbles briefly over the exertion then straightens.

She then goes to another and stomps on his fingers. He cries out briefly. She turns, and her eyes fall on the leader. With fury in her step, she trudges over and kicks him in between his legs. He moans loudly in pain, but she doesn't seem satisfied with the result. Pausing, she studies her once attacker. Standing over him, she looks into his eyes.

"What's wrong with you?" she asks. He's nonresponsive. She pulls her arm back and lets it fly, striking him hard against his face. The slap leaves a red welt covering his cheek. He still doesn't respond. She shakes her head and grabs her clutch purse that she spots in the thin grass and pulls out her phone. She dials 911 and walks over to the attackers observing them. Her eyes flick from one laceration and broken bone to another. After one ring, she hangs up.

"How am I supposed to explain this to the cops?" She packs her phone back in her purse and talks to her attackers. "As much as you lowlifes deserve it, all nine of you have broken bones and bruises like you've been in a massive street fight, and I only have a couple of marks on me. I've no idea how." Her unsympathetic eyes continue to study them. "In fact, I'm not even going to call you an ambulance." She turns on her heels and starts walking toward the path lining the edge of the river, calling over her shoulder, "Good luck, jerks!"

After witnessing the spectacle, I'm certain this girl would've fought back if she'd had the chance. I feel a touch of pride as I watch her walk away. One of our perpetrators coughs, taking my attention away from the retreating girl.

I turn to Ben and Yellow, who are standing next to me. "What do you think of these guys fighting? Did something seem strange to you?"

"Yeah!" Yellow blurts out. "They kept coming back even after crippling injuries."

Ben nods. "It was a little unsettling. I was fine fighting them, but it was a little sinister."

"Good, so I wasn't the only one who noticed," I say. I walk over to the group and grab one of the left wrists while asking, "Did you notice this?" I'm looking up at Ben and Yellow and twisting the wrist toward them.

They'd strange looks on their faces.

"The inside of their wrists?" Ben asks. "Yeah, they have one like everyone else."

I frown and look down at the wrist I'm holding. The skin is blank. Baffled, I grab the other wrist. It's also unmarked. I go to the next man and pick up his wrist. Blank. I try his other one. Blank. I see the leader and dash over to him and pick up his left wrist. I definitely saw it on his wrist. Nothing. I check his other wrist. Again nothing.

I stand straight and look at Yellow and Ben. "Are you telling me you didn't notice the tattoos at all?"

They shake their heads.

"I'm not really a tattoo guy," Ben says and smirks.

"Me, either, wisecrack," I retort playfully. "But these tattoos were all the same, like these guys are in some kind of gang, and now they're gone."

"Sorry. I didn't see them. I was too busy looking at their faces. What was the tattoo?" Yellow asks.

"It was a circle with an upside-down pentagram inside, finished with the details of a goat's head. Doesn't look like much, but it's the sign of Satan."

"Is that bad?" Yellow asks.

"If taken seriously, it can be. To many Devil worshipers and other fast-growing occult groups, it's their symbol. These men and women have seen and experienced powerful supernatural forces. And they're in bondage to them." I look around at the perpetrators. "I don't know if this was part of the play here, but it's not to be laughed at."

"I didn't know you were such an expert in occultism." Ben raises an eyebrow at me.

An element of embarrassment hits me. "I'm not. I just happened to have a couple of friends obsessed with the spiritual life in high school. Some of the knowledge rubbed off in the end." I give off a half-chuckle tinged with embarrassment. "Now look at me."

"Yeah, you're an angel with a rebel streak." Ben grins.

I scowl at him playfully. "Hmmm!" I cross my arms. "I just follow my heart, I don't rebel." I look at our perpetrators. "We can't just leave them here. Either I can see if I can heal them enough to walk out of here by themselves, or we can call them an ambulance and let them explain how they got all those injuries."

"I vote for calling the ambulance," Yellow says.

Ben looks uncertain. "I don't know. I'm a little on the fence." His eyes pass over the males. "Some look tormented enough."

Knowing what my conscience insertion will probably do to my perpetrators, with Ben's perpetrator not faring much better, I know what I want to do. "I vote that I try to heal them. I think they'll suffer enough."

Yellow groans. "Fine," she says. The sound of disappointment fills her voice.

I kneel in next to the one with a broken knee. I hold both hands around it and picture it healing in my head. A light shines from my hands. Underneath my palms, I feel eerie movements as the pieces of bone find their way back to their correct places. I flinch as the kneecap slides under my hand. Once I've finished healing the major wounds on this man, I make my way to the next.

A thought crosses my mind. Maybe now Ben would like to try this. I look up at him. "Hey, Blue. Do you want to see if you can heal, too?"

Ben casts a quick look at Yellow. She places a hand on his shoulder. "Go on. Go try at least. I won't be mad if you can do it."

He comes over and kneels next to me. "What do you do?"

"I just place my hands or touch the wound and imagine it healing and going back to its original form. Why don't you try a small wound first?"

He places his hand on a bruise that's growing. His palm lights up over the area. After a minute, he pulls his hand away. The bruise is still there.

"I guess you can rule me out, too," he says, although he seems to be taking the news better than Yellow did.

"Give it another go," I say. "Maybe you just need a little practice."

"I don't think so, but I'll humor you." He smiles at me with a hint of cheekiness in his eyes.

Finding a smaller wound, he gives it another go. A moment later he pulls his hand away and looks at the result. "Nothing."

I frown as I fill with sorrow. "That's a shame."

Not wanting to waste any more time, I start back at work. I watch with awe and disgust as bones slide back through the skin automatically, then line up to heal, and the skin seals itself and heals. I cherish this new gift I've discovered.

When finished, I stand and face the other two. "We should go."

I see them nod before I'm about to take off. Then a thought hits me. "Hey, Yellow." She looks at me.

"What was your last human name?"

"What?" she gasps. "I can't tell you that; I'll be in so much trouble."

"Only we'll know," I say. "We won't tell anyone else."

She shakes her head. "No. I'm not doing it. I'm not giving in to your rebellion."

I can't help but smile. "Our rebellion?"

"Yeah. Oh, I don't mean it nastily, but you keep getting into trouble, and I don't want to do that."

"I know Blue's name, and he knows mine, but we found out by accident." It's half a lie. "It'd be nice to know yours, too."

Her eyes expand. "I'm not doing it. I'm not spending any time in the abyss."

"I'm not asking you to. Blue's last human name was Ben. I now call him that in private. My name was Aurora, and this's what Ben calls me." She reaches up like she's going to cover her ears. I grab her hands gently. "I know, how about we use a fake name instead of calling you a color? It's the same thing, really. I hope you'll use our names, but I'll understand if you don't. A color just seems so . . . impersonal."

Her face warms a little. "What would you call me?"

I look at Ben and smile. "Ben mentioned the name Cindy, and I think it suits you." I look back at her. "The name's bright and bubbly, just like you. What do you think?"

Her face lights up with excitement. "Actually, I love it!" A somber cloud soon snuffs out the light.

"What's wrong?" I ask.

Her brow creases with deep lines. "Please don't get me into trouble for this."

"Trust me. We've no intention of getting you into

trouble." I place an arm around her shoulders and turn my head to look at Ben. "So what is it, teleporting or flying back?"

A smile spreads wide across his face. "You have to ask?"

I laugh. "Flying it is then."

CHAPTER SIXTEEN

Flying back to base with Ben and Cindy, I relish the wind lifting me higher. So far, this's my favorite part of being an angel. I flap my wings, pushing myself above the clouds and into the thin air, where no parachutist or bird is capable of going. I follow my urge and pump my wings. With each stroke, they lift me higher and higher. It's so peaceful up here—not a soul in sight. It gives me a chance to think.

My mind passes over the shared mission we had today. It was an odd mission; completely different from any other we've done. Not only did we do this together, but there were also strange things about the perpetrators. They weren't normal. Each violator before these was easier to defeat and certainly did not come back to fight after a crippling blow. My mind ticked over why this would be.

A strong gust of wind charges through my hair and blows it in my face. I twist to face the other way as I progress higher.

Thoughts of the tattoo enter my head. My instincts are telling me that there's something about that tattoo. I can't quite put my finger on it. What's more, why'd it disappear? As I ponder over this, flapping some more, I remember how I didn't do an innocence check before inserting the consciences. A small lump of guilt twists in my stomach. It grows every moment I think about the perpetrators. Those males were eviler than the ones I'd dealt with in the past. It made it hard at the time to feel compassion, but because of the innocence I'd seen in their past, don't they deserve a chance, too? I'm now not so sure I've done the right thing, and this lump is starting to dig a hole through my intestines.

Flapping in big, strong strokes, using my wings at full capacity, I'm mesmerized as I watch them folding and touching in front of me, showing off their golden-yellow color in the sun. I touch my wings together behind me, then bring them forward in a swift motion, tip touching tip. This motion is so relaxing, so revitalizing, and it helps work out the lump of guilt. There's nothing I can do for the males now. I can only use what I learn from this experience in the future.

When I feel I've flown high enough, I look back and Ben and Cindy are following me. I can see the joy that I'm feeling on their faces. I smile and wait for them, hovering in one spot.

"What took you so long?" I jeer when they reach my level. Cindy's golden-blonde hair shimmers in the sun, with the yellow in her clothes sparkling brightly. She looks dazzling.

"Oh, were we following you?" Ben teases. The

sparkle of the sun on his well-defined torso catches my eye. I struggle not to examine it when he turns to Cindy. "We were just going for a leisurely flight. Weren't we Cindy?"

She nods. "Uh, ha. Like we want to follow you." She throws her hands out to the side.

"So that means that you won't follow me when I do this." I turn my head downward and fold my wings in tight to my body and allow myself to fall. The wind is whistling past my ears, becoming louder and louder as I fall. I can feel the pressure on my face and skin. The faster I go, the tighter I pull in my wings. I watch the ground rapidly approach. This 's an adrenaline junkies dream, and I know that Ben and Cindy love to do this, too.

Tucking my chin into my chest, I tilt my head to see if they've taken the bait. In the distance, I can see two little figures piercing the sky, looking like two small meteorites. Turning to look in the direction I'm heading, I try to smile but end up with my lips pushing out like a parachute. Laughing inside, I picture how ridiculous I must look.

I still have a fair distance to go, so I wrap my wings around me and begin to spin around and around like a whirlwind, heading faster toward the ground. I then tuck my chin in and I follow with my shoulders. My body flips, and I tuck my legs into my chest and do a triple summersault, then straighten out again.

When the ground becomes a little too close for comfort, I change my position by bringing my head back a little. This movement causes my whole body to flatten against the pressure of the wind. I'm only feet away from the ocean. To stabilize, I flap my wings and turn my body upright, and I wait for Ben and Cindy. I don't need to wait long. With a massive gush of wind, they're by my side.

"That was so fun," Cindy exclaims. A smile is spread across her face from ear to ear. "Wasn't it Ben?"

Ben doesn't need to answer. His face beams from excitement.

"Do you want to do that again?" he asks both of us.

"I'd love to, but we have to get back," Cindy responds.

"Always the responsible one, hey, Cindy," I tease.

"Someone has to be, and it isn't you," she laughs.

I turn and look over the ocean and see the island in the distance surrounded by crystal clear, blue water. "We're almost there. We've all done well today, so let's get it over with."

As we approach the island, I wonder if Archangel Michael will be addressing us this time. It's hard to imagine him getting hurt; however, I know war is war. It's about death. The demons must be able to kill angels.

The thought is discomforting. I hope dying three times is enough. I'm hoping there won't be a forth in this spiritual world.

The small grassy plain below is empty. It's not surprising. Even though it's close to the end of the day, it's probably not time yet. We land, unintentionally scaring away a small group of seagulls. They give off squawks of disapproval as they leave. To fill the time, I make my way toward the ocean. It's such a pretty area.

On a perfect weather day like this, the water is a beautiful pale color of blue and transparent. It's like looking into a blue-tinted fish tank, except one hundred times better. The sea life includes many different breeds and sizes, and they live in the stunning, colorful coral.

Behind me, I hear Cindy and Ben's footsteps. The ocean here's wild and untamed by humans, always an attraction. It's a privilege to train here. When we make it to the water's edge, the sun is beginning to set. The sky is picture-perfect with an array of different yellows, oranges, reds, and blues. It's a breathtaking view, even though we can't see it set over the water because the mainland of Australia lies in between.

Selecting a large rock not far from the water's edge, I sit to take in the scenery. Ben and Cindy choose a rock on either side, and we sit in silence, admiring the view. The ocean breeze pushes my hair gently from my face. I can feel the slight saltiness as it touches my skin. I revel in the beauty and the sounds of the birds and the waves lapping up against the rocks.

After several minutes of listening to nature, Cindy says, "It's so peaceful here." She's always one to talk first, but I hear edginess in her voice.

"It was," I say with a big grin. "Until miss chatterbox couldn't handle it any longer."

She squints her eyes at me, trying to feign annoyance. "Well, I'm getting nervous, and you know what I'm like when I'm nervous," She splutters. "It's getting late and none of the archangels are here yet." Her wings flap involuntarily, lifting her off her rock. "It's nearly dark, for goodness sake."

"I'm sure it'll be fine, Cindy," Ben reassures her. "The archangels have been around since the beginning of time. I'm sure they can handle themselves."

Cindy doesn't say anything as she hovers above the ground. Her forehead remains in a frown as she places one arm across her stomach and chews on the other hand's nails. She begins to pace while flying slowly, back and forth, back and forth above the rocks and water.

As much as I understand her concern, it's starting to get on my nerves. My peace is now completely gone.

Rising to my feet, I say, "Come on. Let's go and have a look on land to see if they're waiting for us there instead of calling for us." I reach out a hand to her, and she takes it. She lifts one side of her mouth in a soft smile, looking relieved to be doing something.

We trek through the native trees of the rainforest, and approach our training grass plain. Violet and Pink, a couple of our training fledglings, are waiting on the plain. I feel bad I didn't get to know them that well when we were training. I had clicked instantly with Ben and Cindy, as Violet and Pink had with others. Even in such a small group, we have our clusters.

"Hey, ladies," Ben calls, giving them a charming smile.

Both Violet and Pink turn and give Ben an adoring look. For a place that isn't supposed to have any sexual attraction, these two look like hormonal teenagers.

"Hi," Pink says, waving while batting her eyelashes. "So lovely to see you again." She approaches him and places an arm through his, stroking the lines in between the muscles on his arm with her other hand. I gawk at him in amazement. He looks to be lapping it up. Violet wanders over and takes his other hand. Her attention seems a little more distracted. She's still too friendly for my liking. Suddenly, I'm no longer feeling guilty I didn't befriend them earlier.

"Ah, what're you doing?" I hiss at him inadvertently, although I can't believe that my best friend has turned instantly into a low-level male escort. Much to my dismay, I feel a surge of jealousy. He's Cindy's and my friend.

He turns and winks at me. "Why don't you join us?"

I shake my head and screw up my nose. Cindy is still standing next to me. "Am I sensing jealousy?" Her eyes study me. I don't respond. "We're not supposed to be involved with others in that way. You know that, don't you?"

I scoff. "Oh, I'm not, believe me. I just don't understand why they're all over him."

She giggles. "Haven't you seen how hot he is? Not to mention he's a real sweetheart."

I'm still not looking at her, and I shake my head. "Nope. I haven't noticed at all."

"Uh huh. I believe you; others wouldn't." I can hear the laughter in her voice. "As for them, it'd be very hard for an angel of humanly love and even an angel of spiritual love to resist his charm, even if it's just a smile." She pauses, watching them for a little while. "Besides, he's not attracted to them; he's just enjoying the attention. After all, he was human."

Despite Cindy's reassurances, I can't bear to watch

any longer. I walk over and pin a smile on my face, which I know doesn't reach my eyes, and I barge in. "Excuse me ladies. We've work to do." I grab Ben's arm and walk away with him, leaving Pink and Violet behind. "What're you doing?" I hiss.

"What do you mean?" He looks at me, his face portraying innocence. "I was just being friendly." I can feel his eyes search my face as we walk away from the group. A smile spreads across his face. "Are you jealous?"

"As if!" The words burst out of my mouth while I continue looking straight ahead.

He nudges me lightly in the ribs. "It's okay, you can admit it. I won't mind, I promise."

I look him straight in the eye. "Okay, I admit it."

His smile grows larger.

"I'm jealous of your friendship."

His smile fades. "Aren't you a little jealous in any other way?" His eyes are giving me the puppy dog look, and I've never been good at resisting puppies.

I nudge him lightly with my shoulder. "You know we aren't allowed to like each other in any other way than friendship. They'll have our skins for sure."

"What, and going completely against their rules set for thousands of years for dealing with perpetrators is okay?"

He has me there, but it hurts me to tell him the truth. "Listen to you trying to encourage me to break the rules."

"I'm only following my instincts, just like you." In the rapidly fading light, his face holds gloominess.

We reach the edge of the plain and enter the rainforest. Darkness fills the sky, and our angel vision takes over.

"Where's all this come from?" I ask.

"You seriously don't know?"

I shake my head and feel horrible for the lie.

"Really? I could've sworn I've caught you checking me out a few times."

The pressure is getting to me. I'm not ready for this conversation. "Ben, it's complicated and you know it." The words come out harsher than I intend.

He straightens and drops my arm. "Yeah, I know. You're in love with your soul mate, true love, whatever—who isn't even your species anymore." His words flood with disappointment and anger.

"But he might be one day." I can see his hurt, but I can't help myself. "He's an Innocent, killed in two lives and living his third. If killed while he's still an Innocent, he'll join us." I'm ashamed of what I say, but it's the way I think.

He looks at me stunned. "I've thought you to be many things, usually positive, but never sick or desperate." He glares at me. "Listen to yourself. You sound like you wish for his murder."

I'm speechless. Shaking my head, I reach for his arm, and he yanks it away. He turns his back toward me. Seeing his hurt causes tears to well in my eyes. I let them roll freely down my cheeks.

"You need to wake up to yourself and what your role is now," he rebukes. "It's time for you to work out who'll be there for you when you need it, even when you think you don't need anyone from this life."

My head rocks back and forth in agreement even though I know he can't see it. "I'm sorry, Ben." The large lump in my throat is making it hard to get the words out. "Please don't be angry. I need you, especially in this life."

His back is still facing me as he remains silent. I give out an involuntary sniffle while studying the contoured lines in his back. He's right. I've caught myself unconsciously admiring him. I'm so caught up on my past lives and hoping to reunite with Ethan, I've denied it even to myself.

The ocean breeze blows cold against my wet cheeks. I reach out again to grab his arm and repeat, "I'm sorry, Ben. I do need you. You know I need you, even if I'm too stubborn to admit it myself." The lines of his back and around his neck soften. Slowly, he turns to face me. He steps closer. I can see a hunger in his eyes that I've never seen before. My tears are no longer falling after being stunned into hiding.

Startled, I take a step away and find my back between my wings pressed up against a tree trunk. He steps forward again into my personal space. He's locked me against the tree. If I really tried, I know I could escape. The look in his eyes is shaking me. I long to be in his arms, yet the mood he's in is terrifying me. I don't want our friendship to end, and I'm not sure I'm ready for this.

He steps closer again. This time we're almost touching. His eyes weld onto mine. He wipes away the tears from my cheek with the back of his hand. That one stroke sends waves of emotions swimming through me. It's so gentle and filled with passion, enough to weaken my body. My lips part as I let out a gasp of pleasurable surprise, and my eyes close for only a moment.

During that split second, he presses his body up against mine, pinning me solidly against the tree. My eyes fly open. His face is inches away from my face. His ocean-blue eyes are inviting me in for a swim, a swim within his love and passion.

His face slowly presses in closer. Anxious for our friendship, I breathe in quickly from panic. I'm comforted by a soft, warm sensation pressing against my lips. It's so soft that I think I've imagined it, except my body has lost all strength, being overcome with pleasurable sensations. My knees crumble as he holds me up. My lips move in unison with his, becoming more relaxed with each movement. His moist warmth grows hungrier and presses harder with each stroke of his lips. He tastes so good—like fresh, warm, crusty bread smeared with honey and the added smoothness of butter.

I reach my hands up and touch his chest softly. His muscles dance underneath my palms as he pulls me closer by the hips.

His hand slides up my side and then curves around to the small of my back. My back arches as it runs up my spine. When it reaches the base of my head, his fingers grab my hair gently. By this moment, I'm completely giving in to him. Our mouths part as he gasps for air. His eyes never leave mine, and I know there's more to come. The hunger is still strong.

The hand that holds my hair pulls gently backward with enough force to tilt my chin slightly. My eyes gaze briefly at the beauty of the trees above as I feel soft, warm bites and kisses start from my chin all along my jawline, until they reach my neck. The heat floods my face with each touch, pulsating through my body to my fingertips and toes. The pleasure has completely caught me unawares, engulfing me and taking over my entire body. I don't know how I'm going to stop.

I'm deep in a trance of passion when a voice sounds clearly in my head. "Fledglings." The voice is stern and strong. It's a tone that screams don't mess with me or the rules—it's the voice of Archangel Michael.

CHAPTER SEVENTEEN

My body stiffens. Ben reluctantly pulls back. His face shows a mixture of guilt and unrepentance.

"What've we done?" I ask. I panic thinking Archangel Michael can read our minds from the base.

"Something we should've done a long time ago." He grins as he reaches out, cupping one side of my face softly with his hand, and running his thumb gently across my lips.

I can't help smiling at him. Even after what we've just done, his boldness startles me.

"Fledglings." The voice sounds in my head, bearing that unrelenting tone again.

"We have to go," I whisper.

He nods and reaches in, sneaking a kiss on my lips. With both hands on his chest, I push him away using enough force to show I mean it. I smile. "You rebel, you. You're not even stopping when our leader calls us."

He smirks. "Some things are worth the punishment."

"Come on. Let's go before he comes looking for us." I turn to walk back to the plain, and Ben follows me. I do everything I can mentally to prepare for an emotionless face when we enter into the clearing. If I can be convincing that nothing happened, then, hopefully, Archangel Michael won't search our memory.

We walk straight and tall as we approach the group. I don't look at Cindy in case she picks up on my emotions. A pang of guilt washes over me when I think of Ethan, but I know Ben is right. As much as it hurts me, that life is over. It's sick entertaining any thought of hope that Ethan will be murdered to join us—if he's even chosen. With my emotions in a whirlwind, I feign goodness, keeping my eyes focused on our leader.

"Where have you two been?" he asks as his eyes scan us without emotion. He stands legs apart and arms behind his back, wearing his Roman fighting skirt that stops just above his knee. He looks and sounds normal, although this time I can see a hint of exhaustion around his eyes.

"We apologize, sir," Ben says. His voice carries sincerity. "We'd taken a walk, fearing we'd missed you for the day. If we knew that you were still coming, we would've stayed. We're keen to hear of your recent battles."

A stunned look passes over Archangel Michael's face. "Oh. I see Archangel Gabriel has been unable to keep their mouth shut. This is not an uncommon trait."

He pulls his hands around to his front, clasping them together.

Sensing that Archangel Gabriel is in for a talking to, I say, "It isn't Archangel Gabriel's fault, sir. We were keen to know your location, as we've never had a meeting without you. We were concerned." I pause. I notice that his mind is ticking over the information. "You look a little tired. It must've been a nasty battle."

I see his head tilt slightly to the front. "That along with other things," he finishes cryptically.

"We'd love to hear about it," Cindy says. "Maybe we can help next time."

"There's no time for storytelling right now, and you are too young and immature to help." There was no room for argument in his voice. "Although some of you are maturing quicker than others, you are all still in the fledgling stage." He gazes at each one of us individually, his eyes unrelenting. "It would be too dangerous."

His eyes land on me, and my remorse rises to the surface. He clearly cares for us, yet I can't seem to stop myself from breaking the rules. I try to hold his gaze despite the betrayal I feel. I'm certain if they overlooked my shortcomings, I could still be a loyal and helpful angel.

He stands up straight again ready to take control. "Come now. It is already late, and you have more missions to fulfill." He points to Pink and Violet. "I will see you two first. Come stand in front of me so I can complete your assessment."

This seems odd to me. Archangel Michael has his ritual, and it always starts on one end of the line and goes to the other. Never does he call us up to him. I have to admit, though, that this isn't an ordinary day.

He goes through the ritual with Pink and then Violet. They receive the all clear and their new missions.

"Now go forth and complete your mission, fledglings. The world is in need of you." They disappear, and he sighs. Although he looks slightly worn, it's only in the eyes. His outer appearance still holds the strength of a warrior.

He looks at Cindy, Ben, and me, one by one. His expression is unreadable. "I hear that Gabriel sent you on an unusual mission."

We nod in unison. "Yes, they did," Cindy agrees out loud for all of us. "Very unusual, indeed. Also, we were all on the same mission. It was confusing at first, but we understood why when we saw what it was." The words were filing out of her mouth rapidly, stopping everyone else from speaking.

"Thank you, fledgling," Archangel Michael cut in.

She acts as though she didn't hear him and continues. "There were nine males, nine. Can you believe that? And they fought like they weren't injured even though they should've given up."

"Yes, fledgling." His voice is a little louder and sharper.

"They just kept coming back and back and back like they were pos—"

"Fledgling." Archangel Michael snaps.

Cindy looks around to see that we're all looking at her shaking our heads. "Oh! I'm talking too much, aren't I?"

"Yes, fledgling." I can see our leader is struggling to hide a smile. He can see that her continuous talking is only out of nervousness and that she's thinking she's telling him something necessary. Once he contains the smile, he says, "I can read your mind, remember? It saves a lot of time, especially at a time like this." He motions for her to come closer. "Now, come stand in front."

"Of course, sir." Before I can blink, she's standing in front of him, and he presses a lit finger to her forehead.

After a few moments, he says, "Good work, fledgling. You have served well."

Cindy smiles, happy he approves, and waits for her mission.

"You may step back now, fledgling," he says to her after seeing her remain in front of him.

"But, sir, I haven't received a mission. Are you unhappy with any part?"

He gives her a stern look. Her face turns pale, and she steps backward.

He indicates Ben with his arm reached out. "Come, fledgling."

Ben steps forward. My stomach has jumped to my throat. It annoys me how he looks so calm from behind. I wonder if he's churning inside with worry. My hope is that our leader is too tired to search any further than our last mission, or else I know I'm in big trouble. A feeling of dizziness overwhelms me, and I realize I'm holding my breath. I concentrate on breathing to keep my mind off the probing and what mischief I've been partaking.

After what feels like forever, Archangel Michael removes his finger from Ben's forehead and says, "Good work, fledgling. You have served well."

I see Ben's chest suddenly deflate. He must've been holding his breath also.

"You may step back," Archangel Michael says to him. Ben looks at him for a stunned moment, then steps back as instructed. I'm frustrated when he doesn't look in my direction to give me any indication of what our leader saw.

I know it's my turn, so when Archangel Michael raises a hand in my direction, I step forward before he asks. I'm keen to get this over. As the finger touches my forehead, I look into Archangel Michael's eyes and concentrate on my breathing. I watch as the unusual battle replays in my head. I feel pride when I see me healing the girl, and I think I see a flash of surprise cross the archangel's face. If I did, it's gone as quickly as it appears. It finishes with me healing the males. I don't know if I've done the right thing there, but I did my best.

When he removes his finger, I can't help but breathe out completely in relief. I look for any sign of emotion on our leader's face. There's none, and I'm not surprised. He's always a hard one to read.

He says, "Good work, fledgling. You have served well. You may step back." I'm not surprised by the last comment, as he'd already said it to the other two. It does feel odd not being given another mission straight-away. Deep down I wonder if we're all in trouble for something we did unknowingly. Unless Archangel

Michael knows how to search the mind without the owner knowing, I'm sure that I've escaped punishment for my bad behavior, for now. But I still feel like we've done something wrong. Like Cindy said, it's always been that if a fledgling has done a good job, they receive a new mission.

After a silence that seems to last for an eternity, Archangel Michael speaks. "You three were given a special mission, which in fact was well above your experience level. When I first found out, I held concern for your safety. I see, though, that this concern was unwarranted. You have served above and beyond your level and experience, and did as well as some of the more senior graduates. For this, I am proud of you."

These are words I haven't heard from his mouth before, and I'm speechless.

"I am also grateful," he continues. "By the three of you completing your mission successfully, unknown to you, you also helped us in the war against the demons."

I frown. "How can that happen?"

"By inserting a conscience into the demons' hosts, you cripple or maim the demon responsible. We can then take charge of the demons and overcome them easier."

"Really?" Cindy asks surprised.

Archangel Michael nods once.

"Then I'm glad we could help," she chirps. A large smile spreads across her face.

"So, if we did such a good job, with respect, why're we not given another mission?" Ben asks. "I'm keen to help in any way I can."

Archangel Michael paces the small distance in front of us. He pauses and says, "Because I need to take the three of you up to headquarters to see if the other leaders deem you suitable for the mission I have in mind for you." He paces a little more in silence, then says, "This mission is possibly a very dangerous one; however, I am not one hundred percent sure."

"How are you not sure?" I ask.

"Because we don't know all the facts. There are possibly many untamed elements."

This mission sounds like my kind of mission, and I'm keen to execute. "Then, let's go," I say.

CHAPTER EIGHTEEN

Archangel Michael pushes off and begins to fly, leading us toward headquarters. Cindy turns to look at us. Excitement and fear spreads across her face. "I get to see the headquarters," she says. Her voice betrays the brave expression on her face.

"You'll be fine, Cindy. You'll have us with you," I say.

"Yeah, and last time you two went to headquarters, you were sent to the abyss. I feel so confident," she says mockingly. After giving us a quick smile, she pushes off and follows our leader.

Ben approaches me, and his arm brushes against me. Tingles spread through my body. He stands in front and looks deep into my eyes, towering over and enticing me to swim in his blue-ocean eyes. I place my hands on his bare chest and push him away playfully.

"We have to go, remember? We have a difficult mission." I say, stepping past him and pushing off. Only a moment later I hear his strong wings flapping behind me, stroking with an even rhythm against the wind. Soon, he's flying next to me. Involuntarily I find myself regularly staring in his direction, admiring the parts that make him special. Occasionally he catches me looking at him, deep in thought. Each time I feel my face turn warm, and he gives me a cheeky grin. Our friendship has taken a completely different turn. I hope it's for the better. I'd hate to lose my dearest friend.

This time our trip to the headquarters seems to go too quickly. I surmise it's because we aren't on our way to a likely punishment. I see the cloud platform not too far ahead.

As we land, Cindy looks around. Her eyes are flicking from cloud to cloud, and her face shows disbelief. She turns to us and asks, "Is this it?" Her whisper travels loudly.

I grin at her surprise. "Yes, it is."

"Are you serious? I expected something flashier than this. Clouds as headquarters, I mean, really?" Her eyebrows rise in astonishment.

Archangel Michael turns around. He's leading us toward the boardroom, and by the look on his face and the rock gaze in Cindy's direction, he clearly heard what she said.

"Fledgling." The usual sternness is bordering on harsh.

Cindy's face turns white before she turns around to look at our leader.

"We're angels, not God. Our quarters are not meant to be flashy, for we're meant to serve, not to think about glorifying ourselves. It will pay you well to know your place."

Cindy drops her chin with her eyes cast down. "I apologize, respected leader. I did not mean it in that way. I did not know what to expect, but I wasn't expecting clouds. Not that there's anything wrong with that." She looks up at his face briefly. "Please don't hold my blabbering mouth against me. I tend to speak without thinking at times."

Archangel Michael's stare remains consistent. "I know, fledgling. Yet, you must learn to hold your tongue and think before you speak. The tongue is but a two-edged sword."

Cindy bows her head. "I'll do my best, great leader."

His eyes gaze past Cindy to us. "Now come." We follow as he passes through the gap in the cloud walls leading into the boardroom. Cindy's face turns a paler shade of white as her eyes fall upon the three archangels standing around the room. I sense myself joining her. With each step, my body is becoming increasingly tense. I can't help thinking that the angels may pick up on some of the mischief I've partaken in during the last few days. If they do, then I may end up in the abyss instead of taking on an important mission.

I look at Ben. As usual when he deals with the archangels, his face is strong and unreadable. I wonder if my face portrays that lack of emotion. I focus on my expression, trying to keep it unreadable as I study Archangel Gabriel's face, marveling at the perfect balance in features between male and female.

Archangel Gabriel's friendly eyes make it an easy achievement and a perfect distraction.

"What is the meaning of this meeting, Michael?" Uriel asks. I turn to face the voice. His eyes pass over me, then Ben, finally studying Cindy with interest. "I believed this was called to allocate distinguished fledglings to the search." His eyes land on me again. "Not troublemakers." There's that Zeus impression again.

Archangel Michael takes a deep breath then clasps his hands behind his back. "Yes, that is right, Uriel. However, I have just assessed their last mission and was delighted, although surprised, to find they exceeded their taught capabilities." He moves his feet comfortably to the width of his shoulders and continues. "As you know, two of them have spent time in the abyss for going against the rules." His gaze passes over the other two archangels. "I am also confident when you assessed the mission that landed them in the abyss, that you saw there is more to them—that their gifts are different from the others. Especially that one," he says while pointing to me.

My brow pushes together. I've no idea what he's insinuating. After a quick thought, I guess maybe he's talking about the healing I did during our last mission. I look from Archangel Michael to Archangel Uriel, and I watch his face as a frown creases his ageless features.

Archangel Uriel fiddles with the cape draped over his white gown and then looks at each one of us in turn. He then faces the other two archangels, Gabriel and Raphael. Archangel Raphael stands with his arms crossed in front of his chest, and Archangel Gabriel stands relaxed, leaning up against the cloud wall. This relaxed look is reflected on Archangel Gabriel's face. Archangel Uriel turns back to look at our leader.

"Do you place your full confidence in their abilities?" he asks Archangel Michael. "Will they put the mission first?"

"I understand your concern," Archangel Michael says, his voice weary. "I have brought them here as my best choice after what I have seen. None of you have the time to complete this mission. I have to go back to the war to check on our warriors, and at the moment there is no one else to commit to the task. I have brought them to let you take a look and decide."

While Archangel Uriel processes the information in his corner, Archangel Gabriel steps forward saying, "I'll be the first to have a look, seeing I was the one that sent them on the mission together. I've been itching to find out how it went." Smiling at me and placing a hand on my forehead, I can see my memories being accessed. Nervous, I focus on studying the blueness in the archangel's eyes.

I'm so nervous that my teeth clamp down on my tongue. After a few moments, the pain turns to numbness.

A voice sounds loudly in my head. "Relax, sweetie." Involuntarily I jump. Archangel Gabriel is speaking inside my mind. "If you don't calm down, they'll look farther than you want. They'll think that you're hiding something." The eyes sharpen with intensity. "Are you hiding something?"

I can't talk back. I don't know how the archangels

talk in our minds. They haven't told us. I assume that it's a gift that only the archangels have. I shake my head enough to be seen only by Archangel Gabriel, even though I know I'm lying.

The voice is in my head again. "Uh huh." Archangel Gabriel nods in understanding while lifting an eyebrow, giving me the impression I'm not believed.

Panic strikes me, and my body turns stiff. It must've shown on my face because Archangel Gabriel says it again, "Relax. Remember, I'm a little more open-minded than the others. It's part of my creative nature. I look more at the heart's intentions than the misbehavior." The eyes turn serious. "But, I'll put you in the abyss if I think that your heart isn't in the right place or you overstep the mark. Last time I looked, this wasn't the case, so relax."

I break eye contact with Archangel Gabriel and look around. Breathing a sigh of relief, I see that the others haven't noticed the private conversation we've just had. The other archangels are busy preparing to read Ben's and Cindy's mind, and Archangel Michael is standing to the side, watching. I look back into Archangel Gabriel's calming eyes. I know I'm lucky to have the lenient archangel reading my mind first. I can tell Uriel isn't impressed with me being chosen for this important task. His disapproval is arousing my interest in the mission. I just need to pass their tests.

In silence, I watch my last mission pass by as Archangel Gabriel views it in my mind. There's no hint of emotion, only a straight face until the part is reached where I heal the injured. I then see a small flicker across the eyes and an eyebrow rise.

The finger retracts, and the probing stops. "Interesting," Archangel Gabriel says out loud, then backs away.

Archangel Raphael moves to stand in front of me, uttering not one word as the probing finger is lifted and placed on my forehead. I let my eyes wander over his dark-brown straight hair, which cups around his handsome face. His expression is serious, making nervous twinges rise within me.

Trying to lower my anxiety, I look beside his face, taking in the light green of the soft feathers of his wings. The color is calming, allowing me to relax enough to look straight into his emerald eyes. There's no emotion in them as I see the mission flick past my eyes again. I expect a reaction of some sort when he sees the part where I heal. Disappointment sinks in when he retracts his finger and backs away without even an eyebrow raised.

Being in between readings, I glance over at Ben and Cindy. They don't look at me. I'm not so worried about Cindy, as I'm sure she hasn't done anything wrong, but when Ben doesn't look my way, I'm not sure what to make of it. I hope that it's a sign that all is well on his part.

A flash of golden brown passes across my peripheral vision. Knowing what's coming next, I focus on becoming more relaxed and turn to face Archangel Uriel.

The finger is raised and placed on my forehead before I've time to breathe in, and the probing is beginning. Trying desperately not to hold my breath, I focus on his eyes. They're the color of liquid honey—a light golden brown. I stare so hard that they seem to begin to swirl. I'm vaguely aware of the warmth that's probing my memory. Parts are paused and watched slowly, taking in each action, thought, feeling. I purposely breathe out when he reaches the final scene. The end passes, and his probing finger remains.

CHAPTER NINETEEN

The tension in my body rises. My stomach starts to turn into clusters of knots as I see the next stage of my life unfold. He uncovers that Ben and I know each other's last human name, and I'm insisting on calling Cindy a name. I swallow—that lump just doesn't want to leave my throat. For the first time, our flight back to base is replayed. I'm flying high in the air —up, up to the highest point, where the birds don't fly —and then performing the death-defying dive back to Earth. He continues the replay—the base, the wait for Archangel Michael—me getting annoyed at the attention Pink and Violet are giving Ben.

He's so close. The stress levels are escalating. Someone make him stop! I scream inside of me. I'm now picturing Ben's and my walk into the forest. My knees are starting to buckle.

Something nudges me backward, and I jump. Archangel Uriel's finger has slid from the middle of my forehead toward my left temple, and the probing light has gone out. Stunned, I take my eyes off the archangel in front of me and look at a movement over his shoulder. With an arm slung across Archangel Uriel's shoulders, Archangel Gabriel's friendly eyes greet me. The nudge originated from a strong, friendly pat on Archangel Uriel's back.

"Well, good to see you're finished here," Archangel Gabriel says. Turning to face Archangel Uriel, my rescuer says, "I'm sure you've seen enough to make your assessment. For a while there, I thought you were viewing her whole journey as an angel. You took forever." The blue angel gown swishes around Archangel Gabriel's feet as the archangel turns to the other archangels and says, "Now, let's make a decision. We don't have a lot of time, and lives are at stake."

Archangel Uriel turns to face Archangel Gabriel and crosses his arms. "I call for a meeting." He turns, and his gaze lands on me and progresses along to the other two fledglings. "In private."

I'm sure my eyes are wide open in shock. I look at Ben, and this time he's looking at me. A worried look greets me as his eyes search my face for answers. Cindy is standing in between us, and I can see her head turning back and forth between the two of us.

Archangel Michael answers, "Agreed. We will hold a brief meeting in private." He turns to face us. "Fledglings, wait at our training ground. We will address you shortly."

"Yes, sir." Our voices are joined in unison.

Immediately I turn to leave. I can't wait to get out of here. A fleeting thought crosses my mind. I wonder if it's possible for an angel to run away. Maybe I'm not cut out for this life, but then an image of Ethan and his brother and other Innocents that I've saved come to mind. I know I can't abandon them. I must stay and continue to save lives, even if I have to face punishment again.

I dive off the platform and allow myself to free-fall. The air sounds like static, and the breeze pushes forcefully against my skin. I revel in it as it massages all the tension away. I drop past a bird, and it darts sideways. The ground approaches quickly, and I flick out my wings to trap the air and slow myself down, gliding the rest of the way to the earth's surface. I hear the flapping of wings behind me, and I know that Ben and Cindy are following. With the slightest thump, my feet hit the grassy grounds of our training area. I hear two similar thumps behind me. I turn to look at my friends.

The instant I'm facing them, Cindy is on to me. "What've you done?" Her voice is high, almost a screech. Her arms have flown out to her sides, and her shoulders rise.

I wish I could tell her that I didn't do anything—that I'm blameless. She'd know instantly that this's a lie. I look at Ben. His face shows no guilt, yet he's as guilty as I am. They mustn't have probed his mind as much as mine.

Cindy's glare is burrowing into me. I turn to her again with my face pleading. "Cindy, I honestly don't know why we were sent here." I step forward and reach out my hand to her, and she moves away. With my history, I don't blame her for accusing me first.

"I'll admit that I was nervous that they'd find something, especially Archangel Uriel. But I promise you the only thing that he viewed that was remotely disobedient was when I was insisting that we name you."

Cindy let out an aggravated groan. "I knew that'd amount to no good."

Ben steps forward and places an arm around her shoulders. "I wouldn't worry about it. The memory showed that you did not want a name because you didn't want to break the rules. I don't see how this would get you into trouble." He looks at me for confirmation.

"That's true Cin—" I begin to say.

"Don't call me that!" she screams. "Because of you two, I'm probably going to be sent to the abyss." She pushes Ben's arm off her shoulders and stomps off into the bushes.

As I watch her go, I collapse onto a rock. Her body language tells me she needs to be alone right now, so I don't follow. Remorse fills me as I observe her retreat. I shouldn't have insisted that she use the name, she wasn't ready for it, yet I don't see how she'd be found guilty.

My attention is diverted when Ben prods me over as he sits next to me. With his body pressed up against mine, my anxiety decreases.

He wraps an arm around my waist. "Hey, she'll get over it. I can't see how she'd be in trouble."

"That's what I keep thinking," I say as I look into his eyes. Even in my despair I can't ignore the attraction.

"Did they see anything in you that we didn't want them to?"

He shakes his head. "They didn't look."

"What, they didn't look past your mission?"

His eyes are sympathetic as he shakes his head.

"Great, so Archangel Uriel has it in just for me," I say disheartened.

"Looks that way." Ben chuckles.

"Thanks a lot."

"I was just kidding." He rubs my leg near the knee, and it sends tingles up my body. "Did they even see anything that we're to be concerned about?"

"I wouldn't think so, other than the name giving. Archangel Uriel was very close to seeing us in the forest, though. He'd have kept going if it hadn't been for Archangel Gabriel interrupting."

"Maybe we should've given him something better to watch." He leans in closer to me, running his hand higher up my leg.

I stand. "You're trouble. In fact, you're more trouble than I am, yet I'm the one getting caught all the time."

He grins and stands with me. "I was in trouble, too, remember?" The sun glimmers on his bare chest, catching my eye. Before I can stop myself, my eyes are traveling over his toned muscles. He takes this as his invitation to move forward.

Realizing what he's doing, I take the smallest of steps backward and shake my head. "Not here, not now. An archangel will arrive here at any moment."

He pouts and somehow makes his eyes look genuinely sad.

I laugh. "Oh, stop it. You know I'm right. Besides, Cindy will get angrier if she busts us."

His pout changes to a smile. "I know, but you can't blame a boy for trying."

Confident that he's going to stop, I sit on the grass. It crackles softly under my weight. Sticks and bits of dirt dig into my palms. Even though it's not like a nicely mown lawn, it's nice to feel nature. I pull my knees to my chest, then wipe my hands on my legs and hug my knees. "I hate waiting."

"I know, me too," Ben says as he sits next to me. "If that's all he saw then I think we'll be fine. They obviously need us for this mission as they can't find anyone else they think is capable." He reaches out and holds my hand.

My hand looks so pale and frail compared to his. He takes it to his lap and clasps the back with his other hand. The warmth and firmness of his hands around mine soothes me. There's always been something about him that's had a calming effect on me even before our personal involvement. He's always looking out for people, not just me. I begin to think maybe this stems from his past, when I realize that I don't know anything about him before we were fledglings.

I bump him lightly with my shoulder. "What was your life like before?"

His brow creases. "Do you mean as a human?"

I nod. "I've just realized I don't know what it was like."

"You know that's breaking the rules, right?"

I exhale loudly. "It's starting to feel like everything is

breaking the rules."

"I didn't mean it like that. What I meant is that you know that an archangel will come here at any moment, and this could land you . . . well . . . us in trouble."

"More trouble, don't you mean? I just want to know more about your past life, especially the last one." I pause, trying to think of a way around anymore repercussions. "Maybe if you just let me see how you died they wouldn't consider it as breaking the rules? It might be seen more as caring."

"Okay." He sounds hesitant, and I see something in his eyes I haven't seen before. He looks uncertain.

"What's wrong? Do you have something you don't want me to see?"

He shakes his head. "It's just a little weird and . . . um . . . embarrassing, not to mention that it's rather gruesome."

His comment causes me to smile. "Hey, we were all murdered. What isn't gruesome about that? I'm certain that none of us died pretty."

His eyes search my face and rest gazing into mine. The hesitation intrigues me more. What doesn't he want me to see?

"You can trust me. I won't tell anyone unless you want me to," I say.

He looks down as he releases my hand and slowly rubs his hands together. I can tell he's deep in thought. After a short pause, he turns to me and says, "All right. I'm not keen on reliving it myself, but I will if it means that much to you." His voice is crackling as though the words are hard to get out.

Guilt builds within me. Once again, I'm asking too much of him. "Are you sure?"

He nods.

Remaining seated, I reach my hand up and touch his forehead. His face has lost its color, and my hand almost matches its tone. His eyes are fixed, almost with a shocked look.

"If you want me to stop, let me know." I mean it. His look is starting to unsettle me. "Do you want to change your mind?"

He shakes his head.

With my finger illuminating, I begin the process. I rewind past his life as a fledgling. I'm familiar with most of that life. Images and feelings flicker past. I'm certain that I need to go further back, so I mentally jump several months of his life. When I slow down the memory, what I see and feel doesn't ring true for what I know of his life as a fledgling, so I begin to watch his memory.

Before my eyes, there's a vision of a fire truck—big, bright, and red—sitting inside a fire station. Over Ben's head, an alarm rings. It's so loud I want to place my hands over my ears. Instead, I watch as he reaches out. His hands are masculine and strong. He grabs a fire hat off the hook before hastily making his way into the truck with the big yellow stripe running horizontally across the side. My eyes catch an emblem in line with the stripe—Queensland Fire and Rescue Service. A smile spreads across my face. I find it amusing to find that he's from Queensland, the same state that I'm from in Australia.

Climbing in with several others, he manages to sit before the truck begins to drive out of the station. On the outside of the truck, the siren is blaring above us.

As we drive, a voice calls out, "We've a possible arson attack in a high-rise building. There are several people reported to be trapped inside."

I look for the owner of the voice. The report is coming from the man in his forties sitting in the front seat. I can't see much of him for his yellow protective uniform is sealed up to his chin, and his head is under a yellow, skirted helmet. The uniform's so big and bulky it's hard to tell if the man is overweight or slim and toned. Ben moves his head. From his viewpoint, I notice that he's in a similar type of uniform, with his arms covered in the same type of material and his hands in big, padded black gloves.

The man continues, "There are no known explosives inside the building, but keep your eyes open for any explosives or gas cylinders. Stick to the usual safety procedures. And, men . . . keep safe. We don't kill ourselves to save others." His eyes are serious and creased with concern.

The emotions I feel are indifferent to his speech. From Ben's reaction, I'm sure he's heard it many times before.

A few minutes pass, and we stop outside a high-rise building. The devastation knocks me immediately with full force. We need to save those people. Charging out of his seat and out the truck's door, he immediately sets up the rescue equipment. With the large hose in hand, he starts approaching the building. It's only six stories high. The two bottom levels are completely engulfed, and people in the higher levels can't pass to safety.

A bloodcurdling scream fills my ears. His eyes scan the building. On the second floor, a lady is completely covered in flames. Taking a chance, she runs to the window and jumps out. Onlookers are standing nearby, watching in horror. A crunch of bones is audible as she hits the pavement. Several onlookers run to her with a blanket laden with water, throwing it on her. Her body remains still, even with the flames extinguished.

Desperate to save the remaining people, he starts running with his colleagues and a hose to the edge of the building and calls for action. Water jets out of the hose as he directs it into the burning building. He doesn't want any more lives lost. When he looks up, there are people standing on ledges and screaming out the windows, waving their hands. A formidable urge rises within him to help them.

Ben calls out to the man who was yelling out the instructions in the truck on the way here. His voice sounds exactly like Ben's voice sounds now, with a smooth baritone ring. "Chief." The man looks over, and Ben continues. "Can we get the ladder over there? I want to climb up and help them." He indicates the people on the higher levels. "Before it's too late."

The chief looks at Ben with concern as he asks, "You really think you can do it?"

Deep down, I can sense that Ben isn't certain, but he's not about to tell the chief that. He just wants to see the people safe; this's all he cares about.

"Yes," I hear his answer.

The chief doesn't look convinced.

"I'm the fittest and fastest. I can do it." Ben tries again.

The chief still looks worried. A siren shrills as a second fire truck screeches around the corner. He glances at the backup then turns back to Ben. "You need to take David with you."

Following Ben's gaze as he looks at David, I can sense he's new to the service and doesn't look too pleased about going into the building. Turning back to the chief, Ben says, "I can do it on my own."

He shakes his head. "Gotta follow safety protocol. Two people go in together." Another scream sounds from the building. "You better make it quick, kid."

"Yes, Chief."

The chief goes to the truck and backs it up to the building, aiming the ladder at level three first. As soon as they secure the ladder, Ben is climbing to the top with a breathing apparatus on his back and hauling the large coiled hose into the window. I'm surprised by the strength I feel passing through his muscles as he drags the heavy equipment up several stories. The ladder is rocking slightly with David climbing behind him. Instantly I'm struck by the intense heat and smoke that hits Ben's body. He pulls his fire mask on, turns around, hooks the buddy line to David, and they begin their search.

With adrenaline pumping, strong emotions flood over me as he walks through the smoke and flicks of fire start to lap around the edges of the room. Fear, devastation, and bravery swelling purely from his desire to save lives engulf me. The feeling is so strong and raw. I begin to wonder if I'm intruding too much into his personal life. I don't want to overstep my mark. After a moment's hesitation, I focus my attention on his eyes to read his real-time emotions. I can see he's not comfortable, yet I think I see trust there.

"Are you okay?" I ask.

He nods, although his eyes still betray his braveness.

"Do you want me to stop?"

He pauses, then shakes his head. I stroke my spare hand through the short dark-brown hair at his temple. He breathes out and seems to relax by my touch.

Focusing back on where I left off, I see the level completely smothered in smoke. Ben starts looking on the floor, following his instincts. It wouldn't be surprising if the residents were lying on the floor unconscious. Crouching and walking in a unique motion with his feet first, he begins searching through the rooms. Each time he reaches a foot out in front of him, it is overextended, and he moves it in a sweeping motion. His foot hits something on the floor. He stops and looks. It's a foot. An elderly lady is lying on the kitchen floor. He scoops her up in his arms with surprising strength and ease. She's unconscious and completely relaxed, making her more difficult to carry.

The strength traveling through his arms surprises me. He's stronger than I expect. He progresses to the window, following David's lead over a clear floor to find the chief waiting for them. He's balancing on the top of the ladder, and behind him is another young member of the team.

Carefully, he passes the lady out the window to the chief. It would be a difficult task for them to carry her down, but with two of them, they should have it sorted. He turns in search of more people. The smoke is getting thicker by the minute, but he continues with David only feet away and attached by a line. Despite his own fears, he's determined that no one will be left behind.

He continues to search feetfirst in a sweeping motion, checking for anything that may be lying in their way in the darkened rooms. Together, they reach the final room. Against the wall is a double bed. I think it may be the main bedroom. As flames begin to tickle around the edges of the room, they enter it. Lying peacefully on the bed is an elderly man. Ben scoops him into his arms and fumbles his way through the smoke toward the window, once again led by David. By the time they get there, the chief is waiting. The leader out of breath but ready to go. Carefully they pass the man through and into the chief's care. With another person safely out, they spin and head to the stairwell.

Once inside the stairwell, Ben catches a glance of David's face. He looks anxious and pale even through his bulky mask. "You okay, Dave?" Ben asks him.

He nods, but his expression says otherwise.

"We'll be out of here soon," Ben says, trying to be encouraging. Ben turns to close the door to the last level and sees that the walls in the apartment are now completely ablaze.

He closes the heavy fire door, and they sprint up the stairs, taking two at a time. Their breathing is heavy, and they labor under all the added weight as they begin to search the next level. They connect the fire hose that Ben has been carrying into the fire booster and unravel it as a guide as they plod their way into the apartment. I hear coughing, and they head toward it. I feel Ben's relief as he realizes at least these occupants are still walking. Ben and David escort them to the window, glad to see that the chief is already there and waiting. I can feel Ben's heartbeat rise and muscles tighten with each passing minute. He turns and looks around the room. There are signs that the fire is developing too quickly to rescue all the occupants, so Ben begins to help them out the window to get them to safety faster.

The heat is intensifying, and he's sweating under his heavy fire clothes. He turns to continue his search for people and catches the look on David's face. Even though David is new to the service, he recognizes the signs that the building is burning too quickly.

Another scream pierces from a level above. "Are you all right for one more?" he asks David. David turns his head up as though looking for the owner of the scream, then looks back at Ben and nods. He doesn't look happy, but hearing the scream seems to trigger his rescue instinct. Grabbing the fire hose as a guide, they shuffle their way quickly back to the stairwell. They unhook the hose, drag it up the stairs with them, and connect it to the booster on the next level.

Using it as a guide they shuffle together, feetfirst through the apartment. A crash sounds from the level below. I'm surprised to see the smoke levels rising quickly around them, making it impossible to see. My senses give the feeling of lost hope, yet Ben is determined to rescue as many people as possible, if not all of them. The dedication of putting others before him is a trait I know he has, but I didn't know he had it at this level. Even as the fear within him rises, he doesn't give up; he is giving of himself completely.

A sound reaches his ear from his left. It was only soft but sounded human. He stops suddenly to pull in that direction and stumbles. The resistance he expected from David's end of the line did not manifest. He somehow ends up on his knees on the hot floor. He turns to look for David. Nothing. All he can see is smoke, thick, gray smoke. He reaches down and feels for the line that connects them. His thick-gloved fingers fumble and find the line. Success. He grabs it and begins to pull. Again, there's no resistance. He pulls faster, and the line comes easily; there isn't the drag there should be with a person attached. He pulls quicker. Suddenly the line stops. He finds the frayed end but not David. The line must've severed somehow.

Panic begins to well for David's safety. Ben stands and calls out. "David . . . David!" He hears a feeble call.

"Ben?"

"You all right?" he calls.

The reply is faint, but the panic was clear. "Yes. You?"

"Yes. Try to make it to the window. I'll meet you there." The roaring sound of the fire is rising, making it harder to hear David's response. Strangely enough, Ben does hear that human sound off slightly in the other direction. Everything inside is telling him to follow protocol and get to the window and out of there. He knows if he does, he wouldn't be able to live with himself. He hears the sound again, a high-pitched squeal of someone in a frenzied state of crying.

"Hello?" he calls out trying to confirm what he heard. The same squeal answers him. Knowing that people in a state of panic do all sorts of stupid things, he has to check. "Hello." He inches his way closer to the sound, with his feet feeling the way first. He goes only a few feet when his feet connect with something. He bends down to investigate. The darkness and smoke are so thick that he can't see what it is, even at such a close distance. Squatting further, he reaches out his hands for the object. It's hard. He's surprised to feel that it's round, and when he runs his hands up it, he can feel it is a cylinder. It's not very tall and feels like metal.

The high-pitched squeal sounds again. He jumps. The sounds are coming from the cylinder. I feel the blood drain away from his face as he feels the hard circle attached to the top and the circular handle. It's a perfect shape for a barbecue gas bottle. Instantly Ben stands. His limbs are turning weak from terror, but he has to move now. Panicking, he rushes toward where he thinks the window is. He's in such a hurry that he struggles to do the proper safety walk. He trips over something and lands face-first on the floor. Pain sears through his right side. It's hit something hard. He pushes off the ground, ignoring the piercing pain. He has to get out of here. His heart is pumping so hard that I can hear it in his ears. His breathing through the apparatus is heavy and rushed, making it hard to hear anything else.

I can sense my body tensing. I desperately want him to get out, yet there's nothing I can do. I stand helpless as he rushes forward, stumbling again. Something pierces his side in between his ribs. He takes a breath, and it hurts with a pain that'd cause another person to pass out. Gritting his teeth, he reaches down and feels something hard sticking out of his jacket. It feels like it could be a big shard of glass. Terror and panic begin to take hold. He doesn't know how deep it is, but he needs to get up, and he needs to leave now. Trying not to breathe too deeply, he pries himself up as fast as he can without passing out from the pain.

He hears a voice. "Ben . . . Ben!" It's faint. I think it sounds like the chief.

Ben breathes in deeply. I can feel he wants to scream out in pain, but instead he calls out as loudly as he can. "Gas bottle!"

I don't know if the chief hears him as I don't hear a response. He continues his struggle to the window, each step is excruciating. It's not long until a force hits him from behind. I want to scream out in pain as I feel what he felt. Suddenly the shard of glass in between his ribs is the least of the pain. It's almost in slow motion as I can feel each piece of skin being ripped off—ripped and torn in small and large chunks through the protective clothing and from his bones. Soon the bones begin tearing, piece by piece, and the remainder of his body is thrown forward onto the scorching hot floor. The strong heartbeat that comforted me earlier falls silent. The arsonist had claimed his first fireman.

CHAPTER TWENTY

Unintentionally, I pull my hands away. The shock of what just happened has caused the involuntary action. My palms are damp, and my heart is pounding. I look at Ben. Moisture is trickling down his olive face, and his eyes are haunted as they study mine. I don't know what to say. It was so graphic and horrific. I'm stunned. I circle my arms around him and pull him close, his head resting against my chest. Wanting to comfort him, I begin to stroke his hair along the temples.

After a while, he lets out a big breath. "I told you it was gruesome."

"And you were right," I say. "I expected a murder, but not quite like that. Since an arsonist started the fire, it is a murder—just not the direct kind." I'm almost ashamed of my words; they seem useless, yet it's all that I have.

A blue flash appears next to us. I look up to see

Archangel Gabriel. An eyebrow is raised, and a curious expression is on the archangel's face. I release Ben, and his eyes search for my distraction.

"Fledglings," Archangel Gabriel's tone is uncharacteristically snappy. "I should hope you two are not up to no good again." A finger is flailing in front of us, as if we were a couple of naughty children. "You've already caused enough trouble today just by being you."

I stand. "I was just comforting him," I say a little too quickly, my voice tense.

The eyebrow rises a little higher.

"He relived his last death; it was rather gruesome, and I saw it." I splutter out the words. Archangel Gabriel's more lenient ways are earning my respect at a rapid rate, and I hate being dishonest to someone I respect.

"Hmm!" A suspicious look crosses the archangel's face. "Diverging into another fledgling's past life is a very risky move. It's not completely frowned upon, though definitely not a good way to earn the archangels' trust. You two are lucky it's me who's come to brief you." Archangel Gabriel shakes their head. "You don't know how hard it was to get you two accepted on this mission, especially you." The archangel is looking at me.

"So we're going then?" I blurt out. With the thought of being allowed to go, I forget about the reprimand.

Archangel Gabriel crosses their arms and raises one side of their mouth. "Hmm, I can see you've learned a lot from your close call."

The memory of Archangel Gabriel stepping in

before the discovery of Ben and my relationship by Archangel Uriel comes flooding back. I look down at the ground. "Sorry, Archangel Gabriel. I'm so keen to go on this mission that I was distracted."

"My dear, you don't even know what this mission is. It's possibly a very dangerous mission."

"Even for an angel?" I ask surprised. I'm starting to feel invincible, since I haven't come across any real danger as a fledgling yet.

"Especially for a fledgling," Archangel Gabriel stresses. "And the other archangels have every right to be concerned about sending a fledgling that doesn't abide by the rules."

"So are we going then?" Ben asks. He stands and stretches his arms toward the sky, exposing his bare chest. His face is still slightly haunted, and he appears eager for a distraction.

Archangel Gabriel gazes around. "Where's the little yellow fledgling? I'm supposed to discuss the final decision with all of you together. I thought you'd be waiting together."

The culpability strikes me again, and I look to the side. "Ah, she's angry with us. She thinks we've gotten her into trouble."

"Over what?" Archangel Gabriel's voice rises, the shock evident.

"Over naming her, even when she said she didn't want to, as it was breaking the rules."

"Are you serious?" Disbelieving eyes study our faces.

Ben nods. "Yeah, she kind of stomped off in a really bad mood."

"Oh, what nonsense. She did nothing wrong. I keep telling these archangels that they need to be more communicative. The lack of communication causes so much anxiety. They never believe me." Shaking their head, Archangel Gabriel goes silent for a moment and looks in the other direction of the island. Their expression is serene as their hands reach up and play briefly with their golden locks of hair.

A few moments pass, and then Cindy arrives, flustered and in a hurry. Her hair flies in her face with a puff of sea breeze. When she lifts a hand to brush it away, it reveals her face is anxious and pale.

"I'm so sorry, Archangel Gabriel. I was just taking a walk."

Archangel Gabriel studies her. "My dear, what's this I hear about you being angry at these two for giving you a name?" The archangel's voice is kind yet straightforward.

Her pale face turns ghostly white. "Oh, am I in trouble, too, for being angry?"

Archangel Gabriel frowns, but then a humor hits the pale-blue eyes, and the archangel laughs. "Oh, my dear. You worry too much. You're not in trouble because they gave you a name, and you're not in trouble for being upset with them. Now, sweetie, relax and listen to what I have to say."

Cindy lets her breath out, and color starts to rise on her face. I watch intensely, waiting to see if she'll look our way. She doesn't. I can only assume that she's still angry with us. My heart sinks. I don't like it when my friends are angry with me. I can only hope she'll forgive me soon.

With hands clasped in front at the waist, Archangel Gabriel begins to speak. "After a lot of convincing on my behalf and a fairly large push from Archangel Michael, you three have the mission."

"Yes!" Ben and Cindy exclaim together.

I can't help raising my eyebrows in curiosity. "Archangel Michael vouched for us?"

"My dear, despite your shortcomings, you'll be surprised how much faith your leader has in you." Raising a pointed finger in a warning, Archangel Gabriel continues sternly, "Do not, let me repeat, do not get complacent in this knowledge. He'll punish you if your rebellion continues." Archangel Gabriel's hand drops back down, and their voice drops back to a normal tone. "He's seen your potential, as have the others, but since you're not under their direct training, they don't have as much tolerance for your shortcomings." I watch as the soft, compassionate eyes turn almost to stone. "Archangel Michael has placed a lot of faith in you. Do not fail him."

I swallow. It's never my intention to be a rebel. I just follow my heart, and at times it leads in an unapproved direction. I make the only promise that I know I can make. "I'll do my best."

Looking a little satisfied with my answer, Archangel Gabriel continues. "The reason they chose you for this is because of your last mission. Did you notice anything different about it?"

"Other than working together?" Ben asks.

"Yes."

"Well, the perpetrators were off somehow. They kept coming back to attack us even after they'd been seriously injured," I say.

"True. Why do you think this is?" the archangel asks.

"They felt evil," Cindy adds. "Much more than any other perpetrator I've dealt with before."

Archangel Gabriel claps their hands together lightly. "Yes, well done. A very strong demon possessed them, stronger than any of the others you've dealt with before."

"We've dealt with demons before?" Ben asks.

"Yes, in every perpetrator."

"Why haven't we been told this?" I ask.

"Because you haven't been required to fight the demon. You've been too immature. Before now, inserting a conscience is the only capability you had for fighting demons. Your last mission stemmed from a stronger demon, and when you inserted the consciences, you forced it out as well as injured it slightly. This hindered its ability to fight strongly. He was also fighting in the war against the archangels, the one that Archangel Michael was involved in when I gave you the mission." The archangel paused to let the information sink in. "This means, when you injured him, it helped the archangels win the war enough for

Michael and some of the archangels to take a quick break. You should be very proud of yourselves. Your leader is. It's why he stood by you to go on this mission. You've proven you're stronger than he's trained you to be."

"So, what's our mission?" Ben asks.

"Ah, yes, the mission. We need to get you started quickly. One of the fledglings hasn't come back from a mission and—"

"What?" Cindy blurts out.

"Yes, my dear." Archangel Gabriel turns to her. "As we said, this may be a dangerous mission, we don't know. The person they were supposed to protect is still in danger. It's not a good sign for the safety of the fledgling."

"Who's the missing fledgling?" Ben asks.

"It's one from your group."

A loud gasp from Cindy interrupts the archangel briefly.

Archangel Gabriel continues, "Which is the reason we need the three of you to go together. Being Michael's students, you're trained well to fight, and if one doesn't return, then we need to send more of you to find them."

"So, who is it that's missing?" I ask again.

"It's so hard to explain seeing you don't have names. Ironic isn't it. You're forbidden names until you graduate the fledgling status, yet if we need to say who you are to others, we have no words to describe you."

"Which is why we've been making up our own," Ben says. "What're the colorings of the fledgling?"

A smirk rises on Archangel Gabriel's face. "The main color is orange. Orange wings and orange clothes."

"Orange, really?" Devastation fills Cindy's voice. "He was a really good fighter, confident, too, and always stuck to the rules."

Archangel Gabriel indicates to Cindy with a hand. "There you have it. It's . . . Orange."

I don't know what to say. I hadn't been that close to Orange, but I'm sure that he's very capable of looking after himself in dangerous situations. I don't want anything to happen to any of us, yet I'm itching to go. I stare expectantly at Archangel Gabriel.

"Well, let's get started," Ben says.

"Right, good," the archangel answers. "First we need you to take care of the Innocent. We're certain that they're still in danger. It may lead you to . . . Orange." The name tumbles out awkwardly, and the nose crinkles. "Anyhow, I can't give you the bean as it's been taken by . . . Orange. No wonder you wanted to give each other real names," Archangel Gabriel says, looking at me then Ben. The brow creases again. "Back to the mission. Because there's no bean, I will give each of you the mission inserted by me."

Moving in front of Ben, the archangel places a hand over his exposed navel. A flash of light leaves the hand into his stomach. The muscles in Ben's abdomen tighten briefly, then relax shortly afterward. Turning to Cindy, the angel executes the same process. I watch as her face tenses for a split second, then relaxes. I'm next in line. Having the mission hand-delivered doesn't look as comfortable as swallowing the bean. I brace myself as Archangel Gabriel's hand rests on my abdomen. A small jolt strikes my stomach. It's uncomfortable, bordering on painful, but subsides quickly.

Next destination—Somalia.

CHAPTER TWENTY-ONE

Mogadishu, Somalia—not exactly the safest city for humans. Invisible, we land with soft thuds on the dirt-ridden street. Looking around, I can't see any sign of the living. Crumpled remains of buildings frame both sides of the street. Some are bulleted with deep gashes, and others have walls missing or are completely gone. The sun is blaring, and I can feel the heat beating on my skin. I notice there are very few trees, and the ones that are still standing are shredded and torn, clinging on to life for a better day.

The devastation is depressing. I look at Cindy and Ben. Their faces are the splitting image of how I feel. How can people live here? We walk through the street, taking in the destruction.

In all three of my lives, the families I grew up in didn't have much money. Because of this, I didn't get to travel before my human lives finished. As for my last life, sure Australia has its crime, but it's nothing like this. The scenery is so disheartening that I'm finding it hard to continue walking down the street. A jolt in my stomach reminds me of my mission and Innocent. I press forward.

We continue toward what looks like the middle of the city. The only way we make this judgment is by the density of buildings. Gunfire sounds up ahead. Prickles run up my back. My thoughts go out to the poor people at the receiving end.

Being in places like this reinforces the need for more angels. At present, there are not enough to protect everyone. We pass an open courtyard. Voices travel out to us, and our heads turn in that direction. It's full of women and children. The women are covered from head to toe in burkas, with only slits in their clothing for eyes or a slightly larger gap showing the top half of their face. Even in this heat their hair is still covered. My eyes travel down to the children. I stop. My feet won't move. They're skin and bone. Clearly there isn't enough food here to feed the citizens of the city.

A woman is wailing at the top of her voice. She's standing and rocking back and forth. I notice that she's holding something in her arms. Wet wells form in my eyes. She's holding a small figure, dark skin exposed to the sun, the flesh taut against bones, and it doesn't move. The world is getting darker.

The healer in me wants to run over and see if I can heal their pain and hunger and restore their bodies.

Ben must've seen my expression, because he grabs my hand and clasps it in both of his. The deep-blue ocean of his eyes is almost spilling over with compassion. He shakes his head. "We're not here for this. It's hard, I know." He reaches over and wipes my face gently, catching the tear that's spilled over the edge.

"We should be stationed here permanently until this devastation is gone," I say.

"And I wish we could stay. But we have our mission first. For some reason, it's deemed more urgent."

As usual, he's my stabilizer. I peer over his shoulder and see that Cindy has been looking in our direction. On her face is a mixture of emotions. I can see by the squint in her eye that she's not quite forgiven us yet, but there's also sadness. I'm sure it comes from seeing people suffering and not being able to help them.

"Come on," she says.

We pick up our speed, following the pull to our Innocent.

"Let's get this mission over with and see if we can get some archangels in here later. This place just doesn't feel right." She visibly shivers. "It feels like pure evil, as if demons are here—many of them. We haven't been trained to fight demons."

"What do you mean it feels like demons?" I ask.

"Can't you feel them?" Her golden-brown eyes open wide.

I shake my head. "I only feel compassion for these people, nothing else."

She looks at Ben. "You feel it, don't you?"

"Compassion, yes. Not demons," he says.

"Seriously? You don't feel it. It's like the feeling from our mission under the bridge but stronger, like there are so many more of them."

He shrugs, holding his palms up. "I didn't feel

anything different then, either. I could see the reactions were different—more intense, nothing else."

Her eyebrows rise as far as possible. "Well let me tell you, this place reeks of demons, and I'm shaking in my boots. How are we supposed to fight these if we come across them? We haven't had any training."

"Cin—" I begin but cut it short from the piercing glare she just gave me. I sigh, then continue. "Have faith in yourself. You're a very talented fledgling. You've proved it by sensing demons."

"But Archangel Gabriel said that Archangel Michael can see your special capabilities, not mine," she snaps while crossing her arms in front of her chest.

"I believe he was talking about all of us," Ben says. "Just have faith in your abilities."

"Just follow your heart and instincts," I say.

"Yeah, a lot of good that does you. You're breaking the rules at every turn," she spits.

More gunfire bursts ahead. "Come on. Let's hurry it up." Ben says. "I'm getting a bad feeling about the well-being of our Innocent."

I had to agree. My stomach was beginning to twist into knots. I spread my wings and lift off the ground. "Let's fly. For some reason, Orange has missed the time slot for the rescue. This could be the final chance to rescue our Innocent."

Ben and Cindy lift off the ground, and we follow the pull in our stomachs with an even more rapid pace. The devastation of the place doesn't look any better from above the city. Many roofs are no longer flat; rather they're caved in on the side or middle, exposing the building to the harsh weather.

We haven't flown for long when I feel the overwhelming pull from a building in front of us. I point to the building. "That one," I say.

Ben and Cindy nod.

It's a couple of stories high. I hone in and prepare to land on the second-level balcony that, surprisingly, is still unbroken. Landing with the softest of thuds, I peer into the adjoining room. I can't see anyone. I take a step inside. The place is bordering on a dump. The furniture is ragged, and the windows are smashed. Ben and Cindy land and follow me indoors.

A bloodcurdling scream fills my ears. I quickly look at Ben. Before he dashes into the room, I catch a glimpse of his face covered with concern. I rush forward, following him, and hear Cindy not far behind. The doorway leading to the next room is open. Still invisible, we enter the room. What I see makes my stomach lurch.

A Caucasian man is in the middle of the room. He's tied to a chair and surrounded by four dark-skinned men. His long dark-brown pants are torn, and his light-blue T-shirt is bloodied. Each of the men surrounding him appears to be local.

He's screaming out in English, "Please, please. I didn't do it. Please." I think I hear an American accent. It's hard to tell with all the stress in his voice. His body shakes as he begins to cry. "Please, I'm just an aid worker trying to help your people with food . . . and . . . and ways of a better life. Please . . . I'm trying to help them get through the war and devastation." His face is screwed up, his lips firmly pouted. Tears and snot are running down his face as the Somalian men ignore his words and prepare the weapons.

One of the men has pulled out a large butcher knife and is holding it up, admiring the blade against the glimmer of natural light from outside. The blade is a sharp contrast against his dark skin.

"Please." The captive begs.

If he hadn't been secured to the chair, I'm sure he'd be on his knees begging.

With a heavy accent, one of the men watching and holding a gun speaks in broken English, "You take food, you lose hand." He stands tall and nods quickly, giving the man with the knife approval to act. Immediately he steps forward. Two other men reach for their prisoner's right hand.

"Please! I didn't do it." The man is screaming. His tears have cut the dirt, leaving pale stripes on his face.

Two other men reach forward, taking the captive's right hand, stretching the limb over a bench. The man with the knife approaches the bench.

In my peripheral vision, I see Ben to my left swiftly fold away his wings and become brighter. His bare torso extends from tight royal blue pants, and he looks completely out of place among men in full-length traditional clothes that cover their bodies except for their lower arms and face. The distraction is enough to buy the victim some time.

Every set of eyes turn to see the strange underdressed man that suddenly appeared out of nowhere.

Ben targets the man with the knife first. His back muscles ripple as he slams his palm forward onto the hand holding the knife, instantly disarming him. The knife clatters to the floor. The two men release their prisoner's arm and they and the leader turn to attack Ben.

I fold my wings away and make myself visible. Cindy follows suit. If seeing an underdressed man appear from nowhere is a shock, they're about to be floored. The thought is almost humorous to me. They're now faced with two fully clothed, yet, by their standards, scantily dressed western women. I'd love to read their thoughts right now. They'd punish the women of Somalia severely for dressing this way, and, what's more, we fight back. I watch their faces, especially the leader, as it transforms from shock to demanding dominance once again.

He steps toward us, reaching over his shoulder for his rifle. I skip sideways, cutting in closer in a split second and plant a high-heeled foot into his stomach. His hand drops, and he slumps forward. At this moment, I see Cindy is beginning to fight another man, and the remaining two males are attacking Ben.

I focus my attention back on the leader. He's clasping his stomach with one hand and has a strange glimmer is in his eye. I pause, wondering where I've seen that look before. The answer doesn't come to me, so I refocus on my opponent in time to see the man's other hand is still sneaking up to the rifle strap. I turn and flick a kick directly on his head on the opposite side of the rifle. A soft thud sounds. The force of the impact causes him to tilt in the direction of the kick, and the rifle strap gravitates off his shoulder, landing on the floor.

He realizes what's happened and reaches toward the floor. I slip forward, tuck my knee under his chest, grab his shoulders, and slam him downward on my knee once, then twice. A groan escapes him with each connection. I move my knee out of the way and thrust his body onto the ground. As he falls, he tries again to reach for the rifle, but he misses it and slams onto the hard floor instead. A faint crack sounds. He lets out a cry of pain and pulls his hand up, bracing it with his other hand.

I reach down, grab the rifle, remove the bullets, and throw it to the other side of the room. It clatters down the wall and onto the floor.

Turning back, I see the man still clutching the injured fist with his other hand. Something on his inner wrist catches my eye. I hold my breath. It's hard to see against his darker skin, but it's there. On his inner wrist is a tattoo of an upside-down pentagram finished with the details of a goat's head inside a circle.

It comes back to me now. I know where I'd seen that look in his eyes before—the group of men under the bridge on our last mission. While he's temporarily distracted because of his hand, I study the eyes of the other men in the room. In each of the attackers there's the same look and the same disregard for pain. Cindy was right, there's a demonic presence in this city.

A horrible thought crosses my mind. If she felt it back at the edge of the city and away from these men, then how many more are hiding here, making these citizens' lives intolerable?

Sensing movement from my opponent, I turn. He's heading in my direction, ready to attack again. He shuffles forward, his legs moving rapidly under his ma'awis. Something shiny catches my eyes. I look at his hands and see that he's holding the knife. When he's almost reached me, I step aside and slam a fist against the back of the hand holding the weapon. It clangs to the floor.

The surprise of being quickly disarmed wears off the attacker, and he swings his other hand around in my direction, slapping me hard across the face.

A strong sting spreads over my cheek and jaw.

"Learn your place, woman," he scorns me.

He raises a hand to strike again, and I reach forward grab his wrist, and flip it over my shoulder. With his elbow turned down, I yank it toward the floor in a swift movement. The crunching of bones fills my left ear, and his yells of pain fill the air. Screwing up my face in disgust I push my elbow back into his ribs with swift jabbing movements. A loud moan escapes his lips with each jab. I then step out and flip around with my heel flying high, it connects with his head. The high heel of my boot leaves a nasty red mark down his face as he falls to the floor unconscious.

Not wasting any time, I step forward, grab him under the armpits, and drag him across the floor away from the others fighting. I kneel down over him and place a hand on each of his temples. Knowing more about the problems the archangels are facing with the demons and the strong demonic presence that Cindy felt in this city, I don't search his memory for innocence. As much as it pains me, I don't have the time, and the demon may be fighting against the archangels. If I can help them, I will. So until we discover a better solution, I insert a conscience into him. I'm glad that his evil eyes remain shut, so I don't have to watch them turn dazed and confused.

When completed, I remove my hands and wipe them on my pants. I don't know why, but they just feel dirty. I've a distinct feeling that I'm being watched. I look up to see the captive staring at me. His face holds a strange look of relief mixed with confusion and a touch of terror of the unknown. His arms are free, yet he's still sitting bound on the chair. I frown, wondering why he hasn't freed himself. He motions with his hand for me to come to him. A thump on the ground catches my attention. The victim will have to wait.

I turn to see the two fighting against Ben have coordinated their attack and have had a moment's victory, slamming Ben down on his back onto the floor. As I move to help him, I notice one of the attackers is limping severely, almost hopping, with blood pouring down the front of his ma'awis. The other has a large gash above his eye with the skin underneath swollen, extending over his eye. The eye that's open has the same look as my opponent had, and despite being badly injured they both are overriding their pain with determination to destroy Ben.

The man with one eye knocks something with his feet, and the dreaded clattering sound fills my ears. The knife. As he reaches down to grab his chance find, I catch a glimpse of his inner wrist. Very faintly against his dark skin I can see the same tattoo. My bet is that the other two will have it as a fashion accessory also.

By the time the man has straightened, with the knife securely in his hand, Ben has hurled himself up ready for action. As the men circle around him the one with the injured leg turns his back toward me, unaware of my approach.

Attacking from the side, I stamp my foot down on his injured leg. The sound of bones cracking and flesh tearing fill my ears. My stomach lurches at the mental image of his leg underneath his saronglike clothing. As he shrieks out in pain, I don't allow myself the luxury of recovering from this image. He's bending forward, grasping at his leg. I jump, twisting my hip and flinging my foot in a roundhouse to his face. Again, the sound of squelching cartilage and cracking bones fills the air, and his body flicks to the floor. Screaming from the pain, he lies on the floor grasping his injuries. My shoes click as I approach him, grab him under the arms, and pull him away from the fight scene. These possessed people just keep coming back until cleansed. I haven't a moment to lose.

As I kneel over him, I can still hear the fighting from Ben and Cindy in the background. I reach down and place a hand on each temple. Another loud thud hits the floor. I look up briefly. Cindy has just taken down her man, and Ben has things under control, so I turn back to my opponent. My hands light up, and I watch as the conscience enters his body. This time I see the flash of his life. I see evil and, again, when he was younger, there was once innocence—a hope for a better life. My heart cries out for the person he used to be. I hate what I'm doing to him, yet, at present I don't have a choice. His eyes become dazed. My work is done, and I release his head gently to the ground.

I look up. Both Ben and Cindy are kneeling over their victims. The fight is over. I look forward to feeling the warmth that's released into our bodies when we've saved an Innocent. This one is even an aid worker—an angel in disguise. A smile lights my face as I think of the reference.

I look at our Innocent. He's still staring at me with the same panicked look. My brow pushes together. He should be relieved. I know seeing us would be a little unnerving, but we're the good guys. Surely he perceives that by now. I walk over to him and reach down to untie his legs and body.

He must've just been in too much shock to untie himself, because I can't find any other reason he did not free his limbs while we were fighting. But then, even untied he doesn't move. I frown. The warm feeling I'm expecting doesn't fill my body. Puzzled, I stand up straight. A high-pitched sound zipping through the air reaches my ears. Something small embeds into my back between my shoulder blades. There's a piercing sting that travels the full extent of my spine. I try to look over my shoulder as I feel my back with my hands.

Cindy screams out, "You've been shot!"

The words stun me, and I stand riveted. Another high-pitched whistling becomes rapidly louder. The same sensation hits my back not far from the other hit. The unexpected force pushes me forward, and I stumble, knocking the chair holding our Innocent over, and he crashes to the floor. I hit the ground close to him with a thud.

CHAPTER TWENTY-TWO

The man scrambles across the ground and hides behind a nearby table. Ben and Cindy are crouching by my side before I can roll over. None of us has been shot before, and we're not sure how my body will react. Although most threatening things to humans wouldn't affect us, we can never be certain. As I roll over on my back, my eyes catch Ben's. They shadow with concern. I push up off the ground, and I hear the pinging of the bullets hitting the floor. My body has expelled them naturally.

"I'm fine, see?" I say to him.

A smile creeps up his face, and he exhales.

Cindy leaps on me and gives me a hug that's a little too tight around the throat. "You're okay."

"Yeah," I choke out the words past her embrace. "Looks like we're bulletproof."

"Psst! Come here," the aid worker calls.

I look over at him, and he looks panicked. When we

don't move, he motions with his hands to come closer. I begin to go, keeping low so I don't attract any unwanted attention from the outside. We still have a human with us and don't need him to get in any more danger. Cindy and Ben follow close behind. When we reach him, he's hugging his knees, not too different from a fetal position, and he's rocking back and forth. His eyes flick from me, to Ben, then to Cindy. With each of us, his eyes travel up and down our bodies, taking in what we're wearing and our looks. He doesn't do this in a creepy way, so his gazes don't upset us. Finally, his eyes rest on Cindy for quite some time. He seems to be studying her eyes and hair, lingering extra long on her yellow clothes.

Cindy becomes impatient. "What'd you want us over here for?"

He licks his lips; his eyes are still nervous. "Ah. You've a friend, right?" His voice was barely louder than a whisper.

We fall silent. Our faces remain blank, and none of us move. We just look at him.

He runs a hand through his hair and licks his lips for the second time. His eyes flick over us individually again, and he nods. "You have a friend. He's the color orange."

This comment pushes Ben out of silence. "What do you know about him?"

"They have him." His eyes were more haunted than I'd seen before. "They have him," he repeats.

"Who?" I ask.

"The others. The others have him." He nods again. "Yeah, they do. He came to help me, and they took him." I could hear his American accent now.

I frown and look at Ben and Cindy to see if they've any idea what he's saying. Their faces looked as blank as my mind. "Who took him?"

"Oooh." He visibly shook from head to toe. "They were horrible. Like demons or something. They made these men look nice."

"How many?" Cindy asks.

"Lots. There are lots of them," he whispers.

The news is disturbing. The archangels were right suspecting that this could be a dangerous mission. But why would the demons want to take Orange?

"Do you know where they took him?" Ben asks.

Something clangs across the floor behind us. I turn to see what made the sound and spot a hand grenade bounce in our direction and stop right behind me. We're still all crouched around the human. My head spins around, and I reach for the man, pulling him to a standing position with me. I catch a glimpse of Ben's eyes and see terror as he and Cindy stand. My heart reaches out to him. He's about to face his biggest nightmare again. We don't have time to do anything other than circle around the aid worker, hoping to protect him from the blast. In unison, we release our wings, wrapping them around the man. I grab Ben and Cindy around the waist and make sure my wings are on the outer edge. The bullets didn't seem to do me any damage, but that could just be another one of my hidden gifts. Maybe other fledglings won't have the same reaction. Maybe the bullets would've pierced through them. I look up. Ben's studying me. I can see the panic ripping at him from the inside. I want to say all will be okay, but then the grenade ignites.

CHAPTER TWENTY-THREE

The force pushes me forward and rips at my skin. Each piece of metal burns as it hits me. It hits my back, legs, neck, and rear of my head. I can feel the metal entering my skin. I grit my teeth as the pain sears through my body. The effects of the explosion last only a short while. The back of me aches, but I can already feel the pieces of metal moving out of my skin. Little tinkles sound as they hit the hard floor. I look up and assess the damage to the others.

I can see a change in Ben's eyes. He's more relaxed and happy that it's over. It didn't turn out as bad as he feared. He looks down, and I follow his gaze, pieces of metal are exiting his legs. I look at Cindy, and it's happening to her, too. There's no blood on the floor at our feet. I observe our human, and there's barely a scratch on him.

Breathing a sigh of relief, we pull apart and give him some space.

"Thanks," he says weakly. His eyes are wide and fixed on our wings.

I turn and look around the room. Every wall and piece of furniture is marked and embedded with shrapnel, making the place look more tattered than before. "We have to get you out of here," I say.

He approaches the door, keen to leave, when Ben places a hand on his arm. "Do you know where they took Orange?" The man jumps at the touch, but then he relaxes, realizing it's nonthreatening.

"I don't know for sure, but I have a suspicion."

"Where's that?" Cindy asks.

"I know it's hard to believe, but this place is heaven compared to the other side of town."

"Are you kidding me?" I ask.

He shakes his head. A look of sadness crosses his face. "Just thinking about the place overwhelms you with a sense of helplessness. It feels like hell on earth."

"Which way is the other side of town?" Cindy asks.

He points toward the north.

A noise sounds from the street.

"Come on, we need to get you out of here," I say.

When we reach the door, I hear a groan from the corner of the room, then a whimper from the other corner. I forgot about the other men. Looking in their direction I see pools of blood, and they're not moving.

I turn to Ben. "Can you transport him out of here to somewhere safe. I need to heal these men before we head to the other side of town."

He looks at the men, then gives me an apprehensive look. "Are you going to be safe while I'm gone?"

Forever my protector. "I'm going to be fine. Besides, I've big bad Cindy here to kick their butts." I smile, and he gives Cindy a curious look.

"That's me, baby." She gives him a wink. "A scary yellow bodyguard."

"You're the one that needs to be careful; you're by yourself." I raise an eyebrow.

He scoffs, then turns to the aid worker. "Now, don't be scared. Just relax, okay. It's not safe for you to leave here by foot. I'm going to embrace you and surround you by my wings and teleport you to a place you see as safe." He studies the man intensely. "Okay?"

The man wobbles his head up and down. He looks as though he doesn't completely believe what he's being told. Why would he? From his point of view, his life has just taken a weird turn.

Ben continues, "Now, think of a safe place you'd like to go. Okay?" He watches our Innocent carefully.

The man nods again.

"All right." Ben steps closer to him, wraps his arms around him, and then encloses him in his wings. It's hard to tell that there's a man underneath, yet I know he's there, encased in blue. They disappear.

I turn to the first of the wounded. I can no longer see the evil in his eyes; only fear and anxiety. I can also see the added damage done by the shrapnel from the grenade. The attackers are lucky we'd unknowingly placed them in a spot slightly sheltered from the explosion. As I approach, he wants to squirm away, but he's too injured. I place a hand on him and begin to heal his wounds. While I'm healing the shrapnel wounds, I also work on the ones that were inflicted by us. I watch amazed that I can do this. I still don't know how, but I'm grateful for the gift.

When he's healed, I move to the next man. This time it's the leader. He's still lying unconscious, unmoving, but I'm certain he's feeling. I touch each wound individually watching the skin and bones return to their normal position and heal. I look at the inside of his wrist. Once again, the tattoo has disappeared. It's such an unusual thing to happen. The tattoos are showing signs they must've something to do with being possessed by a demon.

As I finish, my mind wanders to Ben. I thought that he'd have returned by now. A small smidgen of worry creeps into me.

I move to the next Somalian. His blood is pooling in patches around him. His eyes are wide and white, a severe contrast to his dark skin. I can see he wants to flee, but he's just watched as I healed his other two colleagues. Desperate to be healed, he begrudgingly allows me to approach. I work on his more serious wounds first. Lifting the hem of his ma'awis high enough to see the wound on his leg, I gag internally at what I see. I don't know how he's not still screaming in pain. The bone of his leg has completely broken and is sticking out of his skin.

I place a full hand on his leg next to the wound and watch it all slowly move back into place and seal, leaving no mark. Once satisfied, I begin to work on his other smaller wounds, enjoying seeing them disappear.

With the healing done, I rise to my feet. I've one

more to heal. I look around the room, still no sign of Ben. It only takes a few moments to teleport somewhere. Where could he be? I try to push the worry down. I look at the charm hanging around my neck. I wish I knew how to enchant it to glow when one of the other two were in danger. The charm of the three angels remains dull and unlit.

Cindy sees me look at my charm and says, "I thought he'd be back by now." I can hear the worry in her voice. She's not helping to calm my nerves.

"True," I say. "Maybe he's taking a quick holiday on the side." I'm trying to lighten the mood. It doesn't seem to be working.

My next patient moans in the corner. Not wanting to be seen by anyone else, I commando crawl past the door. It's not that I'm injured; I just don't want to have any more unwelcome disturbances. I reach the man's side, kneel over him, and begin to heal his wounds.

Behind me, Cindy calls out, "Finally!"

Curious, I turn my head to look at what she's talking about. Ben is back. On his face is an amused smile.

"Where've you been?" I ask.

"You noticed." He smirks.

"Um, yes. You disappeared for quite a while for a simple teleport." I say. "Did you take a holiday on the side?"

He tilts his head to the side. "Kind of."

I frown.

"What do you mean, kind of?" Cindy asks.

"Well, you know how I said to him to picture himself in a nice safe place?"

I nod.

He chuckles. "That's what he did. I ended up in California on the beach under some palm trees."

A smile creeps across my face. "I'm sure it'd be a lot safer than here." I lean over and finish healing the last couple of places.

"Did you leave him there?" Cindy sounds stunned.

Ben nods. "That's what he wanted. To be honest, I don't blame him. After what he's been through here, he'd need to get away from the place."

I stand. "I agree. I don't want to be here, and I'm not even human." A warm feeling passes all over my body, the conclusion that our Innocent is safe and our mission to protect him is complete. I take a final look at the men lying in the room. They still look haunted from the effects of their conscience. "Ready to go find Orange?"

"Let's do it!" Ben says.

We turn invisible and fly out the balcony door. Below us is the display of ruins and devastation. The thought that the other side of town is worse than here, is hard to believe.

I can hear the sound of our wings flapping, almost in unison, as I observe our surroundings. A gust of sea breeze hits us, catching under our wings.

On the right-hand side, the city is lined by the Indian Ocean. I'm surprised to see the buildings along the ocean are still whole, with some looking quite attractive. Inland from the north, burned cars are sitting next to battlegrounds. Not far from there are long lines of makeshift tents set up for refugees and displaced people. These sites are heart-wrenching. The conditions that these people are living in are ghastly.

As we pass this area, I notice the conditions are getting worse. Trees are sparse, and there are bodies lying in the streets surrounded by armed men that look like peacekeepers. It looks as though a standoff with the rebels has just ended; the rebels coming in second best. Farther up are buildings on fire. Thick columns of dark-gray smoke billow up to the sky. The air seems thicker and feels strange against our wings.

"I don't like the feel of this," Cindy says.

"What is it?" I ask her.

"The feeling is stronger than before. I can't believe that you can't feel it." She looks baffled.

"It's clearly your gift, not ours," Ben says.

"Can't you even feel the change in the air?" she asks.

"I can feel something, but I thought it had to do with the fires down below," I say.

Shaking her head, she continues, "That's not the smoke; that's different."

"Okay," I agree, not knowing what else to say. I try to open my senses to see if I can feel it. I don't perceive anything different. I look down, trying to spot anything that is off. Everything looks much the same, and the circumstances are slowly getting worse as we head farther north, away from the ocean. Evidence of people running around in the streets dwindles. There's been no sign of movement for quite some time now. It's disheartening to see so many buildings ruined. They would've been beautiful buildings, looking at what remains of them. It's such a waste.

Something moves below me. Looking down, I see a wild dog tearing at the flesh of a lifeless body. The spectacle is repulsive, but I've a quick look at what may've caused the death and see several other people lying not far away, each one as lifeless as the other. Cindy was right that they need an army of angels to move in here to protect the innocent people. I can't find the cause of death. It looks like the bodies have been there for a few days. A crow calls out in the distance. The sound comes from behind us. Looking back, I can see we've already flown a fair way.

"Any sign of Orange or a place that they might be holding him?" I ask the other two.

Ben shakes his head.

Cindy speaks, "Between all the evil I can feel ahead, there's a faint angelic pull mixed with it. Can't you feel that, either?"

I shake my head. "I don't feel anything other than the illness in my stomach from looking around at the devastation and waste of life. I'm flying blind, hoping I'll see something shortly."

"I can sense something up ahead, and it's a feeling similar to being around you two or other angels, but it's extremely faint and surrounded by evil. It's all I have for a navigator. I hope I don't lose it," Cindy informs us.

"It's something at least. It could prove helpful in finding Orange. And to think you were upset that you didn't have a special talent. This one is proving extremely useful," Ben says.

"If it's what I think it is," Cindy stresses. A worried look crosses her face.

"You have my confidence," I say. "They chose the three of us for some reason. Let us know when you feel a change."

Some of the worries edge off her face, but she realizes she has a large responsibility. Even though we're looking, she's the only one that can sense them. As we continue to fly, my wings feel heavier with each stroke. It reminds me of my human years when I exercised on an Olympic trainer and it'd hit the hill climbing setting. Each step gradually became harder.

A weird sound comes from the distance ahead of us. I peel my eyes to look for the source, when we're hit by the salty smell of ocean water and pushed by a gust of ocean breeze. When the wind passes, my wings became heavy again, and I scan the horizon ahead of us, listening for the sound. The buildings are more crumpled in this area.

"Over there," Cindy calls out. She's stopped flying and is hovering in the air.

I stop and look at her, seeing she's pointing off to her left. While hovering, my eyes follow her finger and fall on a clearing in the middle of several tall buildings. At first glance, I can't see anything different about the clearing. It looks like several other places we've flown over that have been destroyed by the violence. Squinting, I study the clearing.

"Are you sure?" Ben asks, hovering close.

She nods. "I can feel an extra-strong pull from there. The angel feeling is also stronger in that direction."

"Lead the way, then," I say. "I can't see anything yet."

She turns and begins to fly toward the area, and we follow. I hear the strange noise again. It sounds a little like the shrill of a cat. When we reach the clearing, we fly over, looking for something unusual. I still can't see anything; not one human, animal, or any sign of Orange.

I turn to Cindy, but she answers before I even get to ask.

"I know, I know. I can't see anything, either," she says. "But it still feels right. I'm sure they're here somewhere. I'm definitely getting a concentrated feeling coming from here."

Not quite sure what to think, I look at Ben. He shrugs and looks back at the clearing. "Maybe we should land and take a look around on foot."

"Sounds like a plan. I still can't see a thing." I turn to Cindy. She looks concerned. "I'm not questioning your ability, although I think it'd be good to have a closer look to see what we're missing."

She turns her head and studies the area again. I guess she doesn't find anything, either, because her head nods slowly. "Okay. I really have a bad feeling about this area, but I can't see a way around it. Besides, my wings are getting tired. The air seems thick here."

Spotting a secluded place in between a couple of buildings, we land. Pieces of rubble from destroyed buildings fall to the ground when our wings forcefully push the air down. Snakes slither away from the sudden intrusion, and cats jump up into holes in the walls to watch the commotion. I did not see these animals from above, and I'm struggling to believe that they suddenly appeared on this small street. As I take a few steps, my heels softly click on the pavement. The sound seems too loud in comparison to the area, and I make an effort to quiet the noise. I don't know why I'm worried about the noise when there's no one around. We press forward.

A stone shoots across my path. My eyes dart toward the noise, then rise to look for the source of the rock when they catch Ben's eyes.

"Sorry," he mouths at me. He'd kicked it by accident as he was looking around the area.

I offer a weak smile as we continue. We've almost reached the clearing when I hear a throat being cleared on the side of our path. All three of us spin toward the noise. None of us had seen anyone approaching or moving, yet there in front of us is an old man sitting on a tall pile of rubble. A bandage smothers his weathered dark-skinned head. Under his raggedy clothes, his body is slouched forward, and his back is humped. In one gnarly dark hand he's holding a long thick stick. Taking in his condition, I assume that it's for steadying himself while he walks. His toe twitches, and I look down. His feet are bare, crusty around the edges, and cracked in several spots. They look painful.

I don't know how I missed seeing him there. I did notice when he'd finished adjusting himself on his pedestal that he was silent and unmoving. For us not to be able to spot him, he must've been sitting as still as a statue before he made a sound.

After he recovers from the surprise, Ben approaches the man.

"Good day," he calls to him in the native Arabic. The man raises his head, and the only visible eye looks at Ben. It's bloodshot and slightly bulging, but the surprise of the intrusion doesn't show on his face. His mouth opens showing off the sparse arrangement of brown and broken teeth. I cringe as his tongue flicks out, doing a round on his cracked lips. They look painful, too.

The man doesn't say anything back to Ben's greeting.

Ben continues in Arabic, "Have you seen a foreign person around here. He wears orange clothes."

Shudders run through my body as the man turns his attention away from Ben, and looks at Cindy and me. His one eye travels up and down both of us while his head shakes continually in unnerving small, twisting movements that don't look healthy.

Cindy steps closer to me and looks as though she'd like to stand behind me out of his sight. She whispers in my ear, "I don't like the feel of this. He's really creepy. The feeling I am getting from him is just wrong."

Mastering my confidence, I whisper in return, "You'll be fine. I'm sure he's just an old man who's been through a lot in this war." Trying to add a little light-heartedness I say, "Imagine what we'd look like if we'd been through what he has lived." My voice doesn't carry the humor I had intended.

Her tense face doesn't relax in the slightest way, and she continues to watch him.

With the eerie feeling remaining, and his eye continuing to assess us, I gaze at Cindy and then Ben. It's then that I realize that their forms are dull. We're not visible to humans. I could swear that this man is looking directly at us. On top of this, our wings are still released, meaning if he can see us, he can also see our wings.

Seeing he hasn't answered Ben, I begin to give the man the benefit of the doubt. He must just be looking in our direction simply by chance. I'm so worked up being in this strange place and near danger that I must be imagining things. It'd mean that he couldn't hear us, either, as humans can't hear us when we're invisible. After a long silence, I almost laugh. I turn again to Cindy and then Ben and say, "We're still invisible. He can't see, or hear us."

Cindy sounds out a nervous giggle as a sign of released tension. His one eye flicks toward her. Before his movement registers, Ben is halfway through a quick, relieved chuckle.

Then the man turns his head to look straight at Ben.

CHAPTER TWENTY-FOUR

Cindy gasps as Ben's chuckle halts halfway. His eyes meet mine with a concerned look. That small snap of relaxation has disappeared. This isn't normal. Tension has taken hold of my body, and I can feel the adrenaline rushing.

A strange cackle leaves the man's body. Even though his mouth is showing humor, it doesn't flow up to his eyes. The creepiness I felt before has escalated. I don't know if he's just imitating us or if he's found something amusing.

The man stands. Using his stick like a staff and with his back still hunched, he hobbles a couple of steps toward us. In my peripheral vision, I see Cindy taking a couple of steps back. I'd like to do the same. We haven't come across a human who could see us in our invisible state before. I hold my ground; after all, he's an old man.

His eye passes over Ben and me, and casts an amused glance at Cindy. Using his free hand, he indicates that we follow him. Without a word, he turns and begins to hobble in the direction of the building that's behind his sitting spot.

I notice one side of the building is caved in, and the area is stone rubble; remains from the walls and ceiling. It looks as though it used to be a two-story building. Only one level partially remains. Along the external walls are deep gashes concentrating around large holes that were once windows. Amazingly, there's still a door that looks fairly whole. Right now, it's closed and decorated with several bullet holes. Unlike the holes in the walls, the holes in the door pass completely through to the other side.

The elderly man staggers toward the door. When he reaches it, he stops and turns around with a concerted effort. I suddenly realize, we haven't taken one step to follow him. He raises his hand and indicates again for us to follow him.

Uncertain, I step forward. We're here for Orange; I only hope the man knows where he is. I hear the rubble crumpling as Cindy and Ben follow me.

After seeing us begin to follow him, he reaches out his free hand and turns the doorknob, pushing the door inward as he steps through. A ginger cat scrambles out the door, pausing on a pile of rubble. Its green eyes follow our every move as we continue walking.

Behind me, I hear Cindy whisper to Ben. "Even the cat's creepy."

When I reach the door, I stick my head through and take a quick look around. All I see is more rubble and a big hole in the side of the bottom level. I don't know why we came through the door; there's nearly as much rubble lying in the path from the door as there is from the gaping hole in the wall. Nothing comes across as dangerous, so I follow the man, mindful of where I step.

I turn to see Cindy and Ben have progressed through the door. I'm trying to read their faces when my thoughts are interrupted by the same strange cackle coming from the man. It doesn't make me feel confident about following the man. He could be playing a personal joke on us and lead us in the wrong direction on purpose. True to the archangels' warning, this trip has been completely different from our other missions. My emotions are conflicting. They told us that this mission could be dangerous to angels, yet everything that's happened to me so far as an angel hasn't injured me. Even with this knowledge I'm not going to let my guard down. Every step I take I can feel my training kicking in and my body readying itself for a sudden attack.

There's no other choice other than to press forward.

The man continues. We pass through what used to be rooms. Semicrumbled walls frame the borders of the fallen rooms. Overhead, the first floor barely hangs on. Only parts of the concrete ceiling remain, being more intact as we press on. He leads us to the farthest wall to another door. I follow as he totters toward it. Another eerie cackle leaves his mouth. I'm wondering if it's more of a nervous twitch than an emotion.

When he reaches the back door, his free hand reaches out and opens it, letting it swing to the outside. Cindy inhales noisily behind me. I gaze out through the hole. On the other side of the door before me lies the large clearing in the middle of the crumpled buildings.

I frown. I'm completely baffled. Why would he lead us through this house to take us to the clearing? We could've followed the path we were already on when we ran into the man. A snake slithers into the house. My human instinct wants to jump away, but my angel side knows the reptile won't hurt me. I stay put as it slithers over my boot while it approaches the other side of the house. As I look out over the clearing, it's still empty.

Cindy whispers, "There's so much evil out there."

I blink and squint trying to see what she's sensing. I still don't see anything.

"Can you feel Orange as well?" Ben asks her.

I turn in time to see her nodding. "The feeling is stronger now."

"Can you see anything?" I ask.

She shakes her head. Her eyes are tight with concern. "No, but I can definitely feel it. It's stronger from here."

I turn and glare through the door. I don't like this. I can't see anything, but Cindy says she can feel it. To make matters worse, the man gives out another one of his creepy chuckles. It makes me think there's a trap waiting on the other side of the door. He steps through the door and indicates that we should follow. With the adrenaline still pumping through my veins, my mind turns to our fellow trainee, Orange. We need to find him and get him to safety. I take a deep breath and step through the door.

CHAPTER TWENTY-FIVE

A sensation passes through me that I've not felt before. Instantly the hairs on my arms rise. A ripple travels from the top of my neck down my back. The air is thick and unpleasant. There's a strange awareness telling me I've just walked into another world. I hear Cindy and Ben right behind me.

"Whoa!" escapes Ben's mouth. "What's that stench?"

Cindy is standing behind me, and I can feel her body tensing. Mine is doing the same. In stunned silence, I let my eyes scan the spectacle before me. The scenery is the same. We've stepped into the large clearing in between the buildings. As before, not a single tree exists. The difference is that in the middle, in the full sweltering sun, Orange is tied to a large wooden post. He's tied upright with his hands bound behind the post. His brilliant orange-red hair is falling toward the ground over his tilted face.

A surge of panic travels through me. He looks lifeless. I want to run to him to see if he's still alive, but surrounding him are a countless number of people, most looking like the local Somalians. There's something different about them, though. They looked human, but my instincts tell me differently. They appear to be unaware of our presence and are strolling around Orange as if they're in a trance. I study them, trying to work out what's off about them. As one of the men, looking to be in his thirties, strolls past, I examine his face. Unexpectedly, his dark-brown eyes flick up, and he looks at me. I jump involuntarily. What I see in his eyes is pure evil.

"They're possessed," Cindy hisses. "They're all possessed."

I don't turn to look at her; I don't feel safe enough to take my eyes off the people before me. To make matters worse, this man continues to look at me as he walks another round of the open area.

On the right-hand side of me, I hear a cackle from the old man. I'm about to sneak a quick glance at him when I see several of the people's heads turn and look at us. Each of the dark, almost black, eyes has that unmistakable look. These people are not controlled by human minds. I cringe.

"Ah, guys," Cindy squeaks. "I'm pretty sure they're going to attack us."

"Piece of cake," Ben says. "These guys will be a cinch." He stands with his feet apart in a ready stance.

"Have you seen how many there are?" Cindy says in a panic. "And they look to be the walking dead."

At that comment, I study their faces and skin. I can't

believe I didn't see it before; pieces of skin fall off their bodies. Some have big, gaping wounds caked with dark, dried blood. It's hard to see these wounds against their rich dark skin. The horrid stench now makes sense.

With the number of possessed people in front of me, and an unmoving fledgling centered in the middle, I don't feel that self-assured, either. But then I remember that the archangels sent us here because they have confidence in our abilities. From this, I can feel confidence building and strength entering my body.

"Cindy," I say without taking my eyes off the circling enemy. "We have the mighty Archangel Michael as our trainer. He's the angel of protection, justice, and strength and is one heck of a fighter. He's taught and trained us well. We'll be fine."

"Remember, we were sent here because they have faith in our abilities," Ben says.

After a brief moment's silence, Cindy steps forward and takes a deep breath. She sets her feet apart in a ready stance. "Well then, we can't just stand here and wait for them, can we?"

"Nope," I say.

Another cackle sounds beside me, and the remaining heads turn to look at us. This laugh is getting on my nerves.

A yellow streak flashes past my nose. Curious, I gaze at the flash just in time to see Cindy connect a running sidekick into the old man's stomach. He folds over her foot. She watches as he falls back hard onto his backside.

"And you, old man, are the perfect place to start," she says.

I hold back a laugh. That's the Cindy I know. It's good to see the turnaround in her attitude. We need all of us to fight these people.

Assessing the situation, I say, "These people haven't done anything other than stare and circle Orange. Maybe, we can go to the center and retrieve him without them reacting."

"Don't know," Ben says. "But it's worth a try."

"Why don't we fly to him?" Cindy asks. "We can all fly together, then get the heck out of here to tell the archangels about this place. It sure beats us taking on all of them at once."

"Sounds like a plan," Ben agrees.

We push off the ground and fly into the middle, with our wings feeling the heaviness of the air. Other than watching us, the people don't react. We land in the center and surround the pole. While Ben keeps an eye on the possessed, I reach up to check if Orange is still with us. His vitals are faint, but still there. It's clear that something's happened to him to drain him of his energy completely.

"He's still with us," I tell the other two.

Cindy starts untying his hands and body from the pole.

"We need to go, now." Ben's voice strains.

I turn from helping Cindy to see that we're being surrounded. The staring continues, but they're progressing toward us.

"What changed?" I ask.

"I don't know. They all turned in unison about the time when Cindy undid the first knot." He notices me straining under Orange's weight, as the final rope unties. He rushes over and scoops Orange into his hands. "Let's go." He pushes off the ground, and Cindy and I follow suit.

I watch as several of them jump up to try to grab our feet. I'm surprised at how far they can jump, as one of the men's hands graze Cindy's ankle. She startles and increases her speed upward. The man that narrowly missed grabbing Cindy opens his mouth. A familiar, horrid scream, the same as we heard before we found this place, pierces our ears. On one side, I see the streak of yellow flash faster toward the sky. Cindy must be pretty jumpy after she was nearly pulled back into the crowd.

Out of reach of their jump, I turn to watch where I'm flying. Screams from below are still filling the air. Flying ahead, Cindy is increasing her speed more as Ben continues up at a steady pace with the unconscious Orange in his arms.

We must be sixty-five feet from the ground, right above the middle of the clearing, when a thud sounds from above. I spot a quick flash ahead. I watch in horror as Cindy stops flying, her body tilts backward, and she begins to fall to the ground. It looks as though she hit a force field, and it's either knocked her out or dazed her.

CHAPTER TWENTY-SIX

This can't be happening. Flipping around, I tuck in my wings and begin to nosedive toward her. I have to try to catch her before she hits the ground. I grit my teeth. Almost there. With my arms stretching out in front of me, I'm positioned to dive deep. I fall hard and fast, gaining speed and inching closer. The breeze is pushing hard against my skin, and the wind whistling past my ears. My fingers reach out a little farther. I can just touch her. The ground is rising at an immense speed. I stretch out farther, and my fingers clasp around her wrist.

Having Cindy firmly in my grasp, I spread my wings, catching the wind underneath them and causing us to jerk with the motion. With the harsh movement, Cindy's eyes fly open. Relief passes over me; she must've just been stunned. She flips over and opens her wings, carrying her own weight.

Below us only inches away, the hands are reaching up trying to grasp us. All kinds of weird noises are coming from their mouths. They're unnatural sounds that I haven't heard a human make before.

Cindy looks below then above to where she was flying only a few moments before. "What happened to me?" she asks.

"You seem to have run into some kind of force field." Ben came lower. Orange is still lying in his arms unmoving. "It knocked you out for a moment."

"Thanks for catching me," she says.

"That's what friends are for." I smile weakly. "You do know I didn't want you to get in trouble by the archangels don't you?"

"Yeah, I know." She gives me half a smile. "I was just stressing. When they're together they really have a way of making you feel like a naughty child, even when you haven't done anything."

I smirk. "I've always been guilty of something, but I agree they do make you feel like a naughty child."

"What're you two gas-bagging about?" Ben has lowered to our level. "Surely you realize it's not the time and place, right?"

"True," I say. "But we do have to discuss one thing."

"What's that?" His eyebrows crease together in puzzlement.

"After watching Cindy run into the force field and fall, I've a hunch that they've trapped us within this area. The force field is clearly invisible, even to our eyes, and is probably the reason we did not see all of these people down here when we were flying above."

"We're trapped. Are you serious?" Cindy's pale face has turned a couple of shades lighter.

"From flying out, yes. But possibly we can still leave through the door that we arrived in, or we'll have to fight our way out to release ourselves from this entrapment." I'm observing the ravenous, possessed humans below. They haven't lost interest in us.

I turn to Cindy. Her eyes are focused. Her look is apprehensive, but the fear isn't there. She, too, gazes down at the mass below and says, "I know one thing for sure, I'm not going down without a fight. These people have caused enough trouble already."

"Now that's the Cindy I know and love." I smile. I turn to Ben, who's still holding Orange. Ben isn't going to be able to fight with his arms occupied. I look over at the door we came through. It's still open. I can see through to the other side. There 's no one near the door except the old man. He appears recovered from his solid stomach kick.

An idea comes to me. "I need you two to keep the audience's attention on you. I'll quickly fly over to the door we entered and see if we can leave that way."

"Sounds great," Ben's voice is enthusiastic. "Be careful."

"Always." I start approaching the door. The old man's one eye is watching me. Even from this distance I can see his head shaking. I watch him out of the corner of my eye as I edge closer. Even though Ben and Cindy are doing their best to keep the other humans' attention on them, I keep my eyes on the lookout for a stray. I don't need any nasty surprises. The door is only a few feet away, so I begin to lower my flight. So far, it's only the old man I can see watching me. His tongue circles his dry, cracked lips.

The telltale cackle sounds loud in my ears. I'm expecting it, but I'm still not quite sure if it's a nervous tic or a genuine evil laugh—possibly a little of both. This place is pure evil and at the moment we're trapped. I don't trust the old man, and I'm not willing to find out if he's any hidden talents. He's six feet away from the door and hasn't made a move. I know he walks extremely slowly, so I take a quick dive at the door. After watching Cindy being stunned by a force field, I'm not taking any chances.

Landing upright on the dirt directly in front of the door, I stick my hand through the entrance. My hand hits something that I can't see and won't go any farther. Cursing under my breath, I try again. It'll not go through.

The old man's cackle sounds again. I give it one last try—still no luck. I close the door. I'm greeted with the old man's face right where the door used to be; his mouth spreads in an ugly grin. Startled, I jump and without even thinking about it, my body moves into the ready stance for a fight. My legs are stable, and my arms are up.

He doesn't move forward; he just stands, staring from that one disturbing eye.

His mouth moves, and I want to be sick. For the first time, he speaks in Arabic, "You can't leave, pretty. There's no way out. Not for you, not for your friends."

He reaches for my wings, and I pull back. My eyes catch a glimpse of the mystery tattoo on the inside of his wrist. It's the same one that I've seen on the attackers of the last two missions. An upside-down pentagram finished with the details of a goat's head inside a circle.

The man steps forward and tilts his dirty dark face toward me and breathes in deeply like he's sniffing me. If I hadn't already been disturbed by this man's behavior, I am now.

"Yes," he says. "Yes. You're the one he wants."

"Who?" I'm surprised that anyone is looking for me, especially in the world of demons.

Ignoring my question, he continues. "I'm the gatekeeper, and I'm not going to let you out. I'll be rewarded well for finding you. Yes, yes, I will." He turns to walk away while letting out another loud cackle.

"Then perhaps I should kill you," I call after him.

He turns around to face me. His eye holds an evil humor. "Then you'll be stuck in here for sure. Kill me and the way out stays sealed until he comes." He turns his back on me again to walk away.

"Cindy was right, you are annoying." I want to kick him in the head and fight him, but I'm not completely sure if he's telling the truth or not.

As I glare at the back of his head, I hear Ben's voice. "Aurora. Look out."

I turn in his direction to see that several dark-faced people with disturbing dark eyes surround me. They're almost upon me.

I bend my knees and push off the ground to take

flight to the middle of the clearing with Ben, Orange, and Cindy.

"What'd the old creepy guy want?" Cindy asks.

"He wanted to let me know that we can't escape here and that some guy wants me—I'm assuming from the underworld." I gaze down at the obsessed crowd below us. They're still jumping, trying to grab our ankles to pull us down. "Oh, he also told me that he's the gatekeeper and that if we kill him, we've no way out of here until whoever it is comes and decides to release us."

"Do you think that's true?" Cindy asks.

"I don't know. I don't particularly want to test the theory unless it's our last resort. We can't leave through the door at the moment, or through the middle."

"You don't have to remind me," Cindy says while rubbing her head.

"Looks like we're going to have to fight," Ben says. "There must be another way." Orange remains in his arms, unmoving.

"Well, I know that I'm certainly not hanging around just for some underworld weirdo to show up because he has it in for me," I say. "I certainly don't want to end up like Orange." I look below at the clearing filled with angry possessed people then look back at Orange. I move closer to him and Ben. "I'm going to have to see if I can heal him. Looking at our welcoming party, we're going to need every bit of help we can get." I flap my wings a few more times while deep in thought. "Cindy."

When I see her look in my direction, I continue, "I

need you to keep an eye on me. It may take a fair bit of my energy."

"Are you sure about this?" Ben's voice leaks concern, and his eyes study my face. "You're going to need all the energy you have for fighting."

"I know. Although if this works, we'll have an extra fledgling on our side, and that should make up for any energy I lose in the healing process." I try to reassure him. "It's a risk I should take for everyone's sake."

He doesn't look happy.

I reach out and run my fingers through his hair. "If it doesn't work and it drains me, we can hold off the fighting for a while until I recover enough." I indicate below. "They can't get us up here, so we can hover while we wait for my strength to return."

The reluctance remains on his face. Eventually, he nods; his mouth is turned down.

"Let's go up a little before you start. That way it'll give us a little dropping space if something doesn't go right," he suggests.

I put on my best smile. "Good thinking."

Pushing down with my wings, I rise with Ben and Cindy to the boundary of the force field. Now that we're at a safer distance from the ruckus below, I reach out a hand to Orange's heart. I don't know what's wrong with him other than he won't wake up. Cindy moves closer to me and is watching me intensely while Ben holds on to Orange just a little more firmly. I can see the strain in his muscles, his arms and chest under the constant weight, but I know he'll not whine—it's not his way.

Now I'm secure as much as possible in the situation, I focus on my hand resting on his heart. I close my eyes for a deeper concentration. Warmth flows down my arm and into my hand as it begins to glow. Through probing his health, my mind searches for an area to heal. It's not a simple external flesh wound so it's different from the other healings I've done so far. As my mind wanders through his body, it searches and probes looking for the point or points of injury. After a while, I still can't find a place of injury. An involuntary frown creases my forehead.

Because I don't find the place or places of injury, I follow my instincts and pump healing light into his body and feel it flow. It's only the early stages of the healing process, but I can already sense a large amount of energy leaving me. The impression I'm getting is that Orange's healing needs are not like those I've healed in the past. I press on, hoping for the best.

I can hear the strange sounds from the crowd below. I do my best to block these out, placing full trust in Ben and Cindy to protect me. The healing energy I'm directing into Orange is leaving my body at a rapid rate. It seems like such a long time has passed, and I don't know if I'm helping. He hasn't stirred.

I'm feeling extremely weak when I hear Cindy's voice. "Aurora, you need to stop." It sounds so distant.

"Aurora, stop. You need your energy. Your face has turned ghostly white." This time the concerned voice is Ben's. It sounds to be at the end of a long tunnel.

I press on without responding. I must heal Orange. We need another fighter on our side. I gather some more of my healing energy and give it a forceful push into Orange. As I do this, I hear voices in the background. I can't hear what they're saying; my head is ringing too loudly from the exertion. I vaguely feel arms scooping under my armpits from behind, then a jerk backward. My connection severs from Orange. I labor to open my eyes, managing to open them to tiny slits.

Before me, I see Ben's troubled eyes studying me. His face relaxes slightly when he realizes my eyes have opened.

"That's it. Breathe deeply and gather your energy," he encourages.

I can still feel arms hooked under my armpits. My eyes open a little wider, and I look to the side. Cindy still has me. It's then that I realize that I haven't been flapping my wings.

"That's right. I've still got you." I can hear the relief in her voice. "Just relax now. We need you to regain your strength. I've got you." I see her golden-yellow wings flick out of the corner of my eye.

Looking back at Ben I gaze down into his arms. Orange is still lying almost lifeless. Disappointment floods over me. I was at least hoping that his eyes would open. I was hoping not to lose all of that effort. As thwarted as I am, I can't allow myself to worry over that now. I did my best, and now I need my strength.

I gaze down below and face the possessed watching us—waiting. I'm reminded immediately of the task at hand, and the adrenaline starts to kick in.

CHAPTER TWENTY-SEVEN

My eyes open wide. I begin to flap my wings.

"No, conserve your energy," Cindy speaks softly in my ear. "I have you."

Behind me, I can still feel her body pressing against mine, and her arms hooked under my armpits. I know that I'm secure. My energy is slowly building, and I follow her advice. Gazing below at the waiting enemy seems to boost my energy more quickly. After a few minutes, I begin to use my wings again, and Cindy releases me.

"Welcome back." Ben's voice sounds relieved, almost joyful.

I'm about to respond when I hear coughing coming from his direction. Curious, I turn to look at Ben. My eyes expand when I see that Orange is moving, and his eyes are open. Ben continues to grasp him firmly under the arms, and I watch as he begins to flap his wings and hold his own weight. Just the sight of him moving boosts me with encouragement and tops up my energy levels. Whatever I did worked.

"What happened?" Orange's voice is croaky, and he looks dazed.

"From what we can tell, you were kidnapped by demons while on your last mission. Somehow you ended up unconscious and surrounded by demonic guards," Ben fills him in.

Orange jerks to life and stiffens. "Oh no. That's right. It was a trap." His eyes flicked to each one of us. "It was a trap to get more fledglings here . . . I think they were after a few specific beings." His eyes landed on me. Is that panic I can see filling his eyes? "And to attract one in particular." He looks away.

By his movements, I'm not sure if he's referring to me or not.

"We're trapped here, aren't we?" he asks.

"It looks that way," Ben says.

"But we're not giving up just by that assumption," Cindy says, sounding more confident than before.

"We're not going down without a fight," I add.

"We were hoping you'd wake, so we'd have your help," Ben says. "So what do you say? Are you up for a challenge?"

"Do you really think I'm going to stand back and watch?" Orange is sounding stronger, and his voice is less croaky.

"Oh, thank goodness," Cindy grunts in relief. "As soon as you two recover, let's get started. This place is seriously creeping me out."

Orange frowns. "What's wrong with you?" he asks me.

"It's no big deal. I used some of my powers excessively, and it drained me." I brush off the question.

Cindy isn't going to let it rest there. "What she means is that she just healed you from whatever had knocked you unconscious."

I squirm. I don't like to boast about special gifts, and I don't know Orange that well.

"You can heal?" His voice raises half an octave as he looks at me in awe.

I remain silent.

When I don't answer, he says, "That's awesome. Can either of you two heal?" he asks Ben and Cindy.

They both shake their heads.

"How do you do it?" His questions are making me uncomfortable, but I understand his enthusiasm.

"I honestly don't know. It just feels natural . . . I follow my instincts."

He reaches forward and grabs my right hand in his as though he's about to shake it. Then he painlessly slaps me on my right arm near the shoulder and lets his hand rest there. It seems like a friendly gesture, so I go with the flow.

"Thanks," he says, looking deep into my eyes.

I can feel the heat rising in my face. I look away from his stare. "Not a problem."

He releases my hand and arm then claps his hands together. "So, are we going to kick these smelly butts or what?"

Now he's talking my language. "Absolutely," I agree.

Ben chimes in, "Let's do it!"

"So, what's the plan?" Cindy asks.

We all look down, assessing the ugly faces gazing up at us. They crowd the middle and the outskirts are almost bare.

"How about we all go to the four corners and hover close to their level to draw them to the outer circle," I suggest quietly. The possessed below don't look very clever, but I don't want to take chances. "Then, when the middle is empty, we all fly in quickly and land together in the center. If we fight facing out and our back facing the center, we can protect each other's backs."

"Sounds like someone's been listening during our training," Orange compliments. "And they say that you're a rebel."

I can't help smirking at his comment.

"Everyone agree?" Ben asks.

"Absolutely." Orange shows off his straight white teeth.

Cindy nods.

"Okay, let's get this over with." I drop my level to hover above the ground. I can hear the strokes of their wings behind me not far away. When I reach just above the dead's reaching height, I hover and begin to move slowly toward the outside of the clearing. It's hard to hide my smile as I watch approximately a quarter of the people follow me outward. Turning around, I look to see if the others are having the same success—they are. My plan is working.

Something touches my boot. I look down to see that one of the possessed narrowly missed grabbing my foot when they jumped for it. This reminds me that I can't underestimate them. Pulling my knees up, I stroke my wings to raise my position and continue to the outside.

The process is slow, and my nerves are getting twitchy. I want this to be over. Looking ahead, I see that the outer edges are not far away. A familiar cackle fills my ears. At the farthest point ahead of me, I see the old man's one eye studying me with interest. I must keep a better eye on him. I don't know what his capabilities are. He looks like a cripple, but I'm not sure anymore.

I push forward, then pause and turn around to see how the others have progressed. I'm pleased to see a large open gap near the post in the middle, where Orange had been tied. Ben, Orange, and Cindy are hovering close to the possessed, taunting and teasing them, and then they turn, ready for our plan of attack.

My energy is almost restored, and I'm ready to go. The others are all waiting for one of us to make a move. With big strokes of my wings, I rise, imitated by the other three. We charge forward in unison, spinning around, so our backs face each other and land in the center. Immediately I stand with my hands raised in front and feet shoulder width and sturdy. I'm ready. After training with Archangel Michael, I'm sure the others are doing the same.

I scan the horizon. Rotting bodies controlled by demons hungry for angel blood are advancing. This is going to be interesting. If mildly possessed people keep coming back after severe injury, what're these going to be like? These are not people anymore.

A few of the attackers heading my way begin to run. Weird gargling sounds are coming from their mouths. One moves slightly in front of the others, and I move forward to meet it. I run. Just before we're about to connect, I turn sideways, jump, and kick out my foot, aiming straight for its stomach. It connects. I sense its skin giving way a little under my heel. The force pushes it backward. It stumbles off-balance and crashes into several other attackers behind it.

Without a moment to lose, I turn and grab the extended arm of the next attacker ready to grab me in a vice grip. Securing the wrist solidly with one hand, I feel the cold, clammy skin. Twisting under the raised arm, I snap the elbow over my shoulder. The bones crunch next to my ear. The attacker doesn't cry out in agony as it reaches out with its other hand to grab me. This isn't right. Usually, the receiver of a broken elbow would be too busy concentrating on their injury, but this isn't a normal situation. As its open palms hit me, I feel the energy start leaving my body.

Reaching up, I grab the hand, securing it with my two hands and pressing my thumbs in between the bones on the back surface. I feel the skin give, and my thumbs dig into the flesh. The foul odor suddenly grows stronger, causing my stomach to turn. It's such a repulsive smell that I want to let go. Instead, I slam my foot down on its knee causing it to drop to the ground.

By now there are several hands reaching out to grab

me. I spin and kick out backward. My foot connects with one in the lower stomach area. I spin back in time to watch it tumble forcefully into several of the other attackers. They fall like dominos as I move on to the next in line.

The possessed are not fighting; they're more interested in grabbing. I've no idea what their intentions are, but I'm not stopping to find out. I lash out with my feet, kicking more away from my immediate area only to find they're replaced instantly with more attackers.

Despite my efforts, I'm surrounded. Arms are grabbing me everywhere, and energy is slipping away. I spin and kick, managing to knock them away, often breaking bones and even dismembering bodies. Being surrounded by so many dead bodies, the smell is overwhelming and repulsive. I need fresh air.

The fighting is taxing, although I'm far from being too exhausted to fight, even with the mystery sapping of energy every time they touch me. Still, there must be another way. I crouch and twist my body. I push off the ground in a spin, before the tiny space above me is taken over, knocking off all the grabbing arms. This maneuver has allowed me to rise high enough above my attackers to spread my wings and hover above them.

Breathing in the slightly fresher air, I study my surroundings. They surround each of the fledglings, exactly as I was. They're all putting up a good fight. I watch each one individually for a moment trying to work out what the possessed have planned once they grab us.

Surrounded, Ben and Cindy are still fighting strong. They seem to be keeping the attackers far enough away from them. I turn to look at Orange and see him being grabbed by several of the possessed. His strength rapidly diminishes. If he doesn't remove the hands quickly, he may be taken again. I cross my fingers for him, but it doesn't do any good. Anxiety tears at my stomach as I watch him crumble to the ground over-shadowed by at least ten of the rotting corpses. At the same time, I hear Cindy call out. It's not a cry of agony, rather a disappointed moan. I turn to see she's fallen to one knee and struggles to get up.

Something wells within me. I don't know what it is, but it's strong, and it's taking hold of my body while I watch my fellow trainees and friends being taken over.

I look in Ben's direction. He's still positioned with his hands ready for the fight and kicking anyone that comes near him. My insides scrunch up as I see several hands reach out and grab him through his defenses and lay an open hand on him. His energy crumbles to half the amount in a matter of seconds.

An additional surge builds within me. This can't happen. I can't allow any of my friends to fall, espe-cially Ben. A cry sounds out. I look to find the owner and see Orange has completely fallen. His eyes are imploring me.

A strength surges in my body so strong that my back arches. A burning begins in my stomach and spreads outward to my limbs.

A moan of distress sounds from Ben. That's the final

trigger. A strong force completely takes over me, and I react out of instinct.

With a couple of pushes of my wings, my body begins to rise and spin like a top. My wings encase me, and I begin to drop. I've a sudden urge to release this built up strength straight into the surrounding earth. Slamming my body on the dirt in a small gap within the possessed, I land in a squatting position and thrust my palm onto the ground. A sonic wave expels from the connection, and a white light expands and ripples out like a nuclear explosion.

I see the bodies fall to the ground, lifeless and unmoving. Worried about my friends, I instantly search the area. There are dead bodies scattered everywhere. I scan over each one until I see a rich color of blue. Taking a deep breath and holding it, I focus my eyes.

Relief passes over me when I see Ben stand, dust himself off, and look at me. His face is bewildered yet grateful. Not giving in to emotion or reasoning, I continue to look for Cindy and Orange. I breathe out a large sigh of relief when I see Cindy sitting in the middle of her lifeless attackers. I scan farther and am ecstatic to see Orange slowly breaking through the bodies piled on top of him.

They're all looking for the cause of their release, and they focus on me. I didn't realize, until that moment that I'm still in my awkward landing position, squatting on the ground with my palm firmly planted on the ground in front of me.

A little shocked over what I'd done, I lift my hand and wipe it on my pants, hearing the small stones and dirt fall to the ground. I stand dazed as I study the area in front. All the bodies are motionless and lying on the ground.

I see movement in the farthest distance. Turning in that direction, I see the old man scurry out the door. I hope this's a good sign, and that we will now be able to leave.

From behind me, an aggravated scream pierces the air. I turn in time to see Cindy running toward an ugly sun-aged man that's moving in our direction. I don't even know how he emerged.

His dark skin is taut over his frail body. His eyes are wide, and his mouth is open. Draped over his shoulders are pale fragments of material that have a similar appearance to a sarong. His feet are bare and knobby. He's hobbling and appears to be struggling with an injury, but he's still moving. I don't understand how all the other bodies have fallen immobile to the ground, and he's still approaching us.

His black eyes turn from Cindy and look at me. Instantly I feel like evil is touching me. On cue, he reaches for me with his long and gnarly hand. He's too far away to be able to touch me, but a sensation of evil grips my body. My feet are welded to the ground; I'm stunned. My eyes move up to his head. Now that he's closer, I can see he has two small twirled horns poking through his curly black hair.

Out of the corner of my eye, I can see Cindy rapidly approaching him. She follows the direction of his hand, and her eyes land on me.

"Aurora move!" she screams.

It is all happening so fast. A flash of blue rushes at me and knocks me to the ground. While I'm falling, I see a streak of black pulse from the man's hand and travel through the spot I'd been standing on only a moment before. Covered in dirt, I turn to see it was Ben who'd knocked me to the ground, saving me from whatever was within that black streak. I scramble to my feet, ready for the next pulse, and Ben does the same. We must stop this strange man. I brace myself for a fight, turning ready to attack, when I see Cindy is already upon him and fighting against him. She boots his stomach, knees, and head. He flinches with each one but doesn't appear to be getting hurt. Ben, Orange, and I are almost by her side when I see the man turn, grab her with an unimaginable strength, and place his hand on her stomach. Her eyes open wide as she struggles with all her strength to fight off his unyielding grip.

I call out, "Cindy!"

Fear fills me like I've never experienced before, her eyes turn to me, watching as we rapidly approach. My body almost halts as a large black pulse leaves the man's gnarly hand and enters her body.

Her body shakes violently, and her eyes close as he throws her to the ground.

CHAPTER TWENTY-EIGHT

I stop. What's this man done? Something deep inside of me wells; he can't do this to my friends. Vaguely I see a streak of blue and orange still heading in the man's direction as I gaze at Cindy's motionless body. A burning begins to rise from the pit of my stomach. At first I think it's anger that I'm feeling, but I'm not so sure. It's a sensation like I've never felt before, even different from the last unusual experience, and it burns with the intensity of the sun.

Welded to the spot, I'm barely aware of the commotion not far away. Even though I want to avenge Cindy, I'm unable to move. The burning increases. A bright light illuminates the surroundings. I begin to wonder if the sun is growing stronger, but in my peripheral vision I'm mindful of Ben and Orange fighting unaffected by heat. I don't know what to make of this sensation.

Faintly, I hear voices. "Aurora, move!" It sounds like Ben but distorted.

I look in the direction of the fighting. Ben and Orange are casting curious glances at me in between attacking the man. A black pulse comes flying in my direction. I still can't move, I can only watch. Strangely, this doesn't send me into a panic. As I watch, it appears to hit me then bounce off.

Ben stands stunned, and I see the man turning toward him. Something in me tweaks. The force that's holding me firm jolts me with energy and a passion for ending this before someone else I love gets hurt. I run the last few feet to this man, who I'm beginning to think may be a demon. His attention focuses on Ben. Ben is fighting well, avoiding direct contact with the hands. He gets hit in the leg and crumbles slightly, long enough for the man-demon to target his hand and prepare to release a pulse.

I knock the hand upward using an uppercut with an open palm . The black pulse escapes and narrowly misses Ben's shoulder. The man-demon cries out in pain. I'm puzzled because I only knocked his hand away and did not attack. My eyes travel to the section of the arm that I had hit, and I see a scalding mark. I look at my guilty hand—it's glowing.

The man-demon begins to attack again. I don't have time to ponder what just happened; I move, following my instincts. I block an arm that's reaching for me. The skin on my arm is glowing. His face flinches as I shove my other hand with open palm onto his stomach. His body thrusts backward, and he throws his head back and lets out a spine-chilling cry.

Taking advantage of the situation, I reach for his

throat. He knocks my hand away before I connect. His black eyes glare at me with hatred, while his face tenses with pain. I can see the contact with my skin has hurt him, so I press on. Out of the corner of my eye, I see Orange and Ben standing aside with their mouths ajar, watching every move.

I step back and tilt sideways aiming a sidekick on the man-demon's knee. I hear bones breaking and the knee angles in such a way that confirms unquestionable damage. A cry escapes his mouth, but it doesn't have the same call of pain as my physical touch does. Mystified, I watch as the knee begins to move back into place and heal itself.

I resort to touching his skin, which has a lasting effect. I reach out for his stomach again, but he flinches back before my hand connects.

A pair of black wings unfolds from his back. Unlike ours, they aren't made of soft feathers but rather of material similar to that of bat wings. The demon flaps a couple of times and rises off the ground. I can see the scalding marks remaining on his body where I've touched him. At his stomach, the patch is large and blistering.

I'm not afraid of fighting in the air, so I squat to push off when I hear a raspy voice.

"I'll be back for you fledgling. You've caused me much pain and destroyed many of my servants. You have much to pay."

Before I can push off the ground, he wraps his wings around himself, and then he spins and disappears. I stare at the spot where he was flying only a moment before. I'm puzzled, yet glad over his sudden departure. My eyes fall to the ground to observe the damage. The lifeless, rotting corpses lie everywhere. Ben has given up staring at me and is kneeling over Cindy.

Orange continues to scour the area, looking for any more threats. His eyes fall on me. "You're glowing, dude. How'd that happen?"

"I don't know," I answer truthfully.

I turn around and look at Ben with Cindy resting in his arms. He's stroking her golden-blonde hair. I hope I can help her. Who knows what was in that black pulse. As I step toward them, Ben looks at me, his eyes are hopeful.

"She's barely breathing." His voice is slightly louder than a whisper.

He doesn't need to ask. Naturally I'm going to help my friend. I kneel down on the dirt. Stones dig into my knees through my pants. I ignore the discomfort. While I place a hand on Cindy's stomach, I notice that my skin is still glowing. I focus on inserting some of that energy into Cindy, hoping it'll push out any darkness from the demon.

I push the white light into her. With this, I feel my energy decreasing, and I become frustrated when I run into a barrier that'll not budge. I focus on the core of the energy source within me. After feeling it intensify and gather, I release it into Cindy, pushing it for a longer period. The barrier doesn't yield. Searching around the barrier for a weak spot or edge, I push and push, but the wall won't give. Feeling the energy being zapped from my body, I pause.

"Are you okay?" Ben asks.

I look at him. His eyes study my face. Nodding, I turn back to Cindy. I have to get through this barrier. I take a deep breath and then another and then close my eyes. The power within is building and stirring. I let it gather and rise in strength. Rubbing my hands together, I feel it circulate from one arm to another, spinning around and building up force. When the force is twirling so much it's making me feel lightheaded, I separate my hands and place them on her stomach.

The white force explodes out of my body and through my hands, pushing firmly against the barrier. This time I feel a slight give in the wall, so I push harder. I'm completely leaning over her, directing my energy into her body. My strength is leaving my body, but I push on. I force another surge into her, and I feel the barrier give a little more.

Faintness takes hold, and my arms and legs are feeling weak—I don't stop. I let the pressure continue to assault the wall. A little more gives way. I hold back, letting energy collect within me again. When I feel enough has gathered, I pull all I have and thrust it at the barrier. I sense the release, and the white light forces through, crushing over the barrier and into her body. With all my might, I hold on a little longer, letting as much white light enter her body as possible. I can feel the last of my energy leave my body, but I give over a little more. I've come this far; I can't give up now.

My legs crumble underneath me. A strange sensation overtakes my body, numbing my brain. I can't open my eyes as the texture of the dirt, sticks, and rocks scrape my skin.

Somewhere far away, I think I hear my name being called. No matter how hard I try, I can't answer. My body shakes as everything turns completely dark.

CHAPTER TWENTY-NINE

A strange feeling runs down my arm. My mind is groggy, and the cause won't register. I take a deep breath. The air that fills my lungs is light and fresh. I release it and take another. It's cool, and something about it is slowly revitalizing me. My body won't move. It feels heavy and uncooperative, so I lie perfectly still and just breathe. That air smells so good.

The sensation runs down my arm again. This time I can tell it's soft and gentle; it has traces of a loving touch. I take another deep breath. Ah, yes! That air is definitively good. With each breath I take, my mind becomes clearer.

A flash of dark and an image of Cindy lying still on the ground crosses my mind. My body jolts. I hear myself cry out, "Cindy!" My muscles stiffen, and I lie rigid and unmoving.

Something touches my hair, and my hand flies up and clasps the culprit.

"Aurora."

The voice is riddled with concern. I take it for begging, and I squeeze my hand harder against the offender.

"Aurora."

This time the voice is whispering softly, the breath brushes against my skin near my ear. Confusion strikes me. The voice sounds like Ben's. I take in a few quick breaths and try to open my eyes. Success. I see my protective arm draped across my forehead. My eyes gaze out from underneath it into the deep-blue ocean of Ben's eyes. He's sitting beside me. My grip instantly softens, and I watch as the muscles in Ben's face relax.

I blink a few times and let my eyes wander. Above me is a blue sky decorated with a few puffy white clouds. I'm clearly no longer trapped in the demon's force field.

"Where are we?" I ask. My voice is husky.

He smiles. "Can you not tell?" His eyes circle the room. "You should be familiar with this place. I know I am."

Tilting my head slightly forward, I take a look around. The furniture is made with puffy white clouds on top of a white-cloud platform. Yes, I unmistakably know where I am. There's only one place that looks like this—the archangel's headquarters.

"Cindy?" I ask. My forehead pinches together.

"She's good. Actually, she's very well and on an ordinary fledgling mission. Orange has returned to normal duty, too. In fact, if you didn't wake up soon, they'd be sending me out to keep working." He smiles, showing off his perfectly straight teeth. A glimmer surfaces in his eye. He lowers his voice softer than a whisper and says, "It's not like I can claim that I'm your boyfriend and be granted complete access to your sickbed while you recover."

I smile weakly. "How long have we been here?"

"A couple of weeks."

I feel my eyebrows rising.

He reaches out and strokes my face. "Missed you."

Right on cue, a voice sounds from the corner of the room, and he pulls his hand away.

"Ah, I see the patient has woken."

I turn to see a gown of green coming toward us. My eyes travel to the face, landing on Archangel Raphael. His somber green eyes study me as I lie motionless. I've never been so glad to see him. It's clear he's been healing me and taking care of my health as I lie unconscious.

When he reaches my cloud bed he says, "I was beginning to wonder when you'd wake up." He observes my vital signs.

I clear my throat. "Thank you for taking care of me," I say. My voice is still on the rough side.

"Oh, nonsense child. Of course, I will take care of you. I may not always like what you do, but I will still take care of you—especially after what you have just accomplished. You did well." He looks at Ben. "You all did well. Despite my reluctance, Archangel Michael was right in sending you." A flicker of emotion crosses his face.

A throat cleared in the corner, out of my range of vision. I turn my head and see Archangel Michael standing in the doorway of the room. When his sapphire-blue eyes connect with mine, I see a softness in them that isn't usually there. He approaches us slowly. His face holds a clouded seriousness, where it used to be set and stern. As he continues to walk in our direction, he casts his eyes down to the cloud floor.

"Yes," he said. "You were the right angels to send." He pauses for a while. He reaches my sickbed and stands at the end. "You all did a wonderful job . . . actually, you exceeded my expectations . . . but, if I had known it was going to be that dangerous for you, I would not have sent you." Another pause, then he looks me in the eye. "For my inability to see how dangerous the situation was, I do apologize."

I shake my head. Archangel Michael is always stern and a leader, but I don't like seeing the regret in his eyes. His talent isn't being a psychic. "You don't need to apologize. It's not your fault. I believe it may've been a trap."

"Exactly," he agrees. "I should have been able to see through that . . . and I'm sorry."

I push myself up almost to a sitting position and repeat. "You don't need to apologize. I thank you for the experience and the faith you placed in our abilities." I can't help a little grin. "Besides almost being killed and meeting some really stinky characters, I enjoyed the experience." I look at Ben. "Didn't you?"

He nods.

"How'd we get out of there?" I ask.

Ben spoke, "Just after you passed out, Archangel Michael descended through the barrier, bringing it down. He brought Archangel Raphael with him, who immediately started work healing you." He places a hand on my arm. "I'm just glad you're all right. I was starting to worry about you."

I smile. It's nice to hear him say he worried. I'm also finding it amusing how restrained he is in front of the archangels.

Turning to Archangel Michael, I ask, "Did you find that demon or the gatekeeper?"

He shakes his head.

I sit up and flip my legs over the side of the cloud bed. "I've a feeling that the demon doesn't like me."

"Demons don't like any angels," Archangel Raphael says emotionless, yet a little too quickly.

Archangel Michael turns to him. "She needs to know. For her safety she must know what she is dealing with."

Curious, I look at Ben to see if he's any wiser. His eyes are again troubled as he studies me.

I frown and look at Archangel Michael. "What do I need to know?"

"Over the last two missions, the perpetrators have been of another level. I am sure you have noticed."

I don't say anything; I just nod, prompting him to continue.

"Each time you insert a conscience, you harm the demon that removed it in the first place."

"Is that how we helped you on our last mission, even though we weren't anywhere near your war with the demons?" I ask.

He nods. "Yes, you weakened that demon, the

demon you just fought, making it easier for us in our battle against him and his minions."

He pauses, then continues. "As you know, you were sent on this mission because I was still busy fighting the war. I had a feeling it may be a more difficult mission, which is why I needed to run it by the top four archangels. Even though you are still fledglings, I was impressed by how you three handled yourselves on your previous mission. You all acted above your level, and we were short of graduated angels to send on this mission."

He takes a deep breath while assessing my reactions. He begins to pace the floor and continues. "While I continued to fight the demons, that particular demon disappeared. It is never a good sign, so I left the other angels to fight the lower demons, and I began to search for him. I took Archangel Raphael with me in case anyone needed healing once I found him. Following the scent of his evil led me to the force field where you were trapped. You had already fought admirably, but he must have sensed me coming and disappeared."

"Is that why he just disappeared after he threatened me? I was hoping maybe I'd caused him enough injury that he needed time to heal." My mind wanders over the last few moments before the demon took off. "He did threaten me before he left." With adrenaline pumping through my veins, I stand up and begin to pace the room not far from Archangel Michael. I stop and gaze out at the blue sky, admiring the shapes of the clouds near us.

"Yes, well, you in particular have caused him the

most damage, and he will not forgive you for that. Your life is in danger. He will not stop until he destroys you." Archangel Michael's voice sounds from behind me.

I turn. "What're all these powers coming out of me? My body seemed to glow in the last fight, and all sorts of other gifts are appearing when I need them. Where're these coming from, and how come the other fledglings don't possess them?"

"These are what are getting you into trouble with the demon. Your gifts are powerful and natural. You are accessing them far more quickly than any other fledgling in the past. Because you have grabbed the attention of this demon, we will need to begin your next level of training and teach you how to use your powers correctly and how to control them. I have seen these gifts in you from the beginning, but I did not expect them to surface so soon. Each of you has your special gifts, just as we"—he indicates Archangel Raphael —"have different gifts."

"What're my gifts?" Ben asks him.

"You will find out at the right time. Your yellow friend is beginning to find out one of her gifts—the gift of sensing the strengths of demons and angels. It is the reason she attacked the demon straightaway. She, very bravely, was trying to protect all of you. Unfortunately, she did not have the training yet to protect herself against demons of that caliber."

"So when do we begin training?" I ask, keen to know more.

"The three of you will begin tomorrow after your yellow friend returns from her mission. I am going to give you today to recoup your energy. You have earned it."

I look at Ben. He's smirking at me despite being watched by the two archangels. I just hope they can't read the mischief on his face. Returning my focus to the archangels, I bow my head slightly as a show of respect. "Thank you." I turn to leave.

Archangel Michael speaks, "Oh, and I hear you have been using your last earthly name, Aurora."

I swallow. I look at him straight-faced and don't say a word. Surely he's not about to go mad at me after everything I've been through and done.

"Fledgling, you must not continue to disobey me or the other archangels. Even with your natural talents and benefits to the society of the angels, you will still be punished."

All the joy I felt only moments before vanishes. There's no use denying his accusations. He already knows. I look down from his gaze toward the floor. "I apologize, great leader. I find it difficult not to have a name for me or my colleagues."

He turns to Ben. "Yes, I have heard that you are also going by your last earthly name." All the friendliness that was there a few moments ago is gone.

I reprimand myself. I've just added Ben into my admonishment. "Please," I speak up. "That was my fault."

"Quiet, fledgling," our leader snaps. I can feel his stern eyes gazing over me and then Ben as he paces in front of us. "For this case, and this case only, you can keep your names."

My eyes instantly shoot up to look at him. Is that a smirk I see on his face?

"You and your colleagues from the last mission have earned it." He's now smiling. "I also think your name is very fitting for you even in this life. A natural phenomenon and the dawn of something new," he rattles off the meaning of my name.

I want to run forward and hug him; instead, I bow my head. "Thank you." I can't hide the smile.

"You are dismissed."

I turn and face the outer edge of the cloudy platform. Ben stands beside me. I open my arms out wide; we both dive into the clear-blue sky, twist into a triple somersault, and finish by spreading our wings and gliding.

I feel so free.

THE END

BOOK 2: THE TAKING

ACKNOWLEDGMENTS

I am touched by the enormous amount of support I have received from my immediate family. My husband has been a helpful alpha reader and at times been a wonderful motivator, with hints of ideas to help me through the blanks. The support from my three sons has also been overwhelming. My older two have devoured the book and asked for more. Thank you also for my youngest son, though too young to read this book at the time of publishing, he has been full of enthusiasm and support. He is reading my preteen series, 'The Sanctum Series'. I love seeing his eyes light up as he tells me about what he is reading.

I would also like to thank my good friend and book enthusiast, Julie Hickson for becoming a beta reader. With her enthusiasm to continue being a beta reader for the next book in the series, is inspiring for an author.

A huge thank you to my editor Ruth at Kirkus for her editing, writing tips, and suggestions.

Thank you to all of my readers who have loved my work, and continue to read my stories. There are many more books to come.

Get updates & notifications of giveaways

FREE DOWNLOAD

Find out more
about the
Gatekeeper...

Sign up for the author's New Releases mailing list and get a free novelette story
about **The Gatekeeper**

Click here to get started: FREE copy of The Gatekeeper
Or visit http://www.katrinacopebooks.com
Sign up for my newsletter and receive updates about my fantasy books and notification of giveaways.

Enjoy this book? You can make a big difference.

Honest reviews of my books help bring them to the attention of other readers.

If you've enjoyed this book, I'd be grateful if you could spend a few minutes leaving a review (it can be as short as you like).

The review can be left on:
Amazon: Fledgling
Goodreads: Fledgling

Thank you very much.

Katrina is an author of several Young Adult and Preteen/Middle Grade novels. Each of her released books reaching the top 100 in certain categories on the Amazon's Best Sellers Rank – a few even as high as number one.

She resides in Queensland, Australia. Her three teen/preteen boys and husband of over fifteen years treat her like a princess. Unfortunately though, this princess still has to do domestic chores.

She holds a 2nd Dan in Taekwondo, which she likes to incorporate the experience into her stories. When she has enough time away from her writing to commit to training, she will be going for her 3rd Dan.

From birth, she has been a very creative person and has spent many years travelling the world and observing many different personalities and cultures. Her favourite personalities have been the strange ones, yet the ones under the radar also hold a place in her heart.

During her last extensive travels, she spent 16 nights in a bomb shelter on a Kibbutz 8 kilometers off the Lebanese border. It was to avoid Katyusha bombs that the resident volunteers decided to name her after (she is still trying to work out why).

PS. Do NOT try to scare her in a dark alleyway even as a joke. Just saying!

Katrina's online home is at www.katrinacopebooks.com

facebook.com/Author.Katrina.Cope

twitter.com/Katrina_R_Cope

instagram.com/katrina_cope_author

bookbub.com/profile/katrina-cope

pinterest.com/katrinacope56

AALIYAH

~~~~~

Young Adult Nordic Myth Fantasy

Valkyrie Academy Dragon Alliance

MARKED

CHOSEN

VANISHED

SCORNED

INFLICTED

EMPOWERED

AMBUSHED

WARNED

ABDUCTED

BESIEGED

DECEIVED
~~~~~